Praise for *Tears Before Exaltation*

"This book is part of a literary production which is very important and deserves both critical attention and analysis."

—Babacar M'Baye, PhD, Professor of English,
Kent State University, author of
The Trickster Comes West

"*Tears before Exaltation* is a suspenseful book that drives the readers in high gear sparking curiosity and a craving for more."

—Patrick Achebe, Author of *Whispering Waves*

"A page-turner that will keep you reading eagerly until the end."

—Consuela Murgia

TEARS BEFORE EXALTATION

Fidelis O. Mkparu

Harvard Square Editions
New York
2018

ISBN 978-1-941861-60-8
Printed in the United States of America

Published in the United States by
Harvard Square Editions
www.harvardsquareeditions.org

Chapter 1

THE WAILING SIREN stopped. The wheels of the ambulance stretcher glided over the wet floor by the entrance. As my shoes squeaked and slid, I held on to the wall and steadied my body against the ambulance. Finding dry areas on the floor, my feet maneuvered as if I was a dancer. I realized the decisions we make can save us, or kill us.

Three Knoxville police officers huddled inside an empty patient room. Walking by, I overheard, "Yep. A scary situation."

In the hallway, two paramedics and a nurse exchanged papers. A body on the bed inside a room remained motionless. I saw no oxygen tubing or blood pressure cuff, just a torso covered in a white sheet, feet in booties. The idea of a suspicious death crossed my mind. When I gave the scene a second glance, the nurse looked at me with neither a smile nor a frown. Prying came to mind. A violation of hospital privacy rules. I knew the consequences. Termination of my employment.

I thought about the quiet demeanor of everyone around the room. No wailing families. Chaplain Benjamin was absent. Death usually brought him out of his small office in the basement. Every time he paced back and forth in the emergency room, I had to wheel a body to the morgue. Nothing seemed right to me. I edged closer to the doorway, risking my employment, to investigate the neglected body on the bed.

"Hi Ben," the nurse said. I jumped. My clipboard fell from my hand. The clank of the metallic portion resonated, but wrapped body remained still. "Did I startle you?" the nurse asked. I hesitated. We bent down at the same time to pick up my clipboard, and our heads almost collided. She reached the clipboard first and handed it over to me. My eyes traveled back to the room with the covered body.

"Thanks," I said, without looking at the nurse.

The covered body in the room rose in bed, sitting up, revealing matted hair and sunken eyeballs. My grip on the clipboard tightened as I took two steps back. The bed sheet slithered down from her shoulders. Skin and bones. No muscles or fat. Her blue eyes, barely open, looked at me. Her mouth was agape, but no words came out. Tears rolled down her face. Her features reminded me of someone I knew, but someone with a fuller face. I walked closer to her bed.

"Water, please." She held out her hand as she pleaded in a whispering voice. My eyes settled on her wrist, it was adorned with a silver, winged ankh bracelet. I remembered the bracelet from the first year of medical school, and the beautiful girl that wore it. A brilliant classmate and a confidant. We were inseparable during our first year of school. I shared a dead body with her for gross anatomy class. A six-month, daily contact as 'cadaver partners'. I took a deep breath and rubbed my eyes. Drug addiction and homelessness crossed my mind. It appeared that anyone could be afflicted with such problems, including medical students like me. My own thoughts scared me.

"Brenda, what happened?" I asked. Looking at her physical condition—significant weight loss since the last time I saw her, three months before—I felt queasy. My hands trembled. When I remembered terminal illnesses that could cause weight loss, my heart raced. The thought of Brenda dying slowly scared me.

The disheveled look was different from what I remembered

of Brenda. I visualized ironed khaki pants, starched, buttoned-down shirts, bobbed hair—a quirky smile. A friendly woman, even if she washed her hands after every handshake. Obsessed with cleanliness. I remembered the first day of medical school during our freshman orientation, when I shook her hand. She retrieved a small bottle of sanitizer from her pants pocket, flipped the cover open, and squeezed a clear liquid gel on her hand. She returned the sanitizer bottle to her pocket, and massaged her hands with the gel for minutes. A protracted cleansing.

I thought about her obsession as I reached out to hold her hand, to reassure myself that I was witnessing a real event. She groaned when our hands touched. Tears rolled down her face, and a childlike, whiny cry came out of her mouth. I watched Brenda in disbelief.

As I looked around the emergency room, my vision became blurry. I saw bodies walking in slow motion. My body felt warm, and the room seemed to be spinning around. I used my free hand to hold the bed railing, an anchor to keep from falling. When I tried to speak, my words echoed in my ears and traveled around in my head. I felt my hands disengage from their secured places, Brenda's hand and the bed railing. They dangled at my sides and felt as if they carried heavy loads. When I tried to move my arms, I could not lift them. My heart pounded. The possibility of having a stroke crossed my mind, and sweat trickled down my face.

Brenda watched me struggle to lift my arms without any reaction. She merely observed.

"Are you okay?" the nurse asked. She felt my forehead with the back of her hand. A strong soap scent emanating from her hand tickled my nose. I resisted sneezing. It reminded me of the smell of formaldehyde, the agent used to embalm dead bodies. The chemical Brenda and I were exposed to daily in the anatomy laboratory.

"I'm not feeling well," I said.

The nurse removed her hand from my face and sighed. "We can't afford to lose you," she said.

"I'm staying," I said.

Looking at Brenda felt like watching a child. A distracted child. She ignored all the activities around her. Avoiding looking at me directly, she lowered her body onto the bed and covered what was left of it—the body of a 23-year-old with no padding. I worried about my own body, how other people perceived how I looked—we were born the same year.

"You know her?" a paramedic asked.

"She's my classmate. A third year," I said.

"Ben's a medical student. Our best orderly," the nurse said.

"Good. We need more information," the second paramedic said.

"If it's okay with her. Ben's not family," the nurse said. A paramedic standing by her side nodded in agreement.

"I'm sorry, Brenda. I should've asked your permission," I said. I felt my breathing rate increase.

"It doesn't matter," Brenda said. She turned on her side and tears flowed into her sunken temple. I wiped her tears with the bed sheet, and felt my own run down my face.

Leaning down to hide my face, I wiped my tears with my shirt sleeve. A feeling of emptiness gripped me, as if my intestines were twisting inside me in revolt. Brenda turned onto her back and looked at me. A few drops of my tears landed next to her eyes and mixed with her own. She lifted herself up and hugged me. We squeezed each other harder than I expected, and the thought of her bones breaking crossed my mind.

"What happened?" I asked. I felt embarrassed asking the question, but I needed to know. My tears could not stop flowing, falling all over Brenda. I reached for a box of tissues. The nurse and the paramedics whispered to each other. Looking at them, I wondered why they were smiling. There was nothing funny about Brenda's condition.

"I don't know. I haven't felt good lately," Brenda said, her words barely audible. I had forgotten what I asked her by the time she answered.

One of the paramedics handed a white polythene bag to the nurse. As she checked the contents of the bag, he placed a folded white scarf in a plastic basket and a sharp-looking surgical scalpel on top of it.

"For the cops," the paramedic said. He picked up the basket and waved to Brenda.

"I want my scarf," Brenda said. She unwrapped her body and threw the bed sheet on the floor. I looked away.

"Stop exposing yourself," the nurse said. She picked up the bed sheet from the floor and covered Brenda's body. "We've got to call your folks," she added.

"Don't call anyone," Brenda said, raising her voice for the first time. She grabbed the bedside rails and pulled her body closer to the foot of the bed. The two paramedics helped the nurse to lift her body back to its original position.

"We're trying to help you," I said.

"I don't need it. Let me go," Brenda said.

"They'll come, if we call. What's their number?" the nurse asked. She picked up her clipboard and retrieved a pen from her pocket. Brenda scowled.

"Ain't giving it. Let me go," Brenda said. She shook her bed railings, making continuous jangling sounds. Watching Brenda's reaction to the nurse's request, I wondered why she did not want her parents contacted.

With the noise from the bed railings still going on, one of the cops came over to Brenda's room. A physician followed, and another nurse joined us, creating a space crowded with rattling noise. The cop walked closer to Brenda's bed. She ignored him.

"No charges," the cop said. Brenda continued to rattle the bed rails. "I need your name and address," the cop added.

Brenda's behavior bothered me. She had changed significantly from the person I remembered. I stepped out of the room and leaned against the wall. The cop walked out of the room with a cell phone held to his ear. He saw me leaning against the wall and walked back into the room. He tried to whisper, but I heard what he said.

"A jogger found her sitting on a bench crying. Don't know. Yes. Yes. Yes. Well, he called because of the scalpel. No one hurt. Okay. Thank you," the cop said. I wondered who was on the other end of the telephone.

"Ben, we need you," a nurse said. She stood across the hall from Brenda's room, waiting. Looking around the emergency room, I saw all the rooms had patients in them. I had wasted time in Brenda's room and neglected my job. My graduation from medical school depended on the income from the job. I walked over to the nurse. "We're taking a patient to ICU," she added. She walked to a patient's room, and I followed. Before I entered the room, I turned to look at Brenda's room. There were no cops or paramedics. One nurse remained in Brenda's room.

* * *

I was rolling a gurney out of a room when a wheel froze. It screeched, making sounds that gave me goose bumps. I pushed the broken gurney to a restful place next to Brenda's, now empty, room. The clock hands stood at noon. Three hours had passed since she hugged me. A goodbye hug. An empty room and limited information. I paused to regroup. Admission or discharge? I could not tell. The sharp scalpel came back to my mind. "No charges," the cop had said. The fear of awful things happening to Brenda took my imagination on a whirlwind trip. Self-inflicted disaster occupied my mind. Brenda was too fragile to hurt anyone, I thought, before I remembered how she'd rattled her bed railings. It became clear to me that she had enough strength left in her.

I walked to a secretary's desk, and hovered over her balding scalp to look at the patients' discharge list. She moved her chair away from me, leaving me with full access to the list. I mumbled, "No entry for Brenda Galant." The secretary looked up and frowned. Privacy issues came back to my mind, which would be a blemish on my employment record. I knew I had taken unauthorized liberties, and I panicked. A dismissal from my job would end my medical education, and my quest to become a doctor.

"Sorry, Lori. Just checking for Brenda," I said.

"You shouldn't. Confidentiality issues," she said. Written on a folder next to the list was, 'No disclosure without patient consent.' I already knew the rules. My willingness to take risks worried me.

"I understand," I said.

While I was talking to the secretary, Brenda's nurse walked by and probably heard our discussion. She turned and said, "Come with me." I looked around. "You, Ben, come with me," she added. I followed her from a distance.

She walked toward the staff lounge and did not look back to see if I followed her. I thought about my interactions with Brenda. Hugging a patient while on duty. Privacy issues violated. Grounds for a reprimand, or dismissal.

"Sit down, Ben," the nurse said. I looked around the room. No witnesses. A nurse and an orderly.

"I'm sorry about this morning," I said. My heartbeat skipped, then took off. On a race with no destination. A futile effort. The Valsalva maneuver crossed my mind. I tried to remember the details. Taking a deep breath with the mouth closed, the nose pinched with the thumb and index finger. When I thought about keeping the cheek muscles tight—and not allowing them to bulge out during the procedure—I worried about accidental defecation. I wondered what would happen to me if I had a bowel movement while trying. The nurse watched me as if she knew what I was thinking. She smiled. I sighed, and smiled back.

"Stay away from Brenda. She's trouble," the nurse said.

"I don't understand," I said. The smile that I had welcomed earlier vacated her face, and a stern look moved in.

"You held her hand," she said. My mind wandered to my first- and second-year interactions with Brenda. For a moment, I had doubts about my sincerity. I brushed it off.

"We're classmates," I said.

"There's more to it," she said.

"I'll stay away," I said. I wanted the discussion to end. I needed my job.

"Please be careful," she said, and left the room. I picked up my backpack, clocked out, and walked toward the exit door. A nurse pushed a surgical tray out into my path. A blood-stained scalpel and gauzes. My pace quickened until I exited the emergency room.

Chapter 2

NOW IN THE SUMMER after my second year of medical school, I was holding down two jobs. One as an emergency room assistant, or orderly. I also worked in the library. I was a 23-year-old man wasting beautiful summer days, but I needed two jobs to survive, and to save for the times I could not work during the academic year. The only resource I had was me.

Sitting in the emergency room lounge, I read my novel and watched my co-workers eat their snacks during a midmorning break. Five minutes before the end of my break, I was the only one left in the lounge. I unzipped my backpack to retrieve my peanut butter sandwich. It was the only meal I could afford, and the one the lunch group criticized most. After repeated negative comments, I had resorted to leaving my snack hidden.

When my four-hour shift was over, at ten, I bought flowers from the hospital gift shop, then walked a block to the church cemetery. Kneeling, I placed the flowers on my parents' graves. I reached inside my pocket for my handkerchief and wiped the dust off the inscription on my father's headstone: 'My journey has ended, but not yours.' The last thing he said to me before his death. I left the cemetery after a five-minute visit.

The parking lot outside my apartment was almost empty. The summer vacation had started, only two cars remained. A university apartment was my home. I had no family left. For the first time in three weeks, I checked my mailbox. I picked up a letter and entered my apartment. An empty pizza box was on the coffee table. I felt too tired to clean up. Sitting on the couch, I opened the envelope.

Dear Mr Ava,

I am pleased to inform you that you have been selected by the committee as the recipient of the Tennessee Medical Scholarship.

It was the only part of the letter I read, before I fell on the floor of my apartment and cried, tears of joy and sadness. Thinking about how much the scholarship money would help me, I cried more. I thought about taking the letter to the cemetery to share the good news with my parents. After opening the door to leave my apartment, I became worried about my plan. A trip to the cemetery to share a letter with two dead people. Mom and Dad. Remembering Brenda's physical state in the emergency room, I worried that I would not know if I was going crazy. I walked into the bathroom to look at myself in the mirror. Searching for clues of insanity.

Returning to the living room, I stood in front of the framed picture of my parents. I remembered their funerals. Mom was an only child, and so was Dad. No uncles or aunties to attend their funerals. My mother was taken away from me by a stroke, and my father gave up on life because of my mother's death. My father wished for his death, said a few words to me before he went to sleep—three months after my mother died—and did not wake up. I was left with no family. Ben Ava, a man alone.

After I reviewed the details of the award letter, I called the office of the 'Awards Chairman'.

"Hello," a sweet voice said to me. A woman's voice with a Southern accent. I was elated, so everything I heard sounded good.

"Hi. I received a letter for a scholarship. I need to see Dr

Crumble," I said.

"What's your name, Hon?"

"Ben Ava. It's about my scholarship."

"Let me ask him." The phone went dead. I whistled out of excitement, but stopped when I remembered that it was a call about something important. My scholarship. I could not afford to lose the opportunity because of bad behavior.

"Bad behavior, Ben," I said to myself, barely audibly. Elation was getting the best of me.

"Excuse me," a male voice said over the phone.

"I'm sorry, Sir. I didn't know you were on the phone," I said. My hands trembled.

"Are you on campus?" Before I could answer, he added, "Come over." The receiver went dead. I dialed the office number again to clarify the location.

I ran from the residence tower to the university medical center four blocks away. It took me less than five minutes. I opened the office door, panting. Sweat dribbled down my face. A middle-aged woman stood by her desk. A smile and a wink, as if she knew me.

"You're Ben?" she asked. I nodded. "Dr Crumble just left. He forgot his meeting with the dean," she added. I watched her eyes look all over me. I knew I was sweating, and hoped she wouldn't form a negative opinion. The secretary telling Dr Crumble that I was not worthy of the scholarship crossed my mind.

"I ran as fast as I could," I said.

"Not your fault. He forgot," she said.

"I guess I have to wait for him?" I asked. I looked around for a place to sit.

"No. You're going to Memphis."

"I know. My letter said so."

"You're leaving today," she stood up from her chair as she spoke.

"Today? Oh my! I don't know anyone in Memphis," I said. I thought about my two jobs and my depleted bank account.

"I'm working on your dorm housing," she said. She paced around her desk.

"I've never been to Memphis."

"You'll love Memphis. Beale Street and the Blues."

"You're right. I'm feeling blue already." The words just came out my mouth. Thinking about what I said, I felt bad. Sabotaging my own future. I watched for a reaction from her, but no frown appeared on her face. I sighed.

"You're funny," she smiled with her mouth open. I was surprised. I'd expected a negative comment from her, and a different reaction.

"I don't have any money," I said. I noticed that I was wringing my hands while speaking. I stopped it and put my hands in my pocket.

"We'll pay for your temporary housing," she said. I sighed again, loud enough that I felt embarrassed. I tried to smile, making a deliberate effort to hide my anxiety.

"How about my apartment? My things?" I asked.

"I'll cancel your lease."

"I can't take all my stuff at once; my car is too small."

"You start a three-month rotation tomorrow, with another student from here. We'll keep your place for two weeks," she said.

"So, I'm going with a classmate?" I asked.

"Privacy issue. Can't tell you."

"I'm messing up again. Need to mind my own business."

"It's privacy protection. The new thing."

"What do I tell my girlfriend?" I asked. She looked at me, shook her head, and sat down.

"Take her with you," she said with a chuckle.

"I don't think so. She can't," I said. My hands came out of my pockets.

"Tell her you're leaving," she said.

My voice was bitter. "I wasn't planning to leave without telling her," I said, offended by her insensitive insinuation.

"I didn't mean it that way."

"I'm running up to the third floor to tell her," I said, walking away from her desk.

She rose from her chair. "A student?" she asked.

"A surgery resident."

"Good luck to you. Enjoy Memphis," she said. She left her desk, and walked toward me.

"I need the luck, Ma'am. And a prayer, too," I said.

Her phone rang twice, but had stopped ringing by the time she reached her desk. I stood by her office door, reluctant to leave. Several things weighed on my mind. What to say to my girlfriend? How would she react to my missing her fast-approaching thirtieth-birthday celebration? I would be moving away from my parents. I worried about leaving their graves unattended. While standing there, I thought about turning down the scholarship, explaining that I could not leave my dead parents. I wondered what my father would have advised me to do. Without the scholarship money, completing my medical school would be difficult. Even impossible. I knew that the thought of giving up the scholarship was irrational. If I continued to deliberate on irrational ideas, I would jeopardize my medical education, causing irreparable damage to my future.

While still watching me, the secretary picked up her phone. She dialed some numbers before she laid the phone down. I was still standing by the door, confused about what to do next.

"Your letters will be ready in an hour," she said.

"Letters?" I asked.

"For your housing and registration."

"An hour? I'll be here," I said. I left the office.

* * *

On my way to the surgical center, I went through the hallway leading to the emergency room. The place I was scheduled to work the following day. Due to the overwhelming exuberance from my scholarship award, I had conveniently forgotten my work schedule. My prior commitment. The thought of going to the emergency room for an abrupt resignation made me feel sick to my stomach. None of the words I recited in my head while standing in the hallway sounded good. The truth about why I needed to quit suddenly did not sound convincing. It was disheartening when the truth did not sound honest. I decided to let the university administration inform my employers about their decision. I walked a few steps to the elevator.

The elevator door slid open as I approached it. I was happy. There was no time available to waste. I entered the elevator and pushed the button for the third floor. My destination: the physicians' surgical lounge.

Exiting on the third floor, I passed several surgery residents, but not the one I was there to see. Deborah. Deb. Everyone seemed to be in a hurry. There was no opportunity to ask any of the surgery residents if they'd seen my girl. I left the lounge to search for the person with all the information, the ward secretary.

Walking to the secretary's desk, my heart pounded. I shortened my step, thought about what to say to Deb, and looked around the waiting area. I stopped walking as the right words to use to explain my plight to Deb continued to elude me. From a short distance away, I saw Kim, the secretary, watching me. Aimlessly standing in the middle of the surgery center's waiting room, I became worried about Kim's opinion on my mental state. A deranged man. I approached her desk without further hesitation.

"Hi Kim," I said.

"Paying us a visit again."

"You know I won't stay away for too long," I said.

"She's doing a case in room five. Just went in." Kim stood up from her chair and took a few steps down the hall. "Looks like everyone has gone in," she added.

"Not my lucky day," I said. I checked my watch for the current time and sighed. It summed up how I felt at that moment.

"Something urgent?" she asked.

"I'm leaving today. She needs to know." I looked around the hallway hoping that Deborah would come out of room five. She did not. Another drawn-out sigh from me.

Kim lifted her telephone and dialed some numbers. "Dr Linger's boyfriend is here. Can she talk?" After her query, her face looked distraught—she held the telephone receiver to her ear. "OK. I'll let him know." She hung up the phone. She looked at me as if she was about to say something, then hesitated. Things did not look good. I was dying from anticipation.

"What did she say?" I asked.

"She'll call you after her case." It was not what I expected Kim to say. I had expected a rebuke from Deborah for showing up during their busy hours. I reasoned that Kim probably withheld hurtful words from Deborah. Whatever Deborah said could not change anything. I was going to Memphis and had to accept the consequences.

"I'll leave a note. Let me borrow your pen. Paper too," I said.

"All yours, Romeo," she said. Her smile made me feel at ease. Observing Kim's exuberance, I felt that things would work out between Deb and me.

"Thanks for the paper and pen," I said.

"Anytime."

"One more thing, I never could write well standing up."

Kim nodded to the chair next to her. I pulled it out and sat down.

I held the pen and looked at the blank paper for over a minute. I wondered where to start to tell Deborah about my good news, and its consequences. Most importantly, my relocation to Memphis. After pondering over her possible reactions to my written words, I resolved that telling her how much I'd miss her would sound insincere. It would be better to start with the good news first, and figure the rest out afterward.

Kim watched me write. As I began my third line she tried to read my note. She smiled when our eyes met. Busted. I adjusted my sitting position to block her view. Instead of complaining about her intrusive eyes, I deprived her of the opportunity to snoop. She stood up and tried to look over my shoulder by walking behind me. She was the only person who could deliver my note to Deb, so I did not complain about her intrusion. When she came closer, I worried about her reading my note to Deb. She was curious enough to do it.

In a hospital environment, gossiping is one of the prescribed hobbies embraced by everyone. No one has developed immunity to it. My worry was justified. It would not bode well for me if Deb learned about my leaving Knoxville through hospital gossip before she read my note. I read the note over.

Hi Deb,

I came by to see you, but you were busy. I received the State of Tennessee Scholarship Award (STSA). I didn't know that the recipients transfer to the Memphis campus when I applied for it. I consider myself fortunate to win the award, but they are sending me to Memphis. I won't be able to do my clinical rotations here.

I leave for Memphis this afternoon. The rush was my fault because I did not check my mailbox for weeks.

Going back to my room to pack. I'll be back at the medical center in an hour to see you. We'll talk then.

I'll be lost without you.

Love,

Ben.

There was no doubt in my mind that it was not the right way to tell Deborah about Memphis, but I had no other choice. How she would react to my note worried me. I read the note many times. Kim watched me. When she put out her hand, I handed her the note. Without hesitating, she walked to the double doors leading to the surgery suites. She handed the note to a nurse walking by. I watched her lips move but could not hear her words. The nurse smiled before she walked away.

"Thanks for everything," I said. Kim smiled.

"You're a good man. Polite. Cheerful," Kim said.

"Stop. My head is getting big," I said. We laughed. Although I complained about her compliments, I wished she would describe me the same way to Deb after she had read my note. I waved to Kim and walked away.

* * *

Later that afternoon, I packed my meager belongings in the trunk and back seat of my Toyota Corolla: a black suitcase, books, pillows, a comforter, loose clothes on hangers, and two pairs of shoes. The one hundred dollars I had withdrawn from an ATM remained in my wallet. According to my calculations, the gasoline to travel to Memphis would require most of it.

It was close to noon when I returned to the medical center. I took the elevator to the outpatient surgery lounge. I looked around the surgery center for Deb. Kim, the secretary, was standing with two nurses when I walked in. They were discussing a piece of paper in Kim's hand and talking. After checking physician workstations and not finding Deb, I approached the secretary's desk. No smiles. The two nurses walked away, and Kim ignored me. I wondered what Deborah had told them. Kim picked up her phone and placed a call. Looking at the frown on her face, I imagined that Kim did not want to deliver Deb's bad news to me. I stepped away from her desk.

I stood against the wall opposite the surgery schedule board. There were four names listed below the staff column and a note: 'Third year medical students to start surgery rotation on July 15.' Three weeks after the Memphis program would start. Ben Ava was third on the list and Brenda Galant was at the bottom. I was happy to see Brenda's name, but sad that I would not get to see her and talk about her emergency-room visit. Most importantly, to discuss the purpose of going to the park with a scalpel and a scarf early in the morning. My thoughts wandered to the privacy issue. Brenda's right to her privacy and my interference. If not contained, my meddling in Brenda's affair would betray me someday.

While waiting for Kim to get off the phone, I thought about the fun I could have had with Deb at the surgery center if I did my surgery clerkship with her. The more I thought about things, the more I began to worry about the effect of the separation on our relationship. My stomach felt queasy. I felt warm all over. My heart pounded.

I whistled, hummed, and moved my body to songs that played in my head while I waited. After I ran out of gimmicks to occupy my mind, I counted my losses. A new life, devoid of my past. Abandoning my parents' graves worried me. No one to place flowers. No roses—her favorite flower—for my mother. I felt like an unworthy son. Leaving Deb made me feel like a quitter. It was not too late to change my mind. I could suffer on without a scholarship, and might not even graduate from medical school anyway. While standing against the wall, internal conflicts consumed me. Closing my eyes to reflect on my future, security of employment and finances, Memphis felt like the best option for me. I decided to accept the consequences of my decision: desolation.

Kim ended her telephone conversation, and pulled out her top drawer.

Deb's rejection of my note went through my mind.

"Did you hear me?" Kim asked.

"What?" Apparently I had been lost in my thoughts.

"Here's a note for you. I'm going to lunch." It was a small envelope, with nothing written on the outside. I accepted it from Kim, and made no effort to open it. I thought about Deb being too angry or heartbroken to write my name. Maybe she had resolved to forget about me. I would be expunged from her brain crevices, a mistake that needed to be blotted out. Stupid thoughts going through my mind while the answer was in my hand. I began to worry about my sanity.

"Where's Deb?" Somehow I regained my senses enough to ask the question.

"In surgery. Said you can scrub in when you return."

"I can't. Have to be in Memphis before eight today," I said.

"You better tell her yourself. No one is yelling at me again," Kim said.

"Was she upset?" I asked.

"Leave me out of it," Kim said and walked away. I stood there wondering what to do. However, the excitement of seeing Deb, even from a distance, engulfed me. It was a beautiful feeling. I forgot about the six-hour drive to Memphis and the outcome of arriving after the housing office had closed. Walking toward her operating room, I opened the blank envelope.

Dearest Ben,

It has been two years since we met. I thought you were everything I wanted in a man. Kind, hardworking, ambitious, and crazy sometimes. It was easy for me to become fond of you. Unfortunately, you are leaving for Memphis when I need you the most. Since Mom died, I've gone through many changes and you have supported me emotionally. I am very grateful for your kindness and love, but you have not asked me to be your woman— you've never said, 'let's live together,' or, 'marry me'.

I'll turn 30 next week. You won't even be here. A long-distance relationship is not good for me at this stage of my life. I need to settle down and have children, before it's too late.

This may not be the right way to end our ~~relationship~~ friendship, but I have no other choice unless you have plans for us. Good luck to you in Memphis,

Deborah

After reading the last paragraph of her note, I stood still in the middle of the busy hallway. Blocking the way. Several nurses maneuvered around me to get to their patients. Each looked back after passing me. I saw their raised eyebrows, some even had their mouths agape. Watching the nurses walk by I thought I knew what they thought about me: a self-absorbed clown. As a medical student, I should know better about the need for an unobstructed passageway in a hospital.

How could they know about my situation? My heart was not openly bleeding for anyone to see, but I was experiencing a physical pain. A broken heart. I felt ashamed standing alone, sweating.

"Ben!" I turned around. Deborah, in green surgical scrubs, walked—with a quickened pace—toward me: face taut and no smile, but beautiful. Curly brown hair barely covered by her surgical cap. I hugged her tight and held on.

"I'm sorry, Deb. I didn't mean to hurt you."

"You're cold." She loosened my grip and took a step back. I reached out to hold her hand, but she ignored my gesture. "A goodbye note? After two years of loving your ass? I deserve better than that," she added.

"You were busy when I came." I lowered my voice. I looked around, concerned that we were being watched. Worried about hospital gossip, I added, "Can we go somewhere private?"

"Abandon my patients? Here's good enough," she said.

"Things have been crazy," I said. I tried again to hold her hand. She hesitated initially before she let me. Forgiven? A chance to make our relationship stronger, even with a six-hour separation. I felt good inside.

"Talk about crazy—Memphis is more important to you. Well, good luck to you."

"I need you, Deb."

"That's my boy. Smooth," a physician standing close to us said. He looked at me and smiled. I ignored his intrusion into our private matter.

"Do I mean anything to you?" Deborah asked.

"You're everything to me," I said.

"I'm getting old listening to words. Commitment, that's what I want." She left me, her last word rolling off her tongue. The double doors swung open, and closed behind her. In less than a minute she was beyond my reach. No hugs or kisses. Not even a proper good-bye. I waited for her return. After a five-minute wait, I left for my car. It had my belongings packed in it for the trip to Memphis. An unfamiliar city, and an unknown future.

I entered my car, and turned the radio on. I sat for ten minutes in the parking lot, wishing that my personal life was not falling apart. When I joined I-40 W, the interstate highway going west—leaving my life in Knoxville behind—I thought I had nothing left to lose, until I remembered my sanity. Losing my mind. The ultimate loss. With no one left in my life who cared about me, fear gripped me. Death came first and took away my parents. Now Memphis had come along, teasing me with financial stability, before it kicked away my anchor. My Deb. The price I had to pay to succeed in life. I imagined that there would be more prices to pay, but I was having doubts about my resilience—could I survive alone?

Chapter 3

STRANGE SOUNDS WOKE ME from my sleep—hurried, whimpering sounds. I wondered if I was dreaming, having a nightmare. The sound continued. Barely awake, I felt disoriented inside a room only large enough for a twin bed and a reading table. It was the type of space I had seen people confined in against their will, comparable to a prison cell. Inside that small space, I felt mentally trapped. The feeling had come over me before I fell asleep.

As my eyes wandered around the room, a full moon appeared, suspended outside my window, watching me in the darkness of my room. Fear gripped me, even though I remembered locking my door before I set the alarm. It was my first night in living quarters chosen for me by strangers, people in the medical school administration.

By the time I was alert enough to reason, the crying had stopped, making it impossible to locate the source. Although I felt happy that the person's pain had been resolved, I became worried when I thought about the other possibility— succumbing to the ailment.

I sat by the side of my bed and rubbed my eyes, as if better vision—seeing through the walls— would enable me to locate the source of the crying. Silence reigned as I placed my hands on my knees, thinking about Deb. My eyes focused on the moon watching me from my window, and curiosity propelled me to the edge of the window. I put on my robe and stood facing Madison Street.

A full moon, and street lights, illuminated a small park across the way. I remembered Brenda and her puzzling early morning visit to a Knoxville park with a scalpel. My eyes searched for things to take my mind away from Brenda. Compared to the full moon, the subdued yellow street lights looked like props on a movie set. On the right side of my window, the street appeared to end at a bridge, with two signs that read 'Entering West Memphis' and 'Goodbye to Tennessee'. The two signs reminded me of my life, roiled by confusion about the direction of my relationship and my exuberance about my academic scholarship, two events that nullified each other. A forecast of my future in Memphis, perhaps. A life of no progress.

While trying to forget about the bridge, and the signs on it, my attention was drawn to the cascades of water below the bridge—a glistening surface with a reflection of the moon that swayed from side to side, each swing opposite the preceding one. I closed my eyes and imagined Deb standing next to me, holding my hand. Kissing me, and bringing stability to my life.

My eyes opened. Still standing by my window, I had forgotten why I was awake. Looking at the river again, it appeared as if it stood still. With dulled vision, I could no longer see it flow. The Mississippi River captivated my clouded senses while I searched for the source of the puzzling sounds. I wondered if I was losing my mind. Weird sounds that woke me up, and a river that was standing still. Trying to alleviate my concern, I decided that, in the dark and from a distance, I should not fully trust my perception. I concluded that the noise I heard was probably a dream. My cry for Deb.

I was about to return to my bed when I noticed a figure standing next to a bench in the park, across from my dormitory on Madison Street. I moved closer to the window, pressing my face against the glass pane to improve my vision. The man undressed and dressed repeatedly. Indecisive, it appeared. I thought about all the things that could have gone wrong in his life. A broken heart and loneliness came to mind. It could be someone just like me.

Emotionally stranded in the park that night, I wondered who was responsible for the stranger. While feeling sorry for myself, and for the stranger in the park, the thought of his cry waking me up crossed my mind. A cry that could transcend the distance between the stranger in the park and six floors above the level of the street, had to be a loud one. Not a whimper. Accepting that the sounds I heard could not have come from the park, I looked around my room and under my bed for an answer. No stowaway, or hidden electronic gadgets. Panic stricken, I could not decide what to do next. Was I losing my mind?

As I wasted time pondering upon inanities, the sign in front of the bank next to the park recorded a temperature of 85 degrees, and displayed the fact that it was 1:15 am. It felt as if I had been standing by my window for hours.

"Somebody help me. Please help me. Please." I heard a female voice, barely audible through the wall.

I was awake, and it was not a dream. Walking to my desk, I picked up my phone. My hands trembled, and my fingers could not steady the phone to dial three numbers, 911. My breathing became shallow and rapid. The pleading stopped, and an eerie silence followed. Things were so quiet that I could hear my breathing. My sweaty hand gripped the phone tightly, but it almost slipped away. A 23-year-old man, a medical student, afraid because of a crying girl.

Remembering my role as a medical professional, I felt the fear being expelled from my body by the profuse sweating. A sudden rush of courage propelled me to my door. I swung it open. After looking around the dark, windowless common living area of the coed suite, as if I could see in the dark, I stepped out of my room. Approaching the room next to mine, I knocked on the door. While waiting for a response, I thought about the risk I was taking—venturing out of my room without concern for my safety. What if someone broke into the dormitory? Whistling, out of fear, I stood waiting by the door as my heart raced. I tried to build the courage to face tribulations.

After a barrage of knocks, I thought about calling campus security. However, my ego stood in the way. The thought of doing heroic things went through my mind. It swelled my head and took away my fear, until I thought about the possibility of dying confronting a dangerous robber. I was standing in the dark, physically vulnerable. The more I thought about my foolishness the more my legs trembled.

The door swung open forcefully. Terrified, I jumped back. A face covered with night cream peered at me.

"I'm Ben. A medical student. Just moved here."

"Idiot," she said.

She turned her lights on and leaned on the door frame. With the lights on, I could see a nightgown hanging from her body. But for the glisten of her sunken eyeballs, she had a twiggy, scarecrow look. She grimaced, a peculiar look on a face covered with white cream.

"Sorry to bother you. I heard cries from your room," I said.

She stepped away from the door frame and held the knob.

"You're nuts," she said.

"I'm sorry, lady," I said.

"Name's Brenda, you retard. Your fucking classmate."

I took a step forward to look at her face, realizing that the voice sounded familiar. Once I realized who it was, I shook my head. The thought of my medical school classmate stalking me crossed my mind, until I remembered the secretary's statement about two medical students being posted to the Memphis campus.

"Brenda! I didn't recognize you. You're here too?" I extended my trembling hand to her. A request. An apology. She ignored my gesture. No handshake. "I heard cries. Thought it came from here," I added.

"You're here to rescue me?" she asked.

"My mistake. I'm sorry," I said, loudly—more loudly than I wanted to. I checked her hands for a scalpel, trying to engage her eyes as I spoke, but she bowed her head, perhaps out of fear or shame.

"I'm grateful you're worried about me. Not like a week ago. You didn't give a shit," she said.

"You're wrong. I did care, but I was confused. Why did you need a scalpel in the park?" I asked. She looked at me with piercing eyes, staring, her lips puckered. Sweat dripped down her forehead. No tears. Just a growl before she closed her door.

"I was working that day. Transporting a patient. You left before I came back," I added, hoping that she heard me behind the closed door.

I stood where Brenda had left me, and lifted my hand several times to knock on her closed door—but could not find the courage to face her wrath, or her scalpel. I believed that she was standing close to her door. I heard her breathing, her panting, and imagined her holding a scalpel ready to charge. I took two steps away from her door.

The closed door separated us. Even her panting stopped. Silence from the other side of the door, and worries on my side. The scalpel and folded scarf occupied my thoughts. Her safety concerned me, as did my own. I took more steps away from her door. My body trembled with trepidation, but, when I heard no sounds coming from her room, my heart felt riddled with guilt. Did she do it? I heard no cry of pain. I sighed.

If she came out of her room, I resolved to ease my guilt, but the thought of easing my guilt made me feel worse about myself. I thought about supportive words to use. Colorful words, delivered with compassion.

From under Brenda's door, I saw her lights go off, heard the shuffling of feet inside. Maybe it was my imagination, but I had heard something. She probably knew I was standing outside her door. Embracing darkness, she shut me out of her life. It was not Deb. Not a love affair. I tried to stop analyzing everything. She had just turned off the light in her room. That was all that had happened. I sighed in relief.

Taking more steps away from Brenda's door, I felt chills, a weakness, and sleepiness too. I opened my door. Going in, I yawned. I sat down and looked at the wall that separated Brenda and me. I had no access to her, physically or mentally. How she would fare for the night depended on her. I felt nauseous.

I turned my desk lamp on, to shed light on my life, my inadequacies. Two envelopes were on my desk. I opened the envelope from the Student Financial Aid office.

Dear Mr Ava,

I am pleased to inform you that you have been selected by the committee as the recipient of the Tennessee Medical Scholarship. After an evaluation of your academic records and non-cognitive skills, the committee members feel that you have the potential to succeed in academic medicine. The committee recommends your transfer to the main campus in Memphis, effective this academic year. You will be assigned a mentor by the dean.

The chairman of the committee extends to you an invitation to meet with him before your third-year clinical assignments.

Please feel free to contact this office if you desire further information.

Very truly yours,

Ollie Crumble, MD, Chair of the Committee

The letter left out my immediate responsibility: keeping watch on my dormitory neighbor, Brenda. I closed my eyes to forget my worries. My thoughts returned to the emergency room in Knoxville. A sharp surgical scalpel and a folded scarf. I survived my meddling in Brenda's life that night. Only time would tell whether my decision not to call 911 was right or wrong. I crawled into my bed and stared at the ceiling for guidance.

While lying in bed, sleep and wakefulness became one entity in me. I could no longer separate dream and reality. I heard another cry, "Please help me. Please." In the state my mind was in, I couldn't figure out who was pleading for help, but one of us needed help that night—Brenda, or me.

Chapter 4

THE FOLLOWING DAY, before sunrise, I walked for a mile on the streets close to the medical center, getting lost in dead ends and finding my way. After crossing a street, I stopped to read a sign on a liquor store: 'The liver is evil, so it has to be punished.' A philosophy and a scientific declaration. The liquor store acknowledged a vice but blamed the liver, instead of the drinker. What twisted logic. It probably supported some of the customers' beliefs: don't blame yourself for your actions—you were compelled to do it. I admired the ingenuity of the business owner. A phrase to encourage the customers to continue drinking without feeling guilty—one guaranteed to boost sales.

I crossed another street and followed a path to the hospital along a one-way street. After climbing steep steps, I found my way to the hospital lobby, a bustling, expansive space. Uncluttered, it was decorated with colorful carpets, sturdy chairs, and tables, all arranged within an array of glass roofs and walls. A welcoming sight.

I stopped at the registration desk. A middle-aged woman was on the phone with her profile turned to me. She glanced at me.

"I'm on hold," she said. She picked up a clipboard and handed it over to me. I took it and looked it over.

"I'm Ben Ava. A medical student, not a patient," I said.

"Badge and locker assignment, next door," she said, and pointed to a room. It was my first encounter with a worker at the medical center, and I felt unwelcome.

After obtaining my badge, I walked to the meeting room

designated in my orientation papers, 'Conference Room A'.

The conference room was littered with empty pizza boxes and leftover doughnuts. Brenda was sitting alone in a desk chair with wheels. An emaciated woman. I wanted to ask if she'd had breakfast. Her blue eyes darted around without looking at my face. Surprised to see Brenda there, I stepped outside to confirm the room number. She watched me with a frown on her face. Returning to the conference room, I pushed the trash aside and sat next to her. She stretched her hands on the desk and fidgeted with her bracelet, a winged ankh. Instead of thinking about the meaning of her bracelet, I remembered a scalpel and a folded scarf, they seemed contradictory. Thinking about Brenda's behavior the night before, I rolled my chair away from her. A safe distance.

Brenda looked at me, sighing repeatedly. She shook her head after her last sigh. Remembering that she'd accused me of indifference the previous night, I avoided looking at her. I fixed my eyes on a clock on the wall. The second hand on the clock stood still. I looked at my watch. Eight o'clock on a Tuesday morning by my watch. Twelve o'clock was displayed on the broken clock. Midnight, or noon. I could not tell. Time stood still for the clock on the wall, the way my life felt to me sitting next to Brenda.

"You hate me, don't you?" she asked. She took her bracelet off and placed it on the table.

A physician, about my height—six-foot-tall with a medium-built frame—walked in with two medical students. He looked at Brenda and me. He shook his head as he looked at the trash on the table.

"We're busy this morning," the physician said. No further

introduction. He approached me and shook my hand. Brenda looked at him, but he ignored her. I read his hospital badge and sighed.

"I'm Ben Ava. This is Brenda. We're from the eastern campus," I said. He nodded at Brenda. I wanted to ask him to shake Brenda's hand, but could not muster the courage. A brave act that could end my medical education, and my desire to become a physician. A risk I could not afford to take.

Brenda's lips quivered. It was difficult to decipher if she was angry. I thought perhaps it was bashfulness, but I knew that I would have been angry if I was her. Rolling my chair around to control my anger, I avoided looking at the physician.

"I'll be your attending for the month. You'll see patients with the residents," Dr Ezekiel Trophy said. He kept his eyes on Brenda while he spoke.

"We haven't met the residents," I said.

"They'll be here soon," Dr Trophy said.

The two students that had come with him sat down. Walking to the end of the conference room, he picked up a phone and dialed. Holding the receiver to his ear, he said, "Dr Trophy here. I want this damn conference room cleaned." He hung up and left. The four of us remaining in the room looked at each other.

"He's temperamental," a medical student said.

"He's a jackass," Brenda said. Her face lit up, eyes bulging.

"No one is like him. The rest are fruitcakes," another male student said. His eyeglasses adorned a pimpled face, and his bow tie clasped a wrinkled collar. He looked at Brenda and added, "Real men are not temperamental."

"He's something, all right," I said. I wheeled my chair closer to the two medical students. "You guys from main campus?" I asked.

"Yes. I'm James Henner," one said. James reminded me of a weightlifter. Physically fit and about my height.

"We're new in town," I said. The other medical student deferred his introduction. A short, pudgy fellow. Looking at me, he frowned. I rolled my chair away from him.

Brenda looked at us from a distance. I had expected her to join us, but she acted as if she had no interest in meeting the boys from Memphis, our classmates. While I was looking at Brenda and making faces at her to invite her into the conversation, James retrieved a pair of earbuds from his pocket. I looked at his music playlist. None of the songs were familiar. James watched me shake my head while looking at his selection of music.

"We'll check out Beale Street. Introduce you to Memphis. Good music," James said. He twiddled with his earbuds, placing a bud in one ear. I was amazed that he could carry on a conversation while listening to music. He rhythmically tapped the shoulder of the student sitting next to him. He pushed James away and rolled his chair closer to me.

"Not from here. Germantown," the other medical student said.

I read his badge, while ignoring his pimpled face. Andrew Smith III. A friendly gem, I surmised. Andrew Smith III sat close to me, but did not make eye contact. Looking at his bow tie, I worked hard to avoid laughing.

"We'll discover Germantown too," I said. James laughed.

"There's nothing in Germantown. Just houses," Andrew said. He pushed James' shoulder, causing the chair he sat in to travel a short distance away from Andrew.

"I'm looking for a good spa," Brenda said. I laughed.

"A spa?" I asked. I could not stop laughing. It did not occur to me that Brenda was the spa type.

"My wife should know," James said.

"You're married?" I asked.

"For a year. Had to. She almost left me," James said. He laughed.

"Can't afford to," I said.

"You have a girl?" James asked.

Before I could answer James' question, two resident physicians walked in. A wiry man about my height, probably in his early thirties, and a healthy-looking woman of average height. I was relieved. The doctors saved me from lying to him.

"I'm Dr Peterson. I'll take two students. The rest will go with Nancy, Dr Nancy Dowd." He looked around the room. I wondered how he would decide who to pick from one girl and three boys. A Germantown boy, two regular boys, and one emaciated girl. A winged ankh girl.

"I'll go with the senior resident," Andrew said, with confidence. He walked to Dr Peterson and offered him his hand. Dr Peterson ignored it. I smiled.

"Brenda, go with Dr Peterson," I said.

"Don't make decisions for me," Brenda said. I smiled because I did not know what to say.

"I'll take the two of you," Dr Peterson said, pointing at Brenda and me.

"The rest of you, come with me," Dr Dowd said.

Brenda scowled as we left the conference room. I smiled.

She probably didn't want to work with me, but she had no choice. Remembering how well we worked together in anatomy class as cadaver partners, I wondered what had happened to our budding friendship.

*   *   *

After our tour of the medical center with the senior resident, we returned to the conference room where Dr Trophy was waiting for us, his coffee mug and laptop were nestled on the table. His left hand caressed the mug, while he maneuvered the laptop mouse with his right. We stood by the door and talked about patients. He ignored us. After a while, Dr Peterson led us to the conference table. The two resident doctors, and we four medical students, sat down across from the attending physician. His eyes focused on his laptop screen. We watched him fondle his coffee mug. Whispers and sighs from us, surprising silence from the attending physician. Watching the resident physicians sit and wait for the attending physician, I began to appreciate the enormity of Dr Trophy's authority.

Minutes passed. I resorted to hand gestures to my classmates. The prince amongst us, Dr Peterson, the senior resident, watched me without intervention, sitting silently with the rest of us. I presumed that only the anointed could speak to the entranced demigod, the attending physician. Our whispers became louder. Dr Trophy ignored us.

"We can come back later," Dr Peterson said. Dr Trophy looked at him for less than a second, then his eyes returned to his computer. Mouse and mug activities resumed, fondling with the left hand, and twirling with the right. We looked at each other. I laughed. Dr Trophy looked at me and frowned.

The look on his face made me feel that I had disrespected his authority. A punishable offense? His eyes returned to his laptop, and I bowed my head.

"Interesting cases?" Dr Trophy asked. His hands moved away from their previous activities. He briefly tapped on the table with his fingers, before closing his laptop, and pushing it to the center of the table. He took a sip from his mug and resumed the fondling. I tried hard not to laugh.

Dr Peterson flipped through the papers on his clipboard.

"Eighty-year-old—failure to thrive. The rest are routine," Dr Peterson said.

"Who's starving the patient?" Dr Trophy asked. A smile on his face. A changed man, I assumed.

"Not sure," Dr Dowd said. Her facial expression was unchanged. If she had a desire to smile like Dr Trophy at that moment, she hid it from us.

"Has a medical student been assigned to the patient? Not the anorexic girl, I hope?" Dr Trophy asked. He looked at Brenda. No one answered. I looked around the room. No angry-looking faces, except for Brenda's. I saw Dr Peterson close his eyes. I thought he would be the one to speak up. An advocate for powerless medical students.

Brenda's eyes shed tears. I remembered our closeness in the past. Spending all day together like we were family. A brother and a sister. I closed my eyes, but I still heard Brenda sniveling.

My anger grabbed my throat and tried to suffocate me. I squirmed, and gasped for air. I seethed, and wiped my sweat. I turned to Brenda. Our eyes met. She wiped away her tears.

Andrew smiled. His pimples staring at me. I thought about

poking his pimples to let the vile pus out of them.

I closed and opened my eyes.

Andrew was still smiling. I thought about more things to do to him. None good.

"I'll wipe that stupid smile off your face," I said to Andrew. He wheeled his chair away from me. Dr Trophy frowned. I had defiled his authority twice. I worried that, the next time I chose to be cavalier, I would not survive.

"My talk is at six. Flanagan's bar and grill. Don't be late," Dr Trophy said.

"Students too?" Andrew asked.

"It's mandatory," Dr Trophy said.

"I'll excuse myself," Brenda said.

"No dice. You need the food," Dr Trophy said. His wife must not often smile, I thought.

"I'll go with you," I said to Brenda.

"I don't need you," Brenda said. Dr Peterson smiled.

"Let's do the rounds," Dr Trophy said.

Dr Trophy pushed his mug away, stood up, and left the conference room. We followed him, taking a stroll behind the attending physician. I thought of a suitable name for him: 'the jackass of medicine'.

A few steps away from the conference room, Dr Peterson's telephone rang. He slowed his pace to take the call, walking behind me.

"I can't stand Dr Trophy," Brenda said. She tried to whisper, but her voice cracked. James, who was ahead of us, looked around.

"He's world-renowned. We're lucky to have him," James said.

"Pile of trash, hates women," Brenda said.

"He's a good old boy," James said.

"He tried to hurt me. I won't let him," Brenda said. Everyone ahead of us turned around.

"You're too loud," I said.

"Fuck you, Ben." Brenda grabbed my coat. I turned to look at her. Her penetrating pair of blue eyes rolled around in their sockets as if she was twisting a scalpel inside my body. I licked my lips.

"Feisty girl. My type of woman," James said. Looking at James' bulk and Brenda's bones, I tried to silence my laugh.

"I'm tired of your crap," Brenda said, pointing her finger at me.

"I am trying to help your ass," I said.

Dr Peterson caught up with us. He placed his phone in his pocket as he passed Brenda and me.

"Medical students, stay close to the attending," Dr Peterson said, when he turned around.

"No one told us," I said.

"It's common sense," Dr Peterson said.

We entered a patient's room. Dr Trophy stood by a woman's bedside. His eyes wandered to the night stand. A cross, a rosary, and a bottle labeled 'holy water'. I thought about the objects. Religious paraphernalia. Instruments of faith, and power. Power beyond that of the demigod, the attending physician. He looked at me, and his face crinkled. Afraid that Dr Trophy could read my mind, I looked away.

"Faith's good, but you need food. A good doctor too. I'm here to help," Dr Trophy said.

"God's first," the patient said. Everyone laughed, except for Dr Trophy, who winced.

"We're God's helpers," Dr Trophy said. The rest of us looked at each other.

He lifted her hospital gown to conduct the physical examination without a formal request and placed his stethoscope on various parts of her body. He gave her instructions on when to breathe. We stood and watched. Having completed the physical examination, Dr Trophy looked around the room and rested his eyes on Brenda.

"Common causes of elderly failure to thrive?" Dr Trophy asked.

"Starvation," Brenda said.

"Third-grade answer. We know they starve, but why?"

"Because of illnesses or physical limitations," I said.

"I didn't ask you. Brenda, tell us why you starve," Dr Trophy said.

"I don't, Sir," Brenda said. Her teeth clenched, and the skin on her face taut.

"How's our patient different from anorexics like Brenda?" Dr Trophy asked. Dr Peterson looked at Brenda and sighed. I looked away.

"I'm not sure what you mean," Dr Peterson said.

"A senior resident? What happened to residency training?" Dr Trophy asked.

"I'm not sure what you're saying. I'm not anorexic," Brenda said.

"Anorexics hate food," Andrew said, his face beaming with a smile. I walked closer to Andrew. His smile faded away.

"Anorexics self-starve, but our patient lacks access to food,"

Dr Dowd said.

"You don't seem to have that problem," Dr Trophy said. Dr Dowd buttoned her white coat. "Ask a social worker to check her living conditions," Dr Trophy added.

"They've been consulted," Dr Dowd said.

"Anorexics hate their body and have low self-esteem. It's a psychological problem. They need intervention. Our patient needs food," Dr Trophy said.

Brenda walked away from the group. I followed her, and James trailed me. After a few steps, she sat on a chair in the hallway. Her tears flowed, and her nose ran. I sat down and put my arms around her. She pushed me, and scooted away. She created space between us. James walked up to Brenda. He placed his hand on her shoulder, rolled his wedding ring around with his thumb. She ignored him. He sighed, and tried to walk away—before turning around, and sitting next to her. His hand patted her hair. She nestled her head on his shoulder. They acted as if they had known each other for a long time. Two strangers. It was difficult for me to accept that she was the same woman that had rejected my attempt at closeness. I felt nauseated and walked away.

* * *

That evening, sitting in the dining area of the bar and grill, I held a glass of tonic water and leaned back on my chair. I watched the attendees come in. They stopped at the pharmaceutical company display tables. After reading drug pamphlets, most of the attendees took the free pens and notepads emblazoned with company logos from the table, before finding a place to sit.

Dr Trophy displayed the summary page of his lecture on the screen. A pharmaceutical company logo, the sponsor of the lecture, graced the page. I looked around the restaurant as more people came in, almost every dinner table had pens and notepads displayed on it. An advertisement for the pharmaceutical company disguised as a lecture. Dr Trophy serving as the paid spokesperson.

Brenda and James sat next to each other. She poured red wine beyond the brim of her glass. James dabbed the spill off the table. I heard her whisper, "Thank you." She lifted the wine glass and sucked it dry.

We waited for the lecture to start, but the wine flowed instead. Brenda guzzled the red liquid as soon as James filled her glass. After more than three glasses, her laugh got louder, and James' face beamed with a smile. He removed his wedding ring and placed it on the table. I became worried about their apparent closeness. The waitress replenished the empty bottles on all the tables. From where I sat, it appeared as if the older physicians congregated at the same table. They had more empty bottles of wine, and wiped their lips after each sip.

James' phone rang. He placed his wine glass on the table and answered it. His voice was a whisper as he placed his wedding ring on his finger. As his voice became louder, he stood up and walked toward the bathroom. Brenda looked at me. She smiled, her first friendly gesture toward me. I transferred to the chair vacated by James.

Brenda placed her wine glass on her lips and held it in place for a while, giving the rim of the glass an intimate kiss. She took a sip and, instead of wiping the glass like the old men at the next table, she licked her lips. I looked away.

"I've got to go," I said.

She held her wine glass up and ignored me. James sauntered back to our table. I stood up and vacated his chair. Brenda fixed her eyes on James.

"Get a ride. You're too drunk to drive," I added.

Brenda ignored me. She fixed her eyes on James. Her new friend. I left the restaurant without listening to the lecture. A pharmaceutical company advertisement disguised as a lecture. A waste of time.

* * *

Lying in bed later that night, my phone rang. I placed my hand on the phone, and it stopped ringing. I wrapped my body tightly with the comforter and drifted back to sleep. The phone rang again. I picked up, and held it to my ear. I heard voices.

"You're ignoring my calls. I'm still at the restaurant. Come get me," Brenda said. It was almost midnight.

"Sucking away bottles of wine. Let James drive you," I said.

"His wife came and got him," Brenda said. I laughed.

"Call a taxi. I'm in bed," I said.

"Fine, I'll lie on the floor," Brenda said.

"Go ahead."

"Please help me," Brenda said. She hung up.

I covered my head with my comforter. It did not stop me from thinking about the Knoxville emergency room. Brenda in the park with a scalpel. Fear gripped me. I jumped out of bed.

I retrieved my housecoat and left my room in a hurry. Barefoot. While walking to my car, I stepped on sharp pieces of rock. I regretted not wearing shoes. I was relieved when I got to the driver's seat.

From the rear-view mirror, I saw a police car follow me as I joined Madison Street. Watching the police car in my rear-view mirror, I became worried that the restaurant had called for police assistance because of Brenda. When the police car came too close to my vehicle, I reached in my back pocket to check for my wallet. In my rush to leave, I could have forgotten my driver's license. My hands trembled. The police car turned into a side street. I sighed. The restaurant was one block away, so I continued my journey without my wallet. A violation of the law.

Brenda was standing in front of the restaurant alone. I reached over and opened the passenger's door for her. She hopped into the passenger's side of my car at 12:15 am. She could not reach the door handle to close it. I stepped out of the car and my feet landed on a pile of vomit. There was filth on my bare feet and the stench filled my nostrils. I cringed. I wiped my feet on the sidewalk before I closed the car door for Brenda. She leaned back as I buckled her seat belt. She blew kisses at me, and her breath made me wince.

Brenda's eyes closed, and I could hear her snoring as the car began to move. Without a driver's license on me, I drove for three blocks with a drunk, snoring female passenger. When I turned the car ignition off at our residence hall parking lot, she opened her eyes. I helped her out of the car and held her arm as we walked to the dormitory. While standing in the elevator with her head resting on my shoulder, she began to snore again. She held on to me when we exited the elevator. When we reached her room, she held her door handle and refused to go in.

"I'm scared. Let me stay with you," she said, her speech

slurred. She squinted and wrapped her arms around my neck. I yelped at her grip. Pain traveled down my neck. I dragged her into the room, unwrapping her clutch. I lowered her onto a chair. She closed her eyes. Catching a whiff of her breath, I remembered my soiled feet. The price I paid that night for Brenda. I worried that I could face more challenges with Brenda as long as we lived and worked together.

Filth, alcohol, and stench. My body needed a cleansing. I retreated to the shower stall. Water dripped onto my body; I picked up a bar of soap and lathered my hair. As soap suds covered my face, I held my breath. While my eyes were closed, I felt a pair of hands touch my chest. My body retracted in automatic recoil.

"Shower me," a slurred voice said. It was Brenda. It had not taken too long for another challenge to present itself.

There was a topless drunk woman in my shower. I froze in my nakedness. As her hands traveled down my body, I cupped my loins in my hands. She wobbled. I turned the water off and covered my waist area with a towel. My hands trembled while I helped Brenda to a couch. When she wrapped her arm around my neck—her naked chest on mine—and slobbered in my ear, my heart raced. I felt a throbbing on my wet ear. The possibility of a false accusation of having sex with a drunk woman occupied my mind, and so did the consequences of such an accusation. Expulsion from medical school. Jail time. The dire warning of the emergency nurse was becoming a reality. I ran into my room.

Retrieving a comforter from my room, I returned to the shared area of our suite. I covered her nakedness with the comforter, but it did not stop me from worrying. Lifting her body up, I maneuvered Brenda into her own room and returned to my own.

Lying on my bed, I regretted my decision not to report the incident to the school authorities. I entrusted my future to Brenda's accurate recollection of everything that had happened between us while she was drunk. With no witnesses, Brenda would have to try to explain her naked body and my comforter in the morning. Whether or not she would believe my version of what happened between us was unknown to me. Apprehension kept me awake all night.

Chapter 5

IT BECAME A HABIT THAT, every morning before I left the dormitory, I opened my door, found the remote control, and turned the television on. I was about to return to my room on a cloudy morning and listen to the weather forecast with my room door open, when I saw, 'Breaking news report' flashing on the screen. I perched on a bar stool to watch a 'live broadcast' of placard-carrying protestors in front of a local mosque. Children, teenagers, adults, and the elderly walked around in front of the mosque with signs that read, 'This is America. Muslims go home.' A man wearing a black suit held up a Bible. Drivers passing by honked their horns. Across the street, pedestrians clapped. I switched the television off.

I left my residence hall and took the backstreet leading to the medical center. Four blocks away from the residence hall, I passed Saint Gabriel's Catholic Church. The bulletin board displayed, 'Love everyone as you love yourself.' I crossed the street and walked to the back entrance of the hospital. On the door, a poster read, 'It is against the law to discriminate against people based on their religion (real or perceived).'

I entered the conference room and sat down. Events from the early morning television program weighed on my mind. I can't remember if I said hello to anyone sitting in the conference room. However, I noted that Dr Trophy arrived five minutes late.

"Any deaths?" Dr Trophy asked.

"None," Dr Peterson said.

"Four new admissions and one urgent case," Dr Dowd said.

Dr Trophy walked out of the conference room without asking us to go with him, but we followed him. While rushing to hand the list of patients to Dr Trophy, Dr Dowd tripped. Andrew laughed. I lifted my leg to kick him, then stopped.

As we approached the first patient's room everyone slowed down. I watched Brenda shuffle her feet with her eyes closed. Watching her lips, she appeared to be mumbling, though she was inaudible over the short distance between us. I looked away. I vowed that her problems should not worry me.

"Mister Hassan is a 50-year-old male with chest pain of two hours duration, minimal EKG changes, and normal cardiac enzymes, admitted for observation," Dr Peterson said. We walked into the patient's room.

A bespectacled man sat by the bedside. He caressed his prayer beads and focused his eyes on an open book on a rollaway hospital desk.

"A damn Muslim," Andrew said. James whispered to him. Andrew lifted a clenched fist. I walked closer to James with the thought of pushing his face onto Andrew's fist.

Looking around the patient's room, I saw Dr Trophy smile. I felt angry.

"*As-Salaam-Alaikum,*" I said. Mr Hassan looked up and smiled. Andrew showed his middle finger to me.

"*Wa-Alaikum-Salaam,*" Mr Hassan said. He nodded twice and shook my hand. "Where did you learn Arabic?" he added.

Dr Trophy sneered. As he moved closer to Mr Hassan, he bumped into me. I retrieved my hand from Mr Hassan and stepped aside for Dr Trophy. I thought about not answering Mr Hassan's question. The cardiac monitor alarm sounded. Dr

Trophy's eyes trailed to the cardiac monitor. He appeared distracted by the sound. The patient was awake and smiling.

"I assume the name Hassan is Arabic, so I took a chance. Well, I only know the greeting. I learned from classmates in college," I said, in a hushed voice.

"You're my brother in God. A good man," Mr Hassan said.

"You're my brother too," I said. Dr Trophy turned to me.

"Kiss and make up, you damn know-it-all," Dr Trophy said. He pushed me aside. "Mr Hassan, tell me about your chest pain," he added.

"I woke up with an elephant sitting on my chest," he said. He grimaced as he spoke.

"A camel, you damn Arab," Andrew whispered, standing behind me.

"You need a stress test. If your religion permits it?" Dr Trophy said.

"I don't think Islam discourages medical care," I said. Dr Trophy looked at me again. He scowled. I wondered when he would snap.

"You're right, my friend," Mr Hassan said.

"You'll get your test, Mr Hussain," Dr Trophy said. I opened my mouth to correct him, but did not. Mr Hassan shook his head. Dr Trophy walked out of the room. We followed.

We returned to the conference room. While Dr Trophy was looking through the list of patients, his phone rang. He stepped out of the conference room to take the call.

Brenda dozed off as we waited for Dr Trophy to return. I moved to the chair next to her and touched her side, the way I used to when she fell asleep during anatomy class. She opened her eyes and kicked my legs under the table.

"Keep your hands away from me. Pervert," Brenda said.

"I watched you booze all night. Booze and sleep go together. Headache too," I said.

"I know you had your way with me," Brenda said.

I looked around the room. No one looked up. I sighed. "You wish," I said.

"Too good for you?" Brenda asked, before she kicked me twice. I moved away from her.

Dr Trophy returned. "Respecting your patients is as important as prescribing the best drugs. Respect is universal, and it fosters trust. Please, try to understand your patients' beliefs, and accommodate their ethnic differences. But, don't kiss anybody's ass like Ben did in the patient's room. This is America. We speak English in this country," Dr Trophy said. Everyone in the room looked at me. He slammed his hand on the table.

Brenda jumped from her chair.

"Didn't mean to offend you, Sir," I said.

"Don't pull crap like that again, or it's over for you," Dr Trophy said. He left the room.

We sat and looked at each other for more than five minutes. No one spoke. Dr Peterson stood up and closed the conference room door. Brenda stood up, scratched her neck, and paced around the room. She walked to the door and looked out. She walked back to her chair and sat down. Her legs wiggled, and her eyes darted around the room. Everyone in the conference room watched her. She stood up, walked to the entrance, and placed her hand on the door. As the door opened, she retreated. She turned around and walked toward us.

While passing me, Brenda said, "They'll kick your ass out."

"Your ass first," I said.

"Watch what you say," Dr Peterson said.

"I'm sorry. I don't know what I've done to Brenda," I said.

"I can't stand you. That's what you've done," Brenda said.

"Don't ever call me to pick your drunken ass up again," I said. Dr Peterson looked away.

"Safer for me. Always looking at my bosom," Brenda said.

"I am? At your flat chest? I can do better," I said.

"Screw you," Brenda said.

"Don't want it," I said.

"Enough. I am not running a kindergarten," Dr Peterson said.

"That damn Muslim is responsible for the craziness," Andrew said.

"You're a bigot, you Germantown troll," I said.

"We're still a Christian country, not a perverted caliphate," Andrew said. He grinned.

"Educate yourself," I said.

"We're here to take care of patients. Not politics or religion," Dr Peterson said. He slammed his hand on the table. I thought about his action. Same behavior as Dr Trophy. I became worried about him.

"I agree," I said.

"Let's get back to work," Dr Peterson said.

James plugged in his earbuds, closed his eyes, and nodded his head. He looked soothed, and walked with his eyes closed. I marveled at his calmness. Brenda shuffled her feet, as always. I concluded that we were a gang of misfits.

"Don't hurt the floor," I said. Brenda looked at me and crinkled her lips. I opened my mouth to say something, but did not.

Dr Trophy's words, 'or it's over for you', echoed in my ears. One mistake, and my future in medicine would be over. I walked past Brenda, hoping to survive another day.

Chapter 6

RAIN PATTERING ON MY WINDOW early the next morning woke me up. Winds howled, and hail spattered. A fear of my window blowing away in the wind, leaving me exposed to the gale, gripped me. My hands trembled. I looked out of my window. Swirls of rain encircled the street lamps and wrung the light poles. Lights blinked. From my window, I could not see the river. With the lights by the river out, the Mississippi was shrouded in darkness. Across from my window, the neon bank clock displayed 2:00 am. I crawled back into bed. Lying face down, I covered my ears with my pillow.

I heard a knock at my door. I blinked and lifted the pillow off my head. The rain had stopped. I closed my eyes. Then I heard three knocks on my door. I sprang to my feet. My heart raced. I held myself still. My hands moistened, and my legs trembled. I looked around my room. The door was locked.

"I'm scared. Let me in," Brenda said. I sighed.

"Stay away from me," I said, loudly enough to be heard.

"Help me. Please," she said. I heard a grumble, and her voice lingered in my ear.

Memories of my encounters with Brenda came back to my mind. Bad memories. Not the anatomy class memories. Vivid images of sharp scalpels and a folded scarf. Her half-naked body on a gurney. I remembered how she had once exposed herself in the emergency room, and the night I picked her up from the restaurant—my heart raced. Something worse could happen if I opened my door to her.

When I heard another knock on my door, I reached for the door handle. My hand slipped trying to turn it—my moist, trembling hand. A sign, I thought. Looking at the door handle, I thought about the consequences of being alone in my room with Brenda. False accusations of inappropriate sexual advances came to mind. That alone could lead to my expulsion from medical school. Standing by my door, thinking about the mistake that I almost made by trying to let Brenda into my room, my eyes focused on the door knob, and my heart drummed away in fear. My door stayed locked. I retreated from the door, and sprawled across my twin bed, my feet and head dangling. I wished the rain could come back and drum away her voice from inside my head. My eyes closed.

I heard a thump outside my room. My door shook and opened slightly. I sprang to my feet and stood by my desk. Brenda lay limp on the floor. I walked over to her, checked her pulse, and lifted her jaw. My face lowered to check her breathing. She coughed on me. I looked away.

"I'm glad you're alive," I said. My heart continued to race. I checked my pulse.

"I'm scared," Brenda said. She reached out to hold my hand. Her eyes dimmed, and tears rolled down her cheek when she spoke. "Let me stay with you," she added. Our eyes met. I could see the fear in her eyes. She wrapped her arm around my neck. I felt the rapid beating of her heart.

"I know you'll get me in trouble," I said. I did not want to turn her away, but I was afraid of what could go wrong, alone with Brenda in my room. One small bed and a desk chair.

"I'll take the chair," Brenda said. I looked at the small chair and looked at Brenda. She peeled the comforter off my bed, sat on the chair, and covered her body with it. "Ignore my crying if my ass hurts," she added. I heard her moan.

"You can have the bed," I said. She unwrapped her body and jumped in, without hesitation.

I pushed the chair away, and spread the comforter on the floor. Looking at the comforter, with Brenda still awake, I decided to pace around the room. As time passed, I heard from my bed the sound of sniffling and snoring. The rainfall returned and sprayed on my window, and the sound of raindrops on the glass took my mind away from the noise coming from my bed. I lowered my body to the floor. My tie dangled on the chair next to me. I thought about Brenda strangling me in my sleep. I lifted the tie from the chair and held it to my chest.

* * *

I heard my phone ring, and felt my joints ache. When I opened my eyes, Brenda was standing over me in her nakedness. She leaned down and gave me the phone, it was still ringing. It was 6:00 am on the phone display, and the caller's name was showing: Deborah Linger. The first early morning phone call from Deb since I moved to Memphis. My mind went through many reasons for her call, and settled on pregnancy. My hand shook, and I closed my eyes.

"Hello Deb," I said.

"Returning your call," Deb said. I had forgotten that I had called her. I took a deep breath.

"I miss you terribly," I said. The only thing I could think of to say when I could not remember why I called her.

"I've been busy," Deb said.

"Me too, but I need you," I said. Brenda knelt next to me, placing her head close to the phone. I wanted to push her away, but I was afraid that she would say something loud enough to be heard. I took a deep breath.

"Focus on your rotation," Deb said. The reason why I called her came back to me.

"Come to Memphis this weekend," I said.

"I can't. I need time away from you," Deb said.

"I love you," I said. Brenda kissed my cheek and blew warm air in my ear. I held my breath.

"I'll take a shower," Brenda said, loud enough to be heard. I tried to mute the phone after she had spoken.

"Screwing around on me?" Deb asked. I looked at Brenda and covered her mouth with my hand. She nodded as if she understood what I wanted, so I turned off the mute and removed my hand from her mouth. "Are you still there?" Deb added.

"Still here. Alone," I said.

"I'm not crazy. I heard her voice," Deb said.

"No one here but me," I said.

"And me," Brenda said, and laughed. "You're busted," she added.

The phone went silent. Then, I heard a dial tone. I made a fist. Brenda looked at my fist and laughed. She put her hands around her neck and squeezed, acting as if she was strangling herself. Angry, I looked away.

"Go ahead. I know you want to. Choke me. I deserve it," Brenda said. Her smile had faded by the time I looked at her. Tears rolled down from her eyes. She wrapped her arms around me and added, "I'm going crazy." As much as I tried to force myself to do it, I could not hug Brenda. My breathing became shallow. While pondering over what to do, she lifted her face up and kissed my lips. Her saliva tasted salty. The swift beating of my heart terrified me, so I loosened her grip on me.

"You need help," I said.

"I can't control my thoughts. It scares me," Brenda said.

"Talk to someone, a psychiatrist," I said.

"Share my feelings? That's bad." She moved away from me and shook her head from side to side.

"You need to, 'cause I worry when you're around me," I said.

"Who needs help? You, or me?" Brenda asked. My alarm went off, and she jumped. I walked over to my table to turn the alarm off. When I turned around, Brenda was gone.

I paced around my room trying to figure out the best thing to do. I called Deb. While the phone rang, I worried about how to explain Brenda to her. The call went to her voicemail, and I sighed. Not having been able to reach Deb immediately, I felt that I had lost her. Permanently.

I sat on the floor and leaned against my bed. Closing my eyes, I thought about Deb. Remembering that I lied to her about having someone in my room, I had doubts that she would ever talk to me again. One option I had was to ask Brenda to call Deb to explain why she was in my room. However, the fear of what Brenda might say worried me more.

While agonizing over my predicament, a siren punctuated the air, blasting the morning quietness. Loud cries followed, from Brenda's room. The siren and screeching, intermixed. The siren sound increased in loudness, muting the wailing next door. It sounded as if the siren purred outside my window, giving three blasts each time. I rushed to Brenda's door and knocked. While I was panicking about Brenda's safety, the siren faded. After my second knock went unanswered, I turned the handle on her door. Brenda was sitting on the floor with her ears covered, screaming. The siren stopped. I looked at the street from her window. No ambulance. The road was empty.

"Please help me. I'm losing my mind," Brenda said.

"I'll call an ambulance," I said.

"Please don't. They'll put me away."

"You need help."

"I know. From you."

"I'm not a psychiatrist. You need professional help,"

"Be with me. Help me."

"I smell trouble. Talk to someone. Get counseling, or something. I can't take care of you."

"Get out of my room. Get out," Brenda said. She stood up and pushed me. I walked out of her room, and she slammed the door.

After I locked the door to my room, I called the crisis center. When someone answered the phone, I hung up. I thought about the story to tell them. I redialed the number.

"Crisis center, how can I help?"

"A friend needs help," I said.

"What type of help?"

"She's losing her mind."

"Suicidal? Is the friend you, Hon?"

"No, Ma'am. I'm not sure," I said. My hands trembled. My thought process scrambled.

"Which one?"

"Well, she's a friend. Not sure about suicidal."

"Let me talk to her."

"She's in her room."

"I'll get one of our counselors to talk to her."

"I am calling from college housing. A dorm."

"Your dorm office can take care of it. Call them."

The crisis center operator hung up. While dialing our housing office, I leaned against the wall and lowered my body to the floor. I pondered over what to do. I closed my eyes, and pressed the telephone against my ear. An announcement came on before the buzzing sound. When my eyes opened, darkness lingered on, and I could not see beyond my face. Stuck in my darkness, fear gripped me. I was losing my mind. Objects formed in front of me. When I reached out, my hand tightly held the door knob of Brenda's room.

"You're back. I knew you'd come for me," Brenda said.

"I know I'll regret my decision. You're with me day and night. Like we used to be, in anatomy," I said.

"I like that. Take charge," Brenda said.

"Until you see a counselor," I said. She leaped up, and hugged me. I held my breath.

Before I decided to superintend Brenda, I knew it would not be an easy process, but once I committed to it, I realized that I could be ruining my life. Looking around her room, images of a scalpel and a folded scarf flashed before my eyes. Two dead dangling bodies, hugging, at the side. Scenarios of potential outcomes constantly flashed in my mind. Fantasies of a deranged mind. Of all the images that flashed before my eyes, the combination of homicide and suicide resonated the most.

I ran to my room and locked my door. Ghastly details of

cutting and hanging kept flashing before my eyes. I became afraid to close my eyes. Tortured by restive hallucinations. I was not sure which one of us needed urgent psychological intervention—Brenda, or me.

Chapter 7

A FEW WEEKS LATER, a van broke down in the middle of Madison Street a few blocks away from the medical center, at 12:30 pm. Drivers crisscrossed around the van, taking turns to get by from each side. A driver failed to yield to another and their cars blocked each other. They sat in their cars and pointed fingers at each other. Their lips moved as they yelled inside their cars, the noises they made staying with them, neither one willing to yield to the other. I turned onto a side street and parked in an overflow lot.

As I stepped out of my car, a few drops of rain fell on my shirt. I quickened my pace. Less than a block away from the medical center, clouds shielded the morning sun. No images of blue skies and cumulus clouds were reflected on the glass hospital building. Today the reflective panes showed no alluring clouds with mountainous aberrations to intrigue me. Deprived of my daily visual stimulation, I struggled with unexpected dejection.

Slush covered the beautiful brick path that led to the side entrance of the hospital. Each step I took, mud covered my shoes and stained my pant legs. Nothing seemed to be going well that day.

Walking down the hall to the conference room, our improvised office, I heard someone cough behind me. I turned around. Brenda and James were a few steps behind me. Brenda smiled as James whispered to her.

"Having a good day? It seems like it. I'm missing out," I

said. Brenda's smile disappeared.

"What's good about it?' Brenda asked.

"I like your dress," I said. She shook her head. James smiled.

"I didn't ask your opinion," Brenda said.

"I'm sorry if I offended you," I said.

"Good guy, Ben. Always ready with an apology," she said.

"I agree. Ben's great," James said. Brenda scowled. "No lunch with us today?" James asked.

"I'm broke. Met with the financial aid office," I said.

"I borrowed. Had my money yesterday," James said. A broad smile on his face.

"While you guys talk about money, I have patients to see," Brenda said.

"Should I call you for a loan, Brenda?" I asked, and smiled.

"Call your bitch. She's got money," Brenda said. She passed me as she spoke.

"Don't walk away now. I'm offended," I said.

"Leave it alone, Bro," James said.

"I try to help her, but she abuses me," I said.

"Babes are like that," James said.

"She comes to me for help but is mean to me. Weird," I said.

"My wife didn't talk to me this morning. Dropped me off. No kiss," James said.

"Going to see my girl this weekend. A surprise," I said.

"Don't do it. Never surprise a lady like that," James said. I thought about what he said and resolved to call Deb before traveling to Knoxville.

* * *

James, Brenda, and I stood on the hospital landing. It was 5:30 pm. This was our daily routine, waiting for James' wife to pick him up. James stood close to Brenda as they gazed at the setting sun. James' earbuds plugged the only access to his brain. He was unavailable for conversation. Brenda whispered words I couldn't hear, to James. I doubted if James heard Brenda with his plugged ears. Although James didn't reply to what she was saying, her lips continued to move. I turned away and watched the traffic.

James checked his watch several times. He paced around, walking from where I stood to where Brenda waited with a smile. The parking meter in front of us read 6:15 pm. James' wife was 45 minutes late. A car screeched as it stopped in front of us.

"She's here," James said, as he ran to the passenger's side. Closer to the car, I heard him say, "Wrong car. I'm sorry, Ma'am." He waved to the driver and returned to us. A woman walked to the same car and opened the passenger's door. The car drove off.

James checked his watch again, while standing next to Brenda. She moved her hand up and down his arm. I became worried about what James' wife would do if she saw Brenda caressing her husband's arm. I moved slightly away from them. Away from a potentially physical conflict between two women. James focused his eyes on the approaching cars and ignored Brenda. His smile was gone. Watching the bewildered look on James' face, I became worried. I approached James.

"I parked down the street. I'll take you home," I said.

"I'll take him home," Brenda said. Her fingers pointing at

me. "He's my friend," she added. She walked over to the space between James and me. I stepped away to make room for her. Physical confrontation with Brenda worried me. I was not sure what she would do to me, if provoked.

"Guys, I'll wait for her," James said.

"She's not coming. Let's go. I'll take you," Brenda said.

"I'll leave. I'm sorry, James. I hope your wife is okay," I said.

"Don't go. Come with us," James said.

"I won't drive if he's coming," Brenda said.

"You don't have to, I'll get my car," I said.

"Don't. I'll get some money from the ATM, then we can go," James said. I walked up the stairs to the hospital lobby with James. Brenda dawdled behind us.

James stood behind a man using the ATM. The man counted his money and walked away. James inserted his card and punched in his numbers. He received a receipt and examined it.

"Ben, something is wrong with my account," James said.

"I've got 20. You can have it," I said. Brenda ignored us.

"I want my money. I borrowed 20 grand. It's gone," James said.

"Machine error. Let's go. Check with the bank tomorrow," I said.

We walked to the garage in silence. Brenda followed behind us. I didn't know what to say to a man whose wife and money were missing.

James sat motionless during the drive to his house. His eyes were fixed on the road, except for when he directed me. Brenda was so quiet in the back seat that I forgot she was in the car with us. A solemn trip to James' place. His matrimonial home.

I stopped the car next to his garage. When we stepped out

of the car, a squirrel escaped from us, trampling on withered, pink rose petals. Brown grass covered most of James' lawn. Across the street, a man watched a woman prune shrubs while their water sprinkler system hummed. Cascades of water, directed away from them, covered most of their green lawn. He exchanged her gardening tools when she lifted her hand. A working system. I waved to them as the man changed his position to inspect his petunia. He nodded, and trained his eyes on us.

We reached the front door. It opened when James tried to insert his key. It was ajar. We walked in.

"Babe, are you okay?" James called. His words echoed in the foyer. A hollow sound.

His living and dining rooms had no furniture. Several areas on the wall showed fresh-looking paint, where, I assumed, photographs or paintings used to hang. The living room contained a carpet with blotches on it and oblong areas that looked new.

James sighed and looked at me. A broken man, his eyes were red with tears, and his lips trembled. I closed my eyes. It was hard for me to look at a man who was falling apart.

James scratched his head as he walked toward the garage. We followed. The floor held a dark spot from motor oil and a broom, but no car or tools. He shook his head. Tears left his eyes and rolled down his cheeks. Brenda clung to his arm.

We entered a wood-paneled kitchen. An envelope lay on the counter. James lifted it, then inspected and opened it. His lips moved, though no teeth showed and no words could be heard. His eyes twitched, and sweat formed on his forehead.

Sweat trickled down to his eyes and joined his tears. He wiped his eyes with his sleeve and dabbed his forehead. As he batted his eyelids, tears flowed down his cheeks. I patted him on the back and squeezed his shoulders. No words could have done better, I thought.

"She left me," James said. He placed his arm on my shoulder and bowed his head. I heard his increased breathing. Fast and shallow breathing initially, then deep. Twice, he held his breath while rubbing his eyes. After an episode of prolonged gasping, he lowered his body to the floor and leaned against the cabinet. Brenda knelt next to him, kissed his cheek, and placed her head on his chest. I looked at them and smiled. Brenda the consoler. An evolving role for her. James looked up and shook his head.

"Not a good way to leave someone you love," I said. I walked to the window and looked out. Brown lawn. Wilted grass. The chances of their dead lawn coming back to life were as good as those of James' wife returning home. Some things are too far gone to be revived. James looked at me. His puzzled look made me wonder if he was reading my mind. I looked away.

"She wanted a new car and a baby. I said no. That's all," James said. Brenda repositioned herself around him, with her arms belted around his waist. Her eyes glistened, and she pursed her lips.

"No good b…." Brenda stopped before she completed the word. I placed my fingers on my lips.

"It's okay Brenda. I'm strong," James said. He kissed her cheek.

"Get your stuff. You'll stay with us," Brenda said. She looked at me. I nodded in agreement.

James rose and walked toward a room. Brenda followed him and held his hand. My heart pounded. At that moment, I realized that they were closer than I had thought. Two unstable medical students in a challenging relationship. The potential outcome worried me.

* * *

Later that evening, across from my room I saw the setting sun, partially hidden by leaves from trees in the park. Empty park benches cast long shadows. On the right side of my window, I saw men and women standing close to a podium. I heard the sounds of music, glimpsed bodies swaying. Beyond them was the river. When the music stopped, I could hear claps, yells, and whistles. I returned to my desk.

Reaching to open my textbook, I heard the sounds of rocking from Brenda's room. The frequency of the rocking increased. Trying to ignore the sound was difficult. I had a suspicion about what was going on next door, until I heard a loud scream. Scalpels and a folded scarf returned to mind. Two dead dangling bodies, hugging, flashed before my eyes. I rushed out of my room.

"Don't stop, Baby. I can take it all. Yes, yes! Oh, yes! Ride it, Baby. Ride me good," Brenda said. The rocking sound became louder. A different picture came to mind. I returned to my room.

After putting my shoes on, I locked my room and took the elevator to the ground floor. I read the residence hall rules on the wall of the lobby. One of the rules stated, 'No overnight guests allowed.' I believed it was my responsibility to notify

Brenda and James about the residence hall rule, but going back to Brenda's room to hear her moan repulsed me. A married James, dumped by a wife, his loan money gone. A vulnerable tool, dishing out pleasure to suppress his own pain.

After I left the dormitory, I walked to the banks of the river. Sitting on a boulder, I watched the dingy river. Uncomfortable on the rock's rough surface, I rose and walked to a path that led to the crowd. A handful of people sat on the grass in front of a platform, which held musical instruments and a few men connecting the wires. Not long after I arrived, an older man with dark sunglasses mounted the stage. He plucked at his guitar strings and swung his head from side to side. He opened his mouth to sing, showing no visible teeth. It was hard to determine if he was smiling.

"My baby's gone. She's gone. Left me all alone. Ugly riverboat took her yonder. Sailing with Captain No-good. Hold on Willie. Let your guitar talk." He plucked taut guitar strings with his bent fingers. He loosened the strings and continued to sing. *"Got me a new woman. Skinny legs, and no ass, but my bed's warm again. I know hell is calling me soon. Yeah! Willie want some of them big hump."* Laughter erupted, drowning his voice and the sound of his strings.

My mind drifted to my two classmates secluded in a small room. Two young people solving their emotional problems through physical means. My own problems came to my mind. I thought about calling Deb. I felt the urge to run to my room, close the door, and call her. In the privacy of my room, I would beg her to take me back and love me unconditionally.

I can't remember how I made it back to the dorm.

Two paces before I opened my door, I turned around and knocked on Brenda's door. No answer, nor the sound of the bed moving. One step from my door, Brenda's door opened. She stuck her head out.

"What?" she asked.

"We need to talk. The three of us," I said.

"It's none of your business," Brenda said.

"He can't stay," I said.

"He is. It's my room. Go to hell," Brenda said. James stuck his head out. I approached them.

"I'll leave," James said.

"You're not. You're mine," Brenda said. She turned around to hold James. Her door opened halfway, exposing their naked bodies.

"You know she's vulnerable," I said.

"Go back to your damn girlfriend. Leave us alone," Brenda said.

"Brenda's right. Not your call, Bro," James said.

"You're married, in case you forgot," I said. Brenda walked toward me, naked and angry, and pushed me. After she had exposed herself, she cupped her flat chest and stepped back into her room.

"Go. Go away," Brenda said. She slammed her door. I could hear them laugh behind the closed door.

* * *

Later that night, the sun had set, but some street light filtered into my room. Thinking about Deb, my heart raced. I thought about her possible response to me. My hand trembled while I thought about rejection. Deb saying no to my request. I lifted my phone. No missed calls showed. I fought the urge to call her, and just held my phone.

I sat at the edge of my bed and dialed Deb's number. The busy signal came on. My hands trembled more. Her phone rang on the third try.

"I get more calls from you now than I used to. Are you okay?" Deb asked.

"I miss you terribly," I said.

"Good," she said.

"That's all? I guess you don't miss me?" I asked.

"Don't go there," she said.

"I was hoping you missed me. Maybe needed me," I said. I heard her heavy breathing but did not hear any words. "Love me the way you used to," I added.

"What's the use? You're in Memphis. I am not going to waste my life anymore," she said. My phone dropped on the floor. I picked it up.

"I'll come home this weekend," I said.

"Not for me, I hope. I have plans," she said.

"Include me."

"I'm seeing someone."

"I guess you don't need me."

"Bye," she said. I heard a dial tone.

Sitting at the edge of my bed it felt as if there was nothing left inside me. My eyes felt warm and swollen, but no tears came. I caressed my phone but could not call her back. Not for two rejections in one day. Looking at my phone's screen, the picture of Deb and me standing in front of a water fountain reminded me of better times. A smiling couple, my hand raised to throw a penny over my shoulder. One penny and one wish. A wish for the longevity of our relationship. It taunted me. I looked around my empty room. Feeling isolated inside its confines, lonesomeness gripped me. Things could not get worse for me. Kneeling by my bedside to pray, I became worried that I would get the opposite of what I asked for. Like the wish at the fountain.

"God, please take care of me. I have no one else, but you," I said. After my prayer, I thought about the opposite of what I asked for. Death.

Chapter 8

A NURSE STOOD in front of the elevator. A full chest and a small waist. Her blue surgical scrubs had black trimming, a blend of navy-blue and black—a different outfit. Her uniqueness interested me, and my eyes sought out more details. Her name tag read Rita. Unlike some of the other nurses, there were no wrinkles or ink spots on her scrub pockets. I watched her push the elevator call button and hold it in. Desperate to get her attention, I cleared my throat. She turned around and smiled. The elevator door dinged and opened. We entered. I stood at a corner, away from the control panel. She pushed the button for the second floor. My plan was to get off the elevator with her.

When the elevator door closed she looked at me, and said, "Sorry. I didn't ask for your floor."

"Same as yours. ICU," I said. She smiled and looked away.

I watched the floor indicator lights. Apart from the physical distance between us, silence separated Rita and me. However, my eyes searched out her distinctiveness. They rested on her chest most. I moved around, trying to contain my desire to start a conversation with her. She smiled. It reminded me of Deb. My eyes went back to her chest. Memories of Deb faded away. One floor before we reached our destination, she tapped her fingernails on the wall. Without forethought, I whistled. She stopped her tapping. Rita moved around. I saw her mouth open twice, as if she wanted to speak, but she closed it without saying anything. I felt uneasy and leaned against the elevator wall.

"You're a third year?" Rita said, as the elevator door opened.

She reached toward my coat and turned my badge around. "I know, it's Ben. You're good with patients. They tell nurses everything," she added, with an emphasis on 'everything'.

"Thank you," I said. We walked toward ICU.

"For what? You deserve to be told," she said.

She walked ahead of me and opened the ICU door with her badge. Inside the unit, a woman in brown scrubs was cleaning the floor with a wet mop. In several areas, there were yellow 'Wet Floor' signs. It was easy to identify dry areas, but I walked with caution. While I focused on the wet floor, taking careful steps, Rita left me behind. I felt disappointed and resolved to take more risks in my life.

I entered room 410, which was the only one without a nurse. The patient in the room had a breathing tube taped to the side of her mouth and connected to the ventilator. Her eyes were closed, and her arms rested at her sides, motionless. I assumed she was sedated, but still I introduced myself. I felt it was respectful to introduce myself, even if she was not aware of my presence in her room. Respect.

Positioned by the patient's bedside, the ventilator churned and occasionally chirped. The numbers displayed on it changed after it delivered each mechanical breath. I inspected the heart monitor and vital signs before I examined the patient. I bent down to listen to her lungs and heart. When I arose, Rita was standing next to me.

"Her lab results look good," Rita said.

"Her lungs still sound wet," I said.

"The lung guy said it's pneumonia."

"She's covered, on three antibiotics."

"And my constant prayers," Rita said. "You're from here?"

Rita asked, as we left the patient's room.

"Knoxville," I said.

"You're not. You don't have a *knoxvul ac-cent*," she said with a southern drawl. We laughed.

"Ma'am, I ain't from the sticks," I said. We laughed more. Together. Ideas came to mind. I suppressed my desire to ask her out. My resolution deferred itself.

"You're okay, Ben. Come to my erection party Saturday," Rita said. Rita, a swinger. I felt disappointed. I looked around the ICU, wondering who had heard her comment, what their opinion of me would be, and if they would label me a perverted medical student.

"Excuse me. What type of party?" I asked. She smiled.

"You've got a dirty mind. Not that kind of party," Rita said.

"What kind is it?" Dr Peterson asked. The muscles on his face tightened, and his eyes were trained on Rita. I heard his breathing rate increase. He appeared distressed. Rita smiled and shook her head.

When I heard a laugh, I looked behind me. Brenda was standing there, next to James. Dr Peterson moved closer to me. He was standing so close to me that I could smell the garlic on his breath. It was evident to me that he was violating my private space. I took two steps away from him.

"Is there something wrong here?" I asked. A short distance away, I saw a nurse tap another nurse on the shoulder and point in our direction. Although I tried to create a comfortable space between us, Dr Peterson moved closer each time, standing like a sentry. I became worried about a physical confrontation between us. The outcome of such a conflict was obvious to me.

Hierarchy is paramount in the medical profession. In the absence of Dr Trophy, he was my supervisor. Rita looked at Dr Peterson, shook her head, and walked closer to me.

"I'm erecting a patio. I'd like you to come," Rita said, ignoring Dr Peterson's frown.

"What should I bring?" I asked.

"You're on call," Dr Peterson said, before Rita could answer my question. He looked at Brenda and James. "You're on call too," he added. The smile fled from Brenda's face.

"You're mean," Rita said, to no one in particular. She walked away.

"Find Andrew, and report to the conference room," Dr Peterson said.

I tried to leave with Brenda and James.

"Stay," Dr Peterson added, it was a command.

"I am not sure what I've done to you," I said.

"You're always flirting with the nurses. I'll write you up," he said. Two nurses walking by heard what he said. They looked behind twice as they walked away.

"Not me. Wrong guy," I said.

"Flirting at work is sexual harassment," Dr Peterson said. Two nurses in a patient's room peeked their heads out to look at us. His choice of words worried me. Accusations of such magnitude had consequences. Dismissal from medical school. An end to my career choice.

"Are you serious?" I asked, raising my voice. I made a fist with my right hand and looked at his face. He looked down at my fist. Insubordination. I knew the consequences.

"Go ahead, punch me, and your ass will be gone," Dr Peterson said.

"I've done nothing," I said.

"Go and see room 403. Present his case to me in ten minutes," Dr Peterson said, before he left the ICU and I walked toward room 403.

I sat in a cubicle next to room 403 and overheard the two nurses inside the room.

"That fool knows that Rita won't go out with him," one nurse said. "He'll destroy that medical student, just to torture Rita," a nurse said.

I coughed, and they stopped talking. They came out of the room, looked at me, and smiled. One of the nurses came up to me.

"He's in love with Rita. That's why you're in trouble. Be careful with him," the nurse said. Another person added to my list of people that could ruin my life. It appeared that my survival in medical school was becoming impossible.

"Good to know," I said.

"Rita likes you," the nurse said. She giggled and walked away.

Weirdly enough, I sympathized with Dr Peterson's feelings. When I thought about it, I felt that I could identify with him. Rita rejecting his romantic interest was almost the same as Deb breaking up with me. A rejection. Remembering being discarded, I winced.

After the nurses left room 403, I was the only one around. Quiet prevailed, even in the presence of beeping heart monitors and buzzing ventilators. Undisturbed for a significant amount of time, I read the entire medical history of my patient without looking up. My eyes twitched, and as I tried to rub them, I felt a tap on my shoulder.

"I'll buy you dinner, if you're free next weekend," Rita said. I looked around the ICU for Dr Peterson. A fear of Dr Peterson, the rejected lover, took hold of me, even in his absence. My heart raced, and my hands trembled. I hesitated before answering Rita's question, and looked around several times.

"I guess," I said. I knew that Rita would mean trouble for me with Dr Peterson, but I could not resist the temptation. An opportunity for happiness, if I survived the repercussions. My hands were shaking. The sexual harassment threat lingered in my mind, along with the fear of expulsion from medical school. I looked at Rita while my brain was roiling with survival reasoning. A beautiful smile, dimples, and piercing eyes decorated her face. A full chest. "Yes. Sounds good," I added. Enchantment had overwhelmed my sense of reasoning.

"We'll have fun, I promise," Rita said.

We exchanged glances and smiles. She covered her mouth to giggle, practicing a kind of timid flirtation. Excitement burbled inside me. Becoming afraid that my elation would manifest itself physically, I crossed my legs.

When Rita departed, my fear returned, but I did not want to rescind my acceptance of her invitation. I wanted to spend time with her, even though I knew I was exposing myself to possible retaliation from her jilted lover, Dr Peterson. My clinical supervisor. A man who could ruin my medical education, and my life.

Chapter 9

THE HOSPITAL GIFT SHOP was located in the main lobby. It was full of trinkets and plastic flowers in display cabinets. Simply worded get well cards. Antiquated photo frames and gardening magazines. Country cooking magazines barely lasted for a few hours on display, but one thing was never missing: Rose. The store manager. A white-haired, elderly woman who wore colorful dresses.

I stopped at the gift shop every morning to purchase the daily newspaper. "Good morning, Sunshine," Rose would say to me. As I left, she would add, "That smile of yours brightens my day. We need more people like you around here." Without Rose knowing it, her words set a standard for me. To be generous with my smiles.

On this day, Rose was sitting on her chair when I entered the gift shop. No greeting or smile. I walked to her desk. She looked away.

"Good morning, Ma'am. It's a beautiful day," I said.

"I'm dying. Liver cancer. They gave me a 50–50 chance with chemo," Rose said. Her eyes moist with tears. "I don't want it," she added.

"You don't give up. You fight," I said. I looked in her eyes.

"Fight? You don't fight alone. I have no one," she said.

"You won't fight alone. I'm here for you," I said. She smiled.

"You're alone too. Never seen you with a girl."

"She left me in Knoxville."

"Find a girl, and I'll take their damn chemo," Rose said. We laughed.

I bought a newspaper. With the newspaper folded and placed under my arm, I proceeded to the elevator. As the elevator filled up, I read the front-page headlines until I reached my floor. Sensationalized facts to appeal to saps adorned the front page. I turned around and took the elevator back down to the main floor, where I had started that morning. One thing that stayed with me that morning was the pact I made with Rose. I thought about Rita. I was ready to risk everything for her.

*   *   *

One of the medical center's glass walls overlooked a one-way backstreet, University Drive. The wall was a part of the hospital's social center, 'The Boiling Pot', the main cafeteria. Hospital workers and visitors congregated in the expansive hall at various times of the day for nourishment. I nicknamed it 'The Mixing Pot'. It was a place I could sit down and read my newspaper when I arrived at the hospital earlier than I expected.

No dew or streaks of dirt were visible on the glass wall that morning. Rays of golden sun dotted some areas on the floor of the cafeteria, displaying the sun's early morning hue. I bought a bagel with scrambled eggs, and sat at a table facing the approaching vehicles and pedestrians traveling down University Drive. Each time I tried to take a bite, I was distracted by events on the street. Even the distorted shadows from the pedestrian overpass on the paved road were intriguing. It was an aberrant art form cast on a busy road.

From the shadows on the road, my fascination drifted to the crows swooping down to peck at road kill. Scavengers that forage on the outcome of miscalculations. Each time a car came along, they demonstrated their instinct for survival and flew away to avoid becoming a feast for others. I thought about ways to survive from the scavengers that prey on medical students. Resident and attending physicians. I thought about the promise I made to Rose. Fulfilling my promise to her could end my medical aspirations. I had to acquire new skills in interpersonal relationships, or perish.

Looking down the street, two blocks away, pedestrians marched silently, trekking in groups. Some of the women clutched their shoulder bags, while others let them swing, choices made without much thought. Like choices we make about our lives; restraint or total freedom in how we live. My eyes left the distant crowd and focused on the privileged crowd. Cars dropped them off or picked them up at the curb, a few steps away from the hospital door. While watching the morning procession, I stuck my fork inside the scrambled Egg Beaters on my plate, a substitute for the genuine product. Like a lot of things in our lives, a compromise. It had its purpose.

As I looked away from the street, Brenda's penchant for fleeting anger toward me crowded my brain. I suffered in self-pity until one of the resident physician's beepers played a musical tune close to my table, bringing me back from my reverie. I looked around. Brenda and James were entering the cafeteria with smiles and confident strides. Then, our eyes met. Brenda's glassy eyes looked through me as her smile faded away. She mouthed words I could not hear. James laughed. Closer to my table, she muttered something, before she looked away. James waved at me, before he hurried to catch up with Brenda.

Amused, I watched Brenda and James join the breakfast line with their trays. Once served, Brenda took her tray to a table eight rows from me, out of earshot. When James emerged from the line, he looked in my direction and adjusted his tray, before he looked around the cafeteria. Brenda beckoned to him. She watched James walk to her table. My eyes moved in their direction, analyzing the new allegiance. When James got closer to Brenda, her smile returned.

James stood next to Brenda, exchanging words before he sat down. Twice, he looked in my direction while standing. I could not help but wonder what he was saying that required him to look toward me. I tried to drink my juice, thinking about their noisy lovemaking sessions, but it would not go down, so I took my food tray to the waste conveyor belt.

Throngs of nurses and hospital attendants filled the hallway leading out of the cafeteria. I felt a chill of loneliness walking to the elevator by myself. Before I could collect my thoughts, the elevator door opened, and I walked in and leaned against the wall. Two medical students and a nurse joined me.

"Which floor?" the nurse asked. The students looked at each other and smiled. I stared at the elevator door in front of me. The nurse turned to me, and asked, "Are you okay?"

"I'm sorry. I didn't realize you were talking to me," I said.

"Where're you going?" she asked.

"ICU, I think," I said. She pushed the elevator button. The students laughed. I looked at them and frowned.

"You're riding for fun," the nurse said. Everyone laughed, including me.

"You're funny. I bet you're a good nurse," I said.

"Working a 12-hour shift, humor helps," she said. The

elevator door opened. I stepped out.

Nurses dashed in and out of patients' rooms, exhibiting a change-of-shift urgency. Vital signs and patients' complaints had to be entered in their electronic medical records. An elderly man stood in front of room 407, observing everyone who passed by the room. I watched Rita hug him, then wipe her tears when they separated. I found a workstation and sat down.

I retrieved the clinical summary of the patient in room 407 and reviewed it. Dr Peterson's last paragraph from the admission history summarized the care plan.

Seventy-eight-year-old female with aspiration pneumonia being treated with antibiotics and advanced Alzheimer's dementia that has worsened, per the husband, over the past six months. Husband discussing with the family and social worker about code status. He is interested in do-not-resuscitate status, but has not made up his mind.

I wished I had read the last paragraph first, before reviewing the entire medical records. I recited the clinical summary twice before walking into room 407.

"Good morning. I'm Ben Ava, a medical student," I said.

"I'm Roger, Ellie's husband. You're too young." His smile and firm handshake surprised me. I had expected a downtrodden man.

"I'll be taking care of your wife with Dr Peterson," I said.

"Ellie needs all the help we can give her," Roger said. He walked to his wife's bedside and held her hand. "A young man is here to see you," he added.

Her eyes opened, and her facial muscles twitched. A smile, I assumed. Her eyes tracked my movement in the room.

Walking closer to her, I said, "Good morning, Ma'am. I'm

Ben. Ben Ava." Her eyelids twitched more as she turned to her husband. He rubbed the back of her hand with his. When he caressed her hand, I saw a twinkle in her eyes.

"He's a student doctor," Roger said. She looked around her room as if she were searching for someone.

"I'd like to listen to your heart and lungs," I said. I rubbed my hands together and placed the diaphragm of my stethoscope on the palm of my hand to warm it up.

"Ellie loves warm hands," Roger said, shaking his head and smiling.

"I'm glad I warmed mine," I said.

"What should I do about Ellie?" Roger asked.

"I am not sure what you mean," I said.

"Machine, or no machine—if she can't breathe? We've been together 60 years. She needs me," Roger said. His eyes swelled with tears, and he sobbed. I put my arms around his shoulder and tried to contain my own tears. Ellie shifted around in bed and triggered her alarm. She mumbled and pulled her intravenous line out. Blood trickled out of the small, exposed hole. I used her bed sheet to apply pressure to stop the bleeding. Roger watched me attend to his wife. A smile on his face.

"Depends on what she wants. Did she tell you before she got worse?" I asked.

Rita rushed into the room with a clinical technician. Two nurses stood outside the room with Dr Peterson. Rita walked to the bedside, moved my hand away from the bleeding site, held the woman's hand, and said, "I'll take care of this little problem, Miss Ellie." She placed an IV tray on the bed, pulled a chair closer, and sat down. After Rita replaced the patient's IV line, she put Ellie's hands in protective covers.

"She's all yours," Rita said. She tapped me on the shoulder as she left the room, a surprise gesture inside a patient's room, with witnesses. I watched Rita walk toward the secretary's desk. When she disappeared from sight, I walked outside the room to meet with Dr Peterson, who was standing two steps away from the door. I thought about Rose and my promise to her.

"You're working your way into their hearts," Dr Peterson said.

"I'm trying. He's really upset," I said.

"I don't mean that. You're into ICU nurses."

"Not me. Just doing my assignments."

"I've been watching you and Rita. Do your work, and leave her alone."

"You're wrong about me," I said. I felt annoyed about his insinuation, but I had limited recourse.

"For your own good, I hope you stop flirting," he said.

"I've done nothing wrong," I said. I smiled, but I wanted to tell him to go kiss a halogen light bulb, or even something hotter than that.

"You've no respect," Dr Peterson said.

"I respect my patients. My coworkers too. Everybody. Who's complained?" I asked.

"Smart-ass. Keep it up, and see where it gets you," Dr Peterson said. He squeezed his lips together, and his face looked flushed. It appeared as if the level of his rage had cut off the oxygen supply to his brain. His eyes rolled up. I felt amused watching him suffer. He exhaled, letting out all the demons in his head.

I felt a tap on my shoulder as I watched the transfiguration of Dr Peterson's face. A whiff of lavender traveled to my nose when I turned around. Rita was standing so close to me that I had a whiff of her peppermint breath. She giggled, exposing her beautiful teeth. Closing my eyes, I inhaled deeply, and felt a tickle from the aroma that emanated from her body. Dr Peterson stood still, watching us in silence.

"Here's my number. I have three days off. Call me," Rita said.

"Busy tonight? I thought about Beale Street. The festival is still going on," I said.

"Sounds like fun. What time?" Rita asked.

"I'll call you at noon, if you're taking a lunch break."

A gurney rolled by. Dr Peterson stepped out of the way.

"Conference room, now," Dr Peterson said. A demand.

"Someone is cranky," Rita said, and laughed.

I became worried.

Dr Peterson frowned, swung his stethoscope around his neck, and walked away. His pace was hurried. I tried to keep up with him. Standing close to him in front of the conference room, I watched his hand shake as he pulled open the door. I reached for the edge of the door to keep it open as he walked in. I could not help but look at my hand to see if it was shaking, too.

"Sit down, Boss," he said. I looked around me, wondering who he was addressing as 'Boss'.

After I sat down, Dr Peterson paced around the room. He mumbled, while reaching into his pocket. When he retrieved his hand, he held up two tickets and approached me. With dilated pupils, he waved the tickets in my face. I raised my hand to knock the tickets down, but I stopped before I could do it.

"I bought these tickets for Rita and me," he said. I wiped the sweat from my forehead and closed my eyes as he spoke. "I was going to ask her out, but you messed it up," he added.

"It's not too late. Ask her," I said. He shook his head and rubbed his lower lip.

"She likes you, and it's your fault for flirting with her."

"You accused me of sexual harassment. Now it's changed to flirting."

"I did not. You're up to no good."

I sighed.

"Because I'm a medical student, you have a license to make up lies about me," I said. He waved the tickets in my face again, they were closer to my face the second time around.

"I wasted the money. Why can't you find your own girl?" he asked.

"I'll report you to the chief resident. I need to be reassigned," I said.

"I'm the new chief. Report to me. You rat," he said, and chuckled.

I could not find the right words to express myself as my body temperature reached boiling point. Beads of sweat dripped down my face. He had the advantage of seniority and authority over me. His evaluation at the end of my rotation would determine my grade in the clinical rotation, a decisive factor in finishing medical school. Looking in his eyes and seeing the sneer on his face, I knew what my fate would be.

Chapter 10

LATER THAT DAY, when I returned to my dormitory, I was excited about going out with Rita. Before I removed my clothes, I placed my wallet on top of the newspaper on my desk. The one I bought from the gift shop after making the pact with Rose. After hanging up my clothes, I returned to my desk to read the newspaper. One of the front-page headlines, 'Worst rate of personal savings in decades', was visible, but my bulging wallet covered the body of the article. I opened my wallet to confirm the amount of money I had for my date with Rita. Two 20-dollar bills and a ten. The remaining money I had budgeted for my monthly groceries. There were seven days left in the month, and I would not receive my monthly scholarship stipend until the first day of the following month. A meager living.

Sitting on my chair, I became worried about having only 50 dollars in my wallet. My eyes roamed around my room. Taking stock of all I had, I wished that I had hidden money somewhere in the room and forgotten about it. After an extensive search, I mentally listed everything in my room. An open closet door in a small space. Four pairs of pants and five shirts on wooden hangers. I gave up on my search for a treasure I did not have, and returned to reality. Even without enough money, I was ready to impress Rita.

I tried to read the newspaper but could not focus. My eyes returned to my closet. I decided against my black pants and a white shirt, to avoid looking like a bus boy at the restaurant.

The brown pair of pants looked good to me. When I thought about my limited funds and the possibility of not being able to pay the bill after my date with Rita, I reconsidered my choice of colors, and had to laugh at myself.

I picked up my phone and dialed the restaurant.

"Butcher Shop, may I help you?" a woman's voice said, a pleasant southern drawl laced with honey. It soothed my twitch.

"Sorry, Ma'am. I'm trying to figure how much a meal will cost," I said, while counting my coins.

"What're you having, Hon?" she asked.

"Meat, potatoes, and vegetables," I said.

"Steak, or chicken?" she asked.

"The cheapest," I said. She laughed. "I'm broke, Ma'am," I added. I laughed.

"Come over, Hon, I'll take care of you," she said.

"There's two of us. How much will it cost?" I asked.

"What's your name, Sugar?"

"Ben Ava."

"Ask for Connie. See you, Sugar." She hung up.

Chills and cold sweats traveled through my body in bursts. I whistled tunes I couldn't recognize and walked from one end of the room to the other, forgetting what I was looking for. My eyes focused on the second hand of my watch to make sure that it was moving. When I looked at my body, I realized I was naked. My pants and shirts remained on my bed. I wiped my body dry and started dressing. Rushing through my dressing ritual, I felt my soaked undershirt. Excitement and nervousness shared my body at the same time. I had less than ten minutes before Rita would arrive. Not enough time to clean the inside of my car. Our first date. I had planned to drive.

*   *   *

Rita parked her car in the visitors' lot before she joined me. I waited to open the passenger's door for her.

Less than a block away from the restaurant, the red light at the intersection turned green. I increased speed, to 35 miles an hour. Rita checked her cell phone and returned it to her purse. She lowered her purse to the floor of the car and used her foot to move it to her desired position, close to the door.

A siren blasted, and an ambulance barely stopped before running a red light at the intersection. My foot slammed on the brake, and I barely missed colliding with the ambulance. My tires squeaked, and Rita's body jerked forward. She recoiled and screamed, completing a trilogy of survival sounds with, "Save us, God!" The ambulance sped away. I remembered my prayer to God, and became afraid for my life.

The red light was on. My lips quivered as I inspected Rita's trembling body.

Looking in the rear mirror, I could see no cars behind me. I reached for Rita's hand and squeezed it with my trembling hand. I heard a series of sighs. Rita scooted closer to me and placed her arm around my shoulders. Her black hair dangled close to my face, and the aroma of ginseng ascended to my nostrils. My eyes blinked, and for a moment I forgot about the near collision. My body came alive. I held my breath, as if it would stop my aroused state. Something in me was still alive, I praised God in silence.

"I'm sorry," I said. I wasn't sure if I was apologizing for the near collision or my arousal.

"It's not your fault."

"Thank you."

"Stop it." She smiled and reached for my hand. We looked at each other and laughed. It felt as if the red light stood still for us.

The green light was on for more than ten seconds before my foot found the accelerator. After two stop signs, we reached the restaurant. At the last stop sign, I made a right turn and parked in the first metered space close to the entrance of the restaurant. I got out of the car.

Rita opened her door before I could come around. She swerved her body to face me and reached for my hand. I pulled her out of the car seat.

"I found me a gentleman. Southern style." She giggled. "It feels good," she added, her drawl intentionally more pronounced.

"Don't bite your tongue," I said. We both laughed as we entered the restaurant.

"Welcome to the Butcher Shop," a lady said. She examined the pin on Rita's jean shirt. "Nice butterfly," she added.

"Thank you," Rita said.

I was about to ask her for Connie when I heard, "You're Ben. God help me if I'm wrong."

"Connie?" I asked. Rita looked at me.

"It better be, Hon," she said. She picked up two menus from a rack.

"You know each other?" Rita asked.

"I called," I said.

"The Butcher Shop? For a reservation?" Rita asked. She laughed.

"Checking out their menu," I said.

"Steak and potatoes. It's Memphis, not New York," Rita

said. We laughed.

"I checked out the prices, too," I said.

"What? You're crazy," Rita said.

"No lovers' spats before steak and bourbon," Connie said. She walked and we followed.

The dining room was full. A long grill separated a refrigerator with four glass doors from the dining area. Bar stools lined a wooden counter next to the grill. Paper napkins folded in triangles, with steak knives and two forks nestled on top, were laid on each table. Connie seated us in front of the chef. Heat radiated from the grill, and grease sizzled as the chef held a metal spatula firmly on a piece of steak. As his steak sizzled, he smiled.

"Thank you, Connie," I said.

"I'll take care of you," Connie said, before she walked away.

"What was that about?" Rita asked.

"I talked to her on the phone," I said.

"About what?" Rita asked.

Before I could answer, I heard the clanking sounds of the chef's metallic spatula. I turned to face the chef.

"If you want steak, point to your choice," the chef said, interrupting the question that had almost rolled off my tongue. He pointed to the refrigerator. Steaks of different sizes hung in rows. Blood dripped from the steaks and fell into the buckets placed below them. I looked at Rita, expecting an expression of shock regarding the meat display. Words like 'gross' crossed my mind.

"How did you know?" Rita asked, her face beaming with a smile.

"What?" I asked, wondering if she had read my mind.

"I love steak. Medium rare," she said.

"I didn't know. I took a chance," I said.

"Top row steaks are 20 ounces, second, 16 ounces," the chef said. He sharpened his knives while talking.

"They all look good," I said. I opened the menu; my jaw muscles loosened, leaving my mouth open. The steak prices were more expensive than I had expected. I swallowed the saliva that filled my mouth. Rita looked at me briefly, then her eyes returned to the menu. I turned to the poultry section, observing the price list. I was hungry and broke. Adding these to trying to impress a girl, I felt miserable. Returning to my menu, I found a reasonably priced 'Double chicken breast'.

"I'll go for chicken," I said to the chef.

"Twenty-ounce steak for you, and a 16-ounce one for your lady," the chef suggested, ignoring my request.

"Twenty-ounce T-bone for me," Rita said, grinning.

"You still want chicken?" the chef asked. He shook his head, and laughed. "Get a manly steak. You're in Elvis' town," he added. We laughed. When I remembered the amount of money in my wallet, I stopped laughing.

"Double chicken breast will do," I said.

"Get a single breast, and mix it with a steak," the chef said.

"I don't want that. I love breasts," I said.

"I bet you do," the chef said, and looked at Rita. Rita tried to contain her laughter and almost choked.

"Not those kind of breasts," I said. Their laughter became louder. "Forget it. I love breasts. All kinds," I added. For some strange reason my eyes wandered to Rita's bosom as I spoke. She buttoned her blouse, and I laughed. I felt that she was setting her boundaries with me. No access to her breasts.

"Steak for the lady, and breasts for her man. God bless America," the chef said.

I could not control my laughter after his statement. I watched Rita to see if she was offended. She stayed composed, which made it difficult to tell how she felt. The chef walked to the refrigerator to retrieve the meat we had ordered. The fear of Rita refusing to go out with me after that night engulfed me. I pulled my chair closer to her.

"I hope you're not offended?" I asked.

"No. I'm used to it," Rita said.

"It's been fun so far," I said.

"I'll tell you how much fun, after a margarita," Rita said. I thought about the cost of her drink and my palms became wet.

"We'll take a drive to the river after supper," I said.

"Which river?" Rita asked.

"Down the street," I said.

"It's the Mississippi, not 'the river'," Rita said. She looked at me, opened her mouth, and hesitated.

"What's wrong? Say it," I said.

"You got a girl back home?" Rita asked.

"Not anymore."

"Good. I can't take any hurt."

Connie returned to our counter and picked up our menus. She looked at us and smiled

"What you having, Hon?" Connie asked.

"Double chicken breast," I said.

"Smart man. What're you drinking, Hon?" Connie asked.

"Margarita for Rita. Jeez. It rhymes. Just water for me," I

said. Connie and I laughed.

"Water? You're getting our special tonight, Hon. Forty dollars for your meals and drinks," Connie said.

"Thank you, Ma'am, but that's all I want," I said. Connie smiled. She left us and strolled to the bar.

After dinner, we drove to the river. The Mississippi. Rita got out of the car and put her hands in her pockets. I felt the distance between us. We walked to a bench and sat down. Alone together, to explore the limits of our first date.

* * *

Gold, red, gray, and other colors in between. The sky glowed from the reflections of the setting sun. Pockets of jagged, mountain-shaped cumulus clouds hung suspended in the sky, reflecting images of gold and red sunlight floating on the flowing Mississippi. As the setting sun darkened, the river looked like a flowing sea of blood surrounded by molten gold. We followed the bank of the river aimlessly. I looked at Rita and offered her my hand, hoping that I would forget my fixation with blood. She hesitated. I watched as her hands found her jeans pockets. She tried to walk but could not walk straight with her hands in her pockets. Either from the effect of the margarita or the mechanics of the human body, she needed two swinging hands to balance.

We passed a couple walking in the opposite direction with a poodle, tethered to a hand by a long leash, its tail wagging and its curious nose to the ground. The dog made short runs to nowhere. Then, she ran around Rita and tied up her ankles with the leash. Rita patted the dog while the owner unleashed her ankles. The dog and its owners walked on. Rita's hand brushed against mine, and she held on. Our fingers intertwined. I was grateful.

"What a beautiful evening. I would've been at home alone," she said.

"I can't imagine that. You're beautiful," I said.

"I got tired of going out with losers."

"Dr Peterson is not a loser."

"Not my type. He wants every nurse."

"Why me? I'm just a broke medical student."

"Money is overrated."

"I wouldn't know. Never had any," I said. I laughed.

Rita looked at me, and her face became solemn. She stopped, and hugged me. I did not expect the hug. My hands dangled by my sides as she squeezed me tight. I could not extricate my hands to hug her.

"Are you okay?" I asked.

"I need to go," she said.

"Sorry if I made you sad."

"It's not your fault."

The sun had set, and the street lights came on. Amber-colored lights, imparting a different feel from the setting sun. As my eyes observed the lights, Rita walked ahead of me. Her action surprised me, forcing me to review everything I'd said to her. Although I felt that the chance of getting another date with her was dwindling, I was not ready to give up. I promised Rose to find a girl, and I felt that Rita was the one.

From a short distance away, I saw Rita standing by the passenger's side, waiting for me. When I reached her, I wrapped my arm around her waist and opened the car door. Instead of getting inside the car, she turned around and hugged me. We held each other and kissed, a wet one, with rolling tongues. Her hug became tighter. I let out a gasp, and laughed. Her grip loosened.

"I'm scared," she said. She closed her eyes. I kissed her closed eyes. "I'm scared of my feelings," she added. She opened her eyes, and looked at me, staring—her lips quivering.

"No reason to be. I thought we had fun," I said.

"We did. More than I expected," she said. We hugged again. Softer than before. Her head rested on my shoulder. "That's what I'm afraid of." Her voice wavered, and we disengaged from our hug.

"I got dumped recently. I'm the needy one," I said. She reached out and held my hand.

She entered the car holding my hand. She held on to my hand and would not let go. I leaned against the door frame and caressed her beautiful black hair. She pressed my hand against her head. I bent down and kissed her for a long time.

"Let's take care of each other," she said.

"I asked God to take care of me. I'll take you for the job," I said.

"I'll be here for you," she said.

"Thank you for everything," I said. I hummed and whistled.

Rita laughed. I closed the car door and whistled my way to the driver's side.

Driving out of the parking lot, I saw a disheveled man carrying several bulging grocery bags. He was wearing a heavy coat, which was unusual for the warm, Memphis, late-summer weather. As I approached the intersection and came closer to the stranger, I thought I recognized him as the same man I had seen from the window of my room, sleeping on a bench at night. A homeless man.

The homeless man turned in different directions while standing in the same spot at the street intersection. One of his bags fell from his hand. He tried to pick up the fallen bag, and the rest fell from his hands. He lifted his face up to the sky and yelled. A poodle ran toward him. The owners yelled out the dog's name, but the dog kept running away from them. Rita and I looked at each other and laughed.

As the poodle approached the middle of the street, an approaching truck swerved to avoid hitting the dog. The driver of the truck lost control of his vehicle and it careened toward us, hitting the driver's side of my car. A loud bang resonated in my ears, followed by a scream from Rita. My body felt limp.

I turned my torso to look at Rita, and a stinging pain traveled from the left side of my chest to my back. My shirt felt warm. Looking at my shirt, I saw a blood stain covered half of it. It looked soaked. I cried out. Rita tore the shirt off my body, folded it, and used the bulk to apply pressure to the side of my chest. I reclined my seat. She kissed my lips, and her tears dripped on my face.

I heard a banging noise on my car door. A man pulled on the door handle. Ambulance sirens resonated from a distance. Rita was crying. Looking around me and, feeling trapped inside my car, the fear of dying gripped me. I closed my eyes and drifted away.

I had the sensation of being in a dark room. Echoes of muffled sounds were swirling around. Sharp pain traveled all over my body before it took up residence in my head. It felt as if someone was drilling holes inside my skull. My eyes watered, but I could not see. Feeling nauseated, I began to see flickers of amber light. I was lying on a bed. A morgue, or a funeral home, crossed my mind. Then I heard a distinct voice.

"You're in the ICU." I looked around a lighted room. Rita was standing next to my bed, her shirt stained with blood. My blood, I assumed. I could see my hands, but I wondered if the rest of my body, which was covered with a blanket, was missing parts.

Chapter 11

A SHARP CHEST PAIN woke me up. As far as my eyes could see, I was alone. I heard sounds from every corner of the room. Beeps and buzzes, as well as laughter and cries outside my room. My eyes trailed outside the door, where I saw blue uniforms and regular street clothes, and nurses and guests walking by: intensive care unit traffic, though none for my room. I was alone. An adult orphan. I had no one to notify, even if I died.

Feeling uncomfortable lying on my back, I adjusted my body. The mattress inflated and deflated. Searching for the bed's control buttons, I found a wired remote close to my feet, just out of my reach. I felt pain reaching for the control buttons, as the pressure in the mattress changed. I tried to adjust mentally.

Cardiac and vital sign monitors hung on a pole by the side of my bed, displaying white, yellow, and red lines. After each painful breath, my eyes wandered. Even when my eyes closed, I could hear the sounds from my heart monitor creating comforting interludes in the rhythmic sounds of my heartbeat, a sign that I was still alive.

Drifting back to sleep, I heard a yawn. Wondering if it was me, I heard a second yawn. I'd thought I was alone. My face turned to the edge of the room where I had a limited view. As I turned steeply, the side of my chest felt as if someone had stuck a dagger into it. Even with the pain in my chest, my eyes saw her. Rita, wearing the same blood-stained shirt. Her eyes were closed, and her hand rested on a pillow. Wrapped around her neck was a blue scrub shirt. Her lips were pursed as if she was smiling. My chest pain worsened, and her face became blurry.

My eyelids felt heavy. Bright lights and distorted objects hung in the room. A voice whispered, drowning out my heartbeat. I felt warm breath on my face and a squeeze of my hand, and heard the sound of a blood pressure cuff inflating. My arm and fingers felt numb. My eyelids could not open. The thought of a stroke crossed my mind. Even death. The opposite of what I wished for. I could sense my breathing rate increase.

"Code blue, intensive care unit, room 401. Code blue, ICU, room 401," the loudspeakers buzzed, followed by a lull.

I remembered the number one being associated with my room. It was my code blue. My death. I tried to wriggle my body. It could not move. My body felt warm. If I could move my body, or open my eyes, it would not be the end. There came another round of announcements. The speaker buzzed, longer this time, then stopped.

I jerked my body around in bed. The mattress deflated, and the intravenous pump alarm sounded. I straightened my arm, and the alarm stopped buzzing.

"I'm still alive," I yelled. Sharp pain traveled all over my body. I felt fingers wrap around my thumb.

"Are you okay, Ben?" a voice asked.

I felt a cold towel on my face. My eyes opened. Rita was looking down on me.

"I heard my code blue," I said. She smiled.

"Down the hall. Not you, silly," she said.

A woman wearing blue scrubs entered the room. As she approached my bed, I remembered her face. Monica. A kick boxer, and a darn good nurse. I imagined she was there to 'kick some butt'. My butt, for yelling.

"CAT scan looks good. Repeat chest X-ray showed no pneumothorax," Monica said. I watched her hands as she spoke. Her legs, too.

"I'm glad. Who's the attending?" Rita asked.

"Don't know yet. His wound isn't bad enough for a trauma team," Monica said.

"So, I'm okay?" I asked.

"You're bruised up bad," Monica said, a grin on her face.

Rita and Monica walked outside the room and whispered. They watched my room as they spoke. I watched their lips but could not make out what they were saying. My chest pain did not improve. Moving my hand around, I felt the dressing on the side of my chest, which was bulky and wet. My fingers came back stained with blood. Monica rushed into my room and inspected the dressing. She took a cordless phone out of her pocket and dialed some numbers.

"Page the thoracic resident for me," Monica said. Her facial skin crinkled as she held the telephone receiver to her ear. "Page the ICU resident on call, too," Monica added.

"Is there a problem?" Rita asked. Having focused on Monica, I did not see Rita return to my room. Rita's question worried me. The thought of dying came back to me. I looked at Rita, the woman I would lose if death came to me.

"I feel okay," I said. My eyes darted to my heart monitor for reassurance.

"You're bleeding. Your temp is high, too," Rita said.

Monica's phone rang. She walked outside the room to answer it.

"Who's on call?' Rita asked, when Monica returned to my room.

"Didn't ask. They're all the same. Bad attitudes," Monica said.

"That's what you think about doctors?" I asked.

"Cocky, dumb residents," Rita said. Monica and Rita laughed. If resident physicians were dumb, I wondered what they thought about medical students. There was no reason for Rita to be with me.

"We'll train you better. You're a good medical student," Rita said.

"I'm not sure about the training part," I said. Monica walked to Rita and whispered in her ear. They looked at me and laughed. I looked around me for a mirror and found none.

I heard footsteps. When I looked around, Dr Peterson, Brenda, and James were in my room. Brenda stayed two paces behind everyone. James gave me a thumbs up, while Dr Peterson approached Monica. He walked by Rita and ignored her. I looked at Brenda and smiled. She frowned.

"He's a trauma case," Dr Peterson said.

"Does it matter? He's your student," Monica said.

Dr Peterson looked at Rita with disdainful eyes. He turned to me and looked at me the same way.

"What's going on with the lover boy?" Dr Peterson asked.

"Don't be disrespectful to a patient," Rita said.

"Get out," Dr Peterson said to Rita. Rita sat down and ignored him. Dr Peterson walked closer to Rita, looking down at her.

"I said, get out," Dr Peterson said.

"You're not my doctor. Get out," I said. I couldn't contain

my anger. I felt around my bed for an object. Something to break Dr Peterson's head with.

My face felt warm, and the rate of the heart monitor's beeping sounds increased. I lifted my hand and it trembled. Pain traveled from the side of my chest to my neck. Dr Peterson looked at me and scowled. I opened my mouth to say more, but no words came out.

Rita walked to my bedside and held my hand. Brenda shrugged her shoulders and walked out of the room. Brenda showed me her middle finger as she stepped outside my room. I opened the palms of my hands to her. James walked to the side of my bed and patted my hand. He stepped outside the room. I heard James' voice rise as he talked to Brenda. Brenda walked away.

"Don't call me about him. Even if he's dying," Dr Peterson said to Monica.

"I'm reporting you for abusing a patient," Rita said to Dr Peterson.

"I hope he was good," Dr Peterson said to Rita. "Ruining your career over a stupid medical student."

"You wanted me to ruin it over you. Egotistical bastard," Rita said.

"I'll show you who's valued here," Dr Peterson said and walked out.

Chapter 12

A KNOCK ON MY DOOR woke me to a dark room, wires across my chest. The vital signs monitors faced the wall opposite me, away from my eyes. I had an interest in the monitors in my room but couldn't reach them, as their screens were directed away from me. Intermittent beeping sounds, at constant intervals, announced the sound of my heart. The lights outside my room were dimmed. I watched the dwindling traffic outside my hospital room. A few men and women in blue scrubs. A rest period for patients. Nothing else to occupy my time. Frustrated and bored, I exhaled.

After I closed my eyes, I felt pressure inside my bladder. My hand reached for the bed railing, the last place I saw a urinal hanging. I could not find the jug by feel, I turned to my side. I saw a figure standing outside my room, whose head almost touched the top frame of the ICU room door. My heart pounded. A hollow feeling settled inside my stomach. While my hands trembled, the figure moved closer to me. I saw a hand and a sickle.

"Ben, can we talk?" a man's voice spoke. I wiped my eyes. The sickle was still present.

"You know my name?" I asked.

"You're one crazy dude. Stop clowning around," the man's voice said.

"You can't take me to hell tonight. I just met a girl," I said.

"What's wrong with you? Are you smoking stuff?" the man's voice laughed.

He pushed the object he held to the side. I blinked twice. My IV pole, with its intravenous bags and tubing, jingled. Not a sickle. I took a deep breath.

"It's James," a woman's voice said. They laughed.

I turned to the female voice. A figure stood close to me. She leaned her face close to mine, blowing out a whiff of peppermint breath. Her fingers caressed my face and settled on my lips, she moved her finger back and forth across the lower one. My eyes flickered from one side of my bed to the other, trying to focus. When my vision improved, I saw James watching Rita caress my lip. My breathing rate slowed down, and I inhaled for longer. Rita placed her lips on mine, and I enjoyed an arousing peppermint taste. It sounded as if there was a doubling in the number of intermittent sounds from my heart monitor.

I had imagined worse things happening to me. I could feel the joy inside me, but my chest hurt. James stepped closer. My vision had improved. His rumpled green scrubs and wire-rim glasses were clearly visible.

"I need your advice," James said.

"He's in pain. Can't it wait?" Rita said.

"I'm dying, but go ahead," I said.

"It's about Brenda," James said.

"Lies, I bet. It can wait," Rita said.

"Privacy, please," James said. Rita ignored him. Rita looked at me, and I smiled. I wanted her lips on mine. Her peppermint breath. My mind wandered, but I remembered what James had said.

"Rita's okay," I said.

"We fight all the time. She's driving me crazy," James said.

"I can't help you, dude. I'm the last person she would listen to," I said. I tried to turn onto my side. My pain did not improve.

Rita shook her head and walked to the corner chair. James stood by my bedside looking at me silently. My pain intensified, and it felt as if hours had passed watching my silent guard, my sentry James.

"My wife wants to come home," James said.

"Good-bye Brenda," I said. He looked at me with a frown. I lifted my hands up, excited. Pain radiated to my shoulder and back. My hands came down. "No more midnight gymnastics in her bed," I added.

"She's unreasonable and crazy," James said. He walked to the foot of my bed and looked at me directly.

"God help you, and me too," I said. Rita laughed.

"Afraid of an anorexic girl, boys?" Rita asked. We laughed.

"She's a bundle of dynamite waiting to ignite," James said.

"She'll light you up. I bet your panties will burn first," I said. I laughed, holding my side.

"I don't wear panties. I knew it was a mistake to talk to you," James said, his face solemn.

Monica entered the room. I wondered where she had been, ignoring all the noise in my room. She walked to the side of my bed and pushed a button on the monitor. The blood pressure cuff inflated on my arm and tightened its grip. My fingers tingled. She walked to the IV pole and pushed it closer to my bed. She then turned to James.

"No visitors after nine," Monica said.

"Leave me alone, Topless," James said.

"Hmmm," I said. I looked at Monica's chest—small

mounds. I wondered what she'd showed James that earned her the nickname.

"Never heard that one. Hiding things from me?" Rita asked.

"High school stuff," Monica said. James laughed.

"You're dead if you tell," Monica added.

James looked at her and mimicked pulling his shirt off. Monica made a fist. Rita raised her eyebrow and grinned. I suppressed a laugh; laughing caused me more chest pain.

"Our super nurse here took her blouse off to save a girl who cut her wrist. Tied her cut wrist and stopped her bleeding," James said.

"It happened before Monica became a nurse. I'm impressed," I said.

"Instinct. That was all I needed. Sad thing is, she died six months ago. Her husband left, and she overdosed. A wasted life," Monica said. James took a deep breath. His smile faded away.

"I didn't know she died. Well, you gave her six more years," James said. He shook his head and left the room.

Rita walked to the sink and washed her hands. She dried them for more than five minutes. Monica pulled out a bottle of hand sanitizer from her pocket and offered it to Rita. She declined and walked to my bedside. I inspected her hands and laughed.

"I didn't know you were dating," Monica said. Rita looked at me and smiled. I exhaled. My chest pain improved.

"Our first date. It was going well until the accident," Rita said. I reached out and held her hand.

"Do I get a second one?" I asked.

"After you recover, I'll think about it," Rita said.

"Lucky you. Unless Dr P. kills you. A dagger to your heart, then his," Monica said. She laughed. She snorted, and stopped laughing.

"You're sick," Rita said.

"No. Just a romantic. I'll die for love," Monica said. The girls giggled.

"Not me. I'll live and love," I said.

"Get some sleep. We'll probably discharge you early," Monica said.

"I'm working tomorrow night. Who's going to watch him?" Rita asked.

The girls looked at each other and laughed. Their laughter got louder. They covered their mouths with their hands. I could not figure out what was funny.

"You have it bad, Girl," Monica said.

"It's not a disease," Rita said.

I looked at the ceiling and the clock on the wall.

"What the heck are you talking about?" I asked. They resumed their laughter.

A man wearing blue scrubs entered the room. His eyes were barely open and the bags underneath them were dark. He yawned as he walked up to Monica.

"Keep your voices down," he said in a whisper. He turned around and left the room.

"Our new supervisor. I can't stand him. He's a prick," Monica said.

"Never met him," Rita said.

"Should have told him you're in love. That you got what you wanted," Monica said. Rita's smile faded away.

"Enough, Monica," Rita said. She looked at me, and added, "I'm sorry about her comment."

"About what?" I asked.

"The story Monica is telling about me," Rita said. Her eyes bulged as she looked at me. It appeared as if she was looking through me. Her lower lip quivered. She walked to the corner of the room and picked up her purse. When she reached the door to my room, she stopped.

"I don't appreciate the innuendo," Rita said, with her back turned against the room. Monica walked to her and whispered words I couldn't hear.

"I'm sorry, Rita. Please don't leave," I said.

"Not your fault. Monica betrayed me."

Monica raised her eyebrows. "I'm happy for you and Ben. You wanted him badly. Now you have him," she said.

Rita left my room without saying good-bye, and Monica followed her. My heart rate increased, and I felt alone in my ICU room. I was afraid that Rita would not return. I thought about the sequence of events. An awesome date, a motor vehicle accident, chest trauma, and a breakup. All in one day. It could have been days. How would I know? Hallucinations occupied some of my time. I wondered about the drugs they gave me for the pain, and what else could go wrong in my life.

Chapter 13

I WOKE TO A VOICE: "Ben, Ben, Ben." An unfamiliar female voice. She called my name with indifference. Not like Rita or Deb. There was no sweetness to the sound. Once would have been enough, I thought. My eyes opened. It was still dark in my room. I had lost a sense of time. A figure standing at the foot of my bed pulled on my toes, giving them a slight twist to the side. Painful. My foot retracted, instead of giving a kick. I moved my hand around the side of my bed, searching for the light control buttons. I heard myself sigh.

The figure walked toward the wall and turned the room lights on. Bright fluorescent lights. I couldn't see. My eyes closed. When I opened them, I saw a female in green scrubs standing next to my bed, smiling with red lips. A pair of sharp surgical scissors and a pack of gauze stuck out of her side pocket. I became worried. She stretched her hand out to shake mine. I remembered to avoid a firm grip. She was a beautiful woman.

Looking at her smiling face did not alleviate my fear. My eyes reverted to watching the sharp object in her pocket. A sharp pair of surgical scissors. She had no scalpel in her possession, but I was still worried. I lifted the blanket and checked my vital organs. Everything seemed to be intact. Nothing I felt I needed was cut off. I sighed. I thought about the silliness of what I had done.

"I'm Eleana. Thoracic resident." I looked around the room, before I focused on the clock. She smiled. "I know it's five. We do our rounds early," she said, reading my mind. I grinned. My jaw hurt. A new place for the lingering pain.

"Do your thing, 'cause I'm leaving soon," I said. I felt helpless. Vulnerable. She reached for my hospital gown. I reached out to cup my loin with two hands. My pain became worse. I clenched my teeth, and stopped. Resident physicians joked about 'sissy' patients. I chose not to ask for help. No pain medications. Sweat covered my face, and my body felt warm. Drug addiction withdrawal and Dr Peterson's involvement crossed my mind. Without knowing what I received for the pain, and forgetting about addiction pathophysiology, my symptoms intensified. Medical knowledge was useless when I was the one sick. My thinking about Dr Peterson drugging me worried me more. My sweating became profuse and my heart rate increased. Seconds felt like days to me. Eleana watched me with patience.

"I'll take a quick look, I promise," Eleana said.

"Very quick, please," I said. Fear of pain-medication addiction stayed on my mind and my desire to leave the intensive care unit became urgent. An escape for survival. Dr Peterson would kill me if I stayed longer. I wrung my hands while watching Eleana. Worried that she was sent by Dr Peterson, I looked inside her pocket for pain-medication syringes.

She tried to pull the dressing off my skin. I gritted my teeth, saw flickers of stars; my facial muscles tightened, and I held my breath. She stopped. It was hard to tell if I screamed. It felt as if she had stabbed me. I searched her hand for a scalpel.

"Bear with me. It won't take long," Eleana said. It had already taken longer than I wanted.

I reached for the bed railing and gripped it tightly. My eyes closed, and I thought about Rita sitting with me at the restaurant. Her tight blouse, and bosom. I licked my lips. My facial muscles loosened.

I heard the sound of footsteps. Squeaky shoes. Monica entered, her face drawn. She took her stethoscope off her neck and walked to my bedside. When our eyes met, she smiled. Eleana stopped applying adhesive pad over the gauze on my chest and walked to the sink. She washed her hands and leaned against the wall.

"Aren't you going to clean up your mess?" Monica asked.

"Did I wet myself?" I asked.

"Not you," Monica said. Eleana threw the paper towel in her hand into the trash can and walked toward the door.

"Dr E., you need to clean up after yourself," Monica said.

"You give nurses a bad name," Eleana said.

"Monica's been good to me," I said.

"You don't know her the way I do," Eleana said.

"Bye. Go find someone's fiancé to snatch," Monica said.

"I'll tell the nursing supervisor," Eleana said.

"Good luck. Our nursing director isn't a man," Monica said.

"Stop the yapping," I yelled. "When am I going freaking home?" I felt pain go through my chest with my yelling, "Ouch, ouch." I missed Rita, her smile and kiss. I worried about not brushing my teeth and my bad breath chasing her away.

My bladder tightened up and was ready to expel its contents. I gripped the bed railings first, before reaching for the bedside urinal. Reaching inside the blanket, I used my hand to direct the flow of urine into the receptacle. Once my bladder was empty, I realized that I had exposed myself.

"Who'll care for you?" Eleana asked.

"Rita will," Monica said. She walked closer to me and whispered, "Don't even look at Dr Eleana twice."

"What did you say?" I asked. She ignored me as she cleared away what Eleana had left behind.

"Once my attending signs off, I'll send you home," Eleana said.

"Sounds good," I said.

The two women eyed each other. A stare. No smiles. As time progressed, their eyeballs bulged, trading piercing looks. I thought about a fist fight between them in my room. Harming me in the process. My body felt cold. I closed my eyes as if to take away my fear. A kick boxer and a trained surgeon. Egos and sharp objects in the hands of those trained to use them. A beeper sounded. Eleana left the room clutching her little sound machine. A relief for me.

* * *

Eleana returned to my room at 5:15 pm with men and women in green scrubs. Some of her team barely had their eyelids open, as if waiting for the last command to shut them. An older man with gray hair and a beaming smile approached my bed, his eyes wide open. He was agile compared to most of the others leaning against the wall. Halfway to my bed, he extended his hand, which I inspected: bony digits. I feigned a smile as I reached out to shake his hand. He had a firm grip that felt like a vise.

"I'm Dr Hollander. You're a lucky bas…" He stopped before he completed his last word and smiled. "Your wound is superficial." His hand rested on my shoulder. Tears rolled out of my eyes as I searched for Rita.

"I'm grateful to God," I said. The tears dripped into my mouth. I wiped my upper lip with the back of my hand.

"Let him walk around the unit before he's discharged," Eleana said. She did not wait for any discussions about her instructions before she left the room.

"No lifting for two weeks," Dr Hollander said. He shook my hand again and left the room.

Eleana returned to my room with a prescription. She walked closer to my bed and extended her hand to me. Her grip was weak, her flesh soft. She helped me to sit up in bed. I stood on my feet. Pain traveled all over my body. I took a few steps to the entrance of my room and returned to my bed.

"Good job," Eleana said.

"Thank you for everything," I said.

"I just dressed your wound. Nothing else to do today," she said. Her smile lingered on. We looked at each other.

"Finally, you're discharged."

Rita in blue scrubs stood by the door. She held the edge of the sliding door, her cross-body bag resting on her hip, her face sullen.

"Come in. I missed you," I said.

Rita walked over to me and kissed my lips. She reached out to hug me. My hands extended, then stopped. Pain traveled to new places on my chest wall. I imagined the way it would feel if I was cut internally. I lowered my hands, and my body trembled. She rubbed my cheeks with her hand.

"I'll take you home," Rita said.

"Home? Whose home?" I asked.

"Yours, silly," Rita said, flashing a smile that made her look more beautiful.

"I don't have a home. A dorm room is not a home," I said.

"Still a home," Rita said.

"I get it," I said. I reached out and held her hand. "You left me," I added.

"I had to think things through. You heard what Monica said." Rita bowed her head as she spoke.

"I heard my name," Monica said as she walked into the room, her hands filled with wound- dressing supplies. She placed them on the bedside table.

"I'm about to tell Ben I'm fond of him," Rita said.

"I'm gathering supplies for him," Monica said.

"Gosh. I'm in paradise. Two women fawning over me," I said.

"That's an insult. We're trying to help you," Rita said.

"Just teasing. Don't run away again," I said.

"Didn't she tell you?" Monica asked. She looked at me and Rita. "She slept in the waiting room," she added.

"I didn't know. I'm sorry," I said.

Rita leaned down and kissed my lips. She squeezed my hand, and I felt her tongue in my mouth, a wanderer in my territory. I granted her tongue free passage. Our tongues rolled around and paused only once. In the process, my eyes closed.

"Can't wait to get home?" Monica asked. She laughed, then added, "Don't do it here."

My eyes opened, my tongue returned home, and Rita sighed. I sensed a protest, as if she did not want to stop. I remembered that I was a medical student and should not break any hospital rules.

"Can't wait to unwrap you," Rita said.

"Like a gift? A damaged one, in case you forgot," I said. I chuckled at the thought of being unwrapped.

"He's discharged. Be gentle," Monica said. She cupped her mouth, but it did not stop her laughter. Rita turned her face to the wall as she laughed too. Giggles, with bursts of coughing.

I lifted my head from the bed and watched their silliness. Squeaking wheels at the entrance of my room attracted my attention. A wheelchair rolled into my room, pushed by a young man in brown scrubs and high-top basketball shoes, barely five foot tall. I wondered if he would be able to push my 190-pound body.

"I can walk," I said.

"Hospital rules. You know what they say," Rita said.

"Let's get out of here," I said.

I sat on the edge of my bed, my pains unabated. It felt as if knives were cutting me up inside. I looked behind to dispel my fear, but the pain intensified. How would I struggle through in the dormitory with my physical limitations? With my head bowed, I reached for Rita's hand. She squeezed mine.

"I'll help you stand, then ease you into the wheelchair," Monica said.

"My pain is worse. I walked earlier. It wasn't this bad," I said.

"I bet it is. We're lucky to be alive," Rita said.

"I'm sorry to put you through this mess," I said.

Rita opened her mouth as if she was about to speak. I looked at her face and my lips pursed. The words I wanted to say stuck in my mouth. Her grip loosened, and her mouth slowly closed. My eyes strayed away from her face. Silence and awkwardness separated us. We sighed simultaneously.

"Are you guys okay?" Monica asked.

No one spoke. I feigned a smile as I stood still, struggling with my pain. A cold feeling came over me, and I felt dizzy. Rita pushed the wheelchair closer to my side. The orderly watched from a distance. I lowered my body onto the wheelchair without moving my torso. When Rita bent down to adjust my footrest, my eyes wandered inside her shirt. For a moment, I forgot about my pain. A warm feeling traveled through my body when I thought about spending time alone with Rita.

Chapter 14

RITA STOPPED HER CAR close to the entrance of my dormitory. She left the driver's door open and ran into the building. She had parked in a no-parking zone. I watched for the campus security. Occasionally I watched Rita's lips move as she spoke to someone behind the reception desk. It appeared as if her hands moved more than her lips. When her hands were not moving, she placed them on her hips. She shook her head as she listened to the person behind the desk. They shook hands before Rita exited the building.

I watched Rita's face as she approached the car, eager to know what she had discussed with the receptionist. She looked around the building before she came to the passenger's side of her car. I opened the door.

"No wheelchair," she said.

"All that for a wheelchair? I can walk," I said. I tried to hide my fear of falling.

"Just trying to make it easy for you," she said.

I placed my legs on the ground and lifted my body out of the car. My pain intensified, but I smiled because Rita was watching me. She extended a hand to me after I closed the car door.

"I'll park the car later," she said. I looked around for campus security.

"I can wait for you. This is a no-parking area," I said. I was worried about the university towing her car and not being able to pay for it.

"You're in pain. I can't let you stand here."

"It's only pain. I can handle it." I tried to laugh, but instead developed a coughing spell. I tried to hold my breath to alleviate the pain. Rita put her hand behind my head and pulled it down. She kissed my eyelids.

We held hands as we walked to the entrance, Rita provided good support as I took measured steps. The sliding door tried to close on us but retracted to the sides. From a short distance away, I saw the number three illuminated above the elevator door. Rita pushed the elevator button. I grumbled. I wanted to take charge, even when I had physical limitations.

"You're like a kid," she said.

"It's my building, and I'm the man," I said. I tried to laugh but settled for a smile. Pain controlled my actions at that moment.

"Really. I'll dump you right here and go home," Rita said.

Enough time had passed, but the elevator stayed on the third floor. I pushed the elevator button three times out of my frustration from standing there in pain. Rita laughed. She probably was not aware of the amount of pain I was in. I turned to the receptionist's area to alert her about the elevator, but she was on the phone with her back turned to us.

Rita kissed my cheek as she watched me rub my forehead. When I sighed, she laughed.

"What's so funny?" I asked.

"I am learning a lot about you. You're impatient," she said.

I snorted.

"It broke down," the receptionist yelled across the lobby.

"I can't walk up six floors," I said.

I was ready to give up and sit in the lobby until the elevator was fixed. Rita looked at me. Her eyes were barely open, and her face looked drawn. She shuffled her feet as she walked around. I wanted to apologize to her, but I was physically exhausted. I turned around and leaned against the wall, which gave me much needed support.

"We can't wait here forever. We can go to my place," Rita said. I thought about Rita taking over my life. Telling me what to do and how to do things. Insecurity.

"The stairway is around the corner. I'll try," I said.

Climbing the steps to my room felt more proper to me than going home with Rita. I wanted her to see me as a resilient man, which I felt would be rewarding for me, and also earn her respect.

We shuffled our feet to the steel stairway door, which I held open for Rita. A young man ran down the steps and through the open door, almost knocking Rita down. He did not apologize. I was not physically able to defend Rita, if necessary. I became more worried.

Rita held on to the railings and ascended the steps, I followed. She stopped multiple times after climbing four to five steps. At last, we reached the sixth floor. We rested at the landing before opening the door to the hallway. A group of young men stood by the elevator. Watching them waste their time waiting for a non-working elevator, I felt elated by my valiant effort. A worthy man. When we entered the common area of my dormitory suite, the lights were off, and the refrigerator hummed in the darkness.

For a moment, I forgot the location of the light switches, either out of tiredness or from the effects of some of the medications. I felt the walls until I found a switch and turned the lights on. Once the lights came on, I saw a body sprawled across three chairs that had been pulled together. An apple and a surgical scalpel lay on a coffee table. I wondered why someone would cut an apple with a surgical scalpel. The body rose, revealing sunken eyeballs and cheeks streaked by drying tears. Brenda picked up the surgical scalpel and stood up. Rita jumped.

"I forgot you live here. Crazy bitch," Rita said.

"What the fuck are you doing?" I said.

"James told you. The bastard left me," Brenda said.

"James the medical student? Can't see the two of you together," Rita said.

"Brenda, that's your problem. I'm in pain right now," I said. Brenda walked closer to me with the scalpel in her hand.

"Put it down. I'll call the cops," Rita yelled.

"Cops? Why?" Brenda asked.

Rita took off one of her shoes and held it up.

Brenda dropped the scalpel to the floor. Rita picked up the scalpel.

"Keep your hands where I can see them," Rita said. She retrieved her phone from her purse.

"You're overreacting. Don't call the cops," I said.

"You'll regret it," Rita said.

"I'm not trying to hurt him," Brenda said. Fresh tears flowed down her cheeks.

"James is married. Forget him," I said.

"What's the scalpel for?" Rita asked.

"To cut my apple," Brenda said.

"You'll cut your hand off," Rita said.

"I'm not a child," Brenda said.

"You act like one," Rita said.

"You've no right to take away my property," Brenda said.

"I'm hurting bad," I said. Rita placed the scalpel on the coffee table. Looking at the scalpel, which was within her reach, I thought about Brenda using it on me. To end my suffering, permanently. When I looked at Rita, I felt the desire to live. To become the keeper of her love and affection. My concern about the influence of pain medications on my thought process returned.

I staggered to my door. Rita followed me into my room. She placed the wound-care supplies on my desk and walked to the window. I sat on the edge of my bed to relieve my pain, and rest. My bed squeaked. The noise attracted Rita's attention. She looked at me. Even though I was in pain, I smiled. Her eyes darted all over my room until they focused on the fire alarm unit above the door. After a sigh, she sat next to me on the bed and bowed her head.

"You need a better place to live," she said. I reached out and held her hand. Her head remained bowed, and her hand lay limp in mine.

"My scholarship is all I have. Fifteen thousand dollars a year and free tuition. Close to your tax bill. I can't afford to move," I said, and laughed.

She stood up and walked around the limited space in my room. She stopped in front of my closet and hesitated before opening the door. A couple of shirts and pairs of pants hung from hangers. I looked away. Although my sense of self-worth was not tied to my material possessions, I could not bear to look at my meager wardrobe in her presence.

"You need more clothes," she said. She closed my closet

door, walked to the window, and leaned her back against it. Watching her walk away from me made me feel that she was trying to create a distance between us, physically and emotionally. I tried without success to restrain the sigh that followed.

"I'm poorer than you probably thought," I said.

"I don't care about your finances." She walked over to my bed and sat down.

"You could do better with Dr Peterson. He makes as much as you do," I said.

She placed her arm around my shoulder and looked in my eyes. I felt her fast heartbeat, and warmth. Her phone rang. She reached for her purse and retrieved the phone.

"Hi." She paused as she listened to the caller. I could not hear what the caller was saying. "I'll be there soon," she said, before she hung up.

"You have to go?" I asked.

"They need me in ICU. Not sure for how long," she said.

"I'll buy more clothes. I promise," I said.

"I'll see you soon, Baby," she said. She kissed my lips and picked up her purse.

My hand reached out to hers. I lifted my body up from the bed and hugged her. She held my body loosely as we left my room. Brenda was sitting on the chair where we had left her, in the shared area of the dormitory suite. Her apple was still on the table, but I couldn't see her scalpel.

"I can find my way from here," Rita said.

"Call me when you're done," I said.

"I plan to," Rita said.

I ignored Brenda and walked back to my room. I took off

my shoes and lay down. My eyes wandered to the bolt lock on my door. It was in the open position. My eyes blinked several times and things became blurry. I felt too tired to get out of bed. In my twilight state, I heard myself snore.

I woke to my door opening. I heard screeching sounds from the door hinges and saw reflections of light. A figure stood next to my bed. I could see no distinctive features as I struggled to keep my eyes open. An outline of a person. A man, or a woman. A shadow. My hands felt limp. I could not reach out to touch whoever was in front of me. As my heart rate accelerated, I heard rapid breathing and smelled pungent breath. Garlic and a musty odor lingered on. My eyelids felt too heavy to keep open. Despite how much I struggled, I drifted back to sleep.

Hearing a loud scream outside my door, I opened my eyes. I heard, "God, please forgive me." There came a moan and a bang on my door. A chilling silence followed, then a thud, as if someone had fallen against the door. My heart raced, and a warm feeling came over me. I jumped out of bed, looked around my room, and picked up a chair. Chest pain overpowered me, and the chair fell from my hand. I struggled to my door with trepidation.

I placed my ear against the door. Apart from my heartbeat, I heard no other sound. I slowly opened my door. Brenda was sprawled on the floor outside my room. Her mouth was open, and blood oozed from her wrist. Forgetting about my pain, I leaned down to listen for breathing, and checked her pulse. A whiff of garlic breath filled my nostrils, my fingers reached out to her neck, and found a bounding carotid pulse. Relieved that her heart was beating—she was alive—I sighed. She mumbled inaudible words.

While I was doing my clinical assessment, she turned onto her side. I tried to restrain her, but she resisted. Her bleeding increased. I walked to my desk to pick up the surgical supplies. I picked up the phone too. My fingers dialed 911 before I thought about my actions. On the first ring, there was an answer.

"How can I help you?"

"There is a student bleeding from a cut. University Tower on Madison. Please hurry," I said. My voice quivered.

Brenda had crawled into my room while I was on the phone. Trails of blood marked her path. I sighed.

"Is she breathing?"

"She is, Ma'am," I said, while leaning down to ascertain my answer. Brenda reached out and grabbed my shirt collar, soaking it with blood.

"Who the hell is on the phone?" Brenda asked. She advanced her grip on my shirt collar, closer to my neck. My legs trembled. I checked her free hand for a scalpel. "I said, who the fuck is on the phone?" she added. Her eyes glistened in the street light that trickled into my room. The fear of Brenda dying in my room—a scandal—worried me. Looking at the newspaper on my desk, I thought about the potential headline and my suspension from school.

"I called 911," I said.

"Sir, what's going on?" the 911 operator asked.

"She's pulling the phone away," I said.

"You fucker. I'll tell them you cut me," Brenda said.

"I'm fucked," I said. My hand trembled. I hung up the phone to collect my thoughts. The phone rang while my hand was still on the receiver. I answered the phone.

"I'm sending an ambulance. University Tower—what's your room number?" she asked.

Brenda grabbed the phone from my hand. I heard an ambulance siren outside my window.

"I ain't going nowhere," Brenda yelled on the phone. I reached for the phone, and she hit my hand with it. "I'm no psycho. No one's locking me up for 72 hours. Your ass is going to jail," she added.

"I'm trying to help you," I said. I wanted to scream at her, but did not. Her threat worried me. My mind drifted to the outcome of a false accusation: a ruined life. My life.

"You fucking idiot. I'll mess you up." Brenda pointed a blood-soaked middle finger at my face. I closed my eyes.

The ambulance siren became louder, then stopped. Sweat rolled down my face. Brenda looked into my eyes and laughed. I wondered if I had made a mistake by calling the ambulance. After reviewing the event, I concluded that I had no other choice available to me for getting Brenda proper care. However, I had to contend with the realization that I'd have to prove my innocence, if she decided to lie about what had happened to her. My hands trembled, and the sweating worsened. Her words, 'I'll mess you up', lingered in my mind. My future depended on the story Brenda would tell.

Chapter 15

BRENDA LAY SPRAWLED on my floor. Her hair was matted into clumps with congealed blood. My eyes wandered to her wrist, which was wrapped with my surgical supplies. Each time she let out a loud puff, I watched her chest rise and fall, forcing the eviction of air from her lungs. An exaggerated action, I concluded. I let out my own puff, a sigh of relief. After all, she was still alive.

Looking around my room, I saw trails of blood on my floor. There were narrow streaks everywhere, and two puddles lay at the edge of my bed. I yearned to unbutton, and discard, my blue pajamas shirt decorated with her blood, marked by her finger and palm prints.

The first to arrive were two campus security officers. They stood by my door, blue notepads pressed tight against their forearms, restrained as if they were in custody. They had not interviewed me about the incident. The way they guarded their note pads made me worry about their opinion regarding the incident. My heart raced.

Paramedics arrived and knelt next to Brenda. One paramedic stretched Brenda's forearm and applied a tourniquet. As he retrieved an intravenous catheter from his bag, Brenda reached for his wrist. She missed the wrist but gripped the sharp end of a needle. Her scream pierced the calmness in the room. I took a deep breath and forgot to exhale. A cold chill traveled over my body. The room spun. I rested my back against the wall. It appeared as if everyone in the room stood still. Distorted sounds resonated in my ears, a hollow babbling.

I lifted my hand to rub my forehead, revealing four blood-soaked fingers, it looked as if I was involved in the bloody situation—the perpetrator. I looked around and placed my hand inside my pocket, hiding the evidence against any false account Brenda might produce.

"What happened?" a campus security officer asked.

My hands trembled inside my pocket. He walked closer to Brenda. I felt relieved. Brenda rolled her eyes and turned away.

"Sir, did you witness the incident?" the other campus security officer asked. He looked at my shirt, and his eyes trailed down to my pocket. I tried to wipe my fingers inside my pocket.

"She came into my room bleeding," I said.

"Did she tell you what happened?" the campus security officer asked.

"She cut her wrist. I tried to help," I said.

"How did she cut her wrist?" the campus security officer asked. He opened his note pad to write.

"I don't know. I saw a cut. Maybe two cuts," I said.

"Was she trying to kill herself?" the campus security officer asked.

"I don't know, Sir," I said.

"Mind your own fucking business," Brenda said. Her eyes remained closed, and I was not sure who she was addressing.

Two Memphis police officers joined the group. Two female officers stood outside my room, wearing blue rubber gloves. No smiles or introductions. They stood silently and watched.

"You saw the blade?" the second campus security officer asked.

"No, Sir," I said.

"You have blood all over you. Are you sure there was no fight?" the campus security officer asked.

"Fight? There was no fight. She was hurt outside my room. I tried to help," I said. My hands trembled, my heart rate increased, and I began to sweat profusely. A guilty look, I couldn't help thinking.

"We need her statement. The truth," the campus security officer said.

I looked around me. The ambulance personnel were there for Brenda, the campus security to protect the university's interests, and the Memphis police for the city's interests. No one was there to protect my interests. Not even Rita. I wondered if she had left me. I turned to the woman lying on the stretcher, Brenda, the only person who could protect me, and she scowled. My body quivered.

"Tell 'em what happened," I said.

I wanted to add 'please' but decided not to, making a decision that hid my desperation.

"Leave me the hell alone," Brenda said. She wriggled on the gurney and pulled out her intravenous line.

"We can't transport you without an IV line," an ambulance attendant said.

"Please cooperate," I said.

Brenda rolled her eyes, her lips taut. She showed me her stretched-out middle finger—a bloody finger.

"Hmm. Lovers' quarrel," I heard one of the Memphis police officers whisper to her partner.

"We're not," I said. The Memphis cop smiled.

"Not what?" Brenda asked. She apparently had not heard

the police officer's comment.

"IV line secured again. We're ready to move," a paramedic said.

"Take the boyfriend with you. He'll tell you why she cut herself," the campus security officer said.

"We can't. No formal complaint against him. We'll complete the suicide-attempt forms in the ER," a Memphis police officer said.

The ambulance stretcher and the Memphis police officers left my room without me. The campus security officer pulled out my chair.

"Sit down. Start from the beginning. We need details," the campus security officer said.

"They'll need me in ER. She'll lie about cutting her wrist," I said.

"So, you witnessed the incident?"

"No. I mean, I think that's what she did."

"Facts only."

My telephone rang. Everyone looked in the direction of my desk.

"Answer it," the campus security officer said.

"Hello," I said.

"I'm on break. Just checking on you," Rita said.

"I'm in trouble."

"Still in pain?"

"No. Brenda cut herself. The campus cops are talking to me."

"I'm sorry I can't be there for you."

"I understand, Babe. I'm okay."

"Another babe," one of the campus security officers said. They whispered to each other and laughed.

I felt anger swell in me as they made jokes about such a serious event. I could not concentrate enough to continue my conversation with Rita.

"I have to go," I said. I switched off my phone.

The officers were still laughing when I walked out of the room. I felt that they were unprofessional.

"You can't leave yet," a campus security officer said.

"Watch me," I said.

"One step further, and we'll arrest you."

"For what?"

"Attacking a fellow student."

"I told you she cut herself."

"We'll see what she tells the Memphis police."

I returned to my chair and sat down. I picked up my phone and scrolled down my contacts' list. Two campus cops hovered over me. My hands rested on my desk. There was nothing left to add to the statement I had given. I wondered if they would arrest me.

Chapter 16

LATER THAT DAY, I entered a crowded Memphis police station, honoring a police invitation. It was warmer inside the building than outside. Sweat poured down my face. When I lifted my arm to wipe my face with my shirt sleeve, my chest pain intensified. My knees wobbled, and my left hip hurt. I tried to stand firm on my two feet, but I needed to rest. Pivoting my body to the right, I looked around the room. An unoccupied chair in the corner looked appealing to me. While I writhed in pain, unable to walk, two other people reached the empty chair at the same time. A shirtless man pushed a young woman aside and sat down. I could not imagine how anyone could be so inconsiderate. The woman muttered some words and stamped her foot. She was helpless. I understood how she felt.

A group of police officers walked by the shirtless man. Watching their dangling guns and handcuffs, I wished they would arrest the man. They glanced at the shirtless man and walked on. The woman raised her hands as if in protest. After the police officers left her area, she huffed. What I saw reminded me that no one is guaranteed fairness. I felt empty inside. I realized that anguish had reached my psyche. Feeling frustrated, I waddled to the reception counter to lean my body against the rough surface, the only support available to me.

A policeman behind the counter answered the questions of a middle-aged man in a black suit. When the man in the black suit turned around, I noticed a red stain on his tie, blood or red sauce, I couldn't tell. He looked at me from my head to my toes, as if I was occupying his space. After inspecting me, he beckoned to a woman seated on a bench. She stood up and approached the counter. She was wearing a short skirt, and her hair was dyed green. Her frame was slim. For a moment, she reminded me of Brenda and the reason why I was in the police station. The woman signed a piece of paper on the counter and left the police station with the man.

I wished that my visit to the station would be as brief as hers, as I approached the cop behind the counter.

"Name?" the cop asked.

"Ben. Sorry, Ben Ava," I said.

He looked through several clipboards until he held one up, and said, "Jane will take your statement."

A police officer stood up from her chair and approached the counter. When she reached the counter, I remembered her face. She was one of the officers who had visited my room. Without looking at me, she drank from a cup, threw the cup in a trash can, and picked up the clipboard.

"You need a lawyer?" Jane asked.

"I'm his lawyer," a voice from behind me said.

I turned around. A young man about my height, black hair, medium build, in blue jeans and a red shirt stood close to me. He extended his hand to me. I hesitated before shaking it.

"I'm Craig. Rita's brother," the man said.

"That's very kind of you, but I don't need a babysitter," I said.

"You need my help," Craig said.

"I don't think so. I can't afford a lawyer," I said.

"I'll help you," Craig said.

"I'll find an empty room while you boys sort yourselves out," the police officer said.

Jane, the police officer, walked down the hall alone, opening two doors. She came out of the second room without her clipboard.

Craig pulled out a business card from his wallet and offered it to me. I looked at the business card and put it in my pocket.

"Call anytime if you need help," Craig said.

"For what? I'm innocent," I said.

"From what my sister said, the young woman is being admitted to the ICU."

"I didn't know."

"I'm not supposed to say, but she's been telling stories."

"That's her problem," I said. I tried to hide my fear. I was afraid of being arrested for Brenda's injury and being dismissed from medical school.

"Next," the police officer behind the counter said. Loudly.

Craig and I stepped aside as the shirtless man approached the counter. He stumbled as he walked. He smelled of alcohol, and mumbled incomprehensible words as he passed by. Three of his fingers were wrapped with blood-soaked Band-Aids. The woman he'd pushed aside followed, several steps behind him. One of the sleeves of her blouse was blood-stained, and her lapel was ripped.

"Back again? Where's your low-life lawyer?" the police officer asked.

"Don't need him," the shirtless man said.

"Boozing and punching your wife," the police officer said.

"Didn't touch her. She hit me first," the shirtless man said.

"You're a damn liar," the woman said.

"Ain't lying," the shirtless man said.

"Tell it to the judge," the policeman said.

I imagined Brenda telling a judge that I cut her wrist in my room. No witnesses to defend me. A jail sentence for a crime I didn't commit. A convicted felon—unsuitable as a physician. My body quaked.

Cop Jane rejoined us as the shirtless man rained down curses on the police officer, and his wife.

It was my first experience of a police station. I wondered how they would decide who was telling the truth, the husband or the wife. I began to worry about my situation, and the effect Brenda's accident would have on my life. A convicted felon, unemployable, and homeless. I resolved to call it an accident, to avoid entangling myself in Brenda's personal problems.

* * *

After I had narrated the details, as I remembered them, about Brenda's incident, I was not arrested. Cop Jane dismissed me.

Leaving the police station, I looked at the clock on the entrance wall and realized that two hours had passed since I arrived. Through the glass front door of the police station, I could see a small stray dog walking down the street. I remembered the dog and the homeless man that caused my accident. My chest pain returned, and I hesitated before leaving the station. Craig caught up with me while I stood by the door watching the dog wag its tail.

"Do you need a ride?" Craig asked.

"I can walk," I said.

"It's late. I'll drop you off."

"I'll call Rita first."

"She's trained you well," Craig said. He shook his head and

smiled. "Good for my sis," he added. My worries about Rita controlling my life returned.

"Sorry, I forgot to tell you; I appreciate your help," I said.

"My pleasure," Craig said.

He reached inside his pocket and retrieved his car keys. He opened the glass door, and I followed him. The dog ran away when we stepped outside the building. Only two police cars and a truck were on the road. We crossed the street to a public parking lot. A police car approached us. A police officer watched us enter Craig's car. My fear of being arrested returned.

The police car trailed us for a short distance before the siren was turned on. Craig stopped his car. I thought about going to prison. Rita leaving me. My heart raced. The police car passed us and turned into a side street. Craig drove to my residence hall. My legs continued to shake after I got out of the car. I stood by the elevator, hesitant to go up to my room; I was afraid of getting into more trouble.

Chapter 17

I PUSHED MY DESK close to the window. It was a moonless night, with subdued stars. Amber street lights filtered into my room, illuminating my bed. Across the street, empty park benches and two stray dogs sniffing each other. The neon sign by the bank registered a temperature of 82, and the time was 1:00 am. A steamy night. I saw a man, the homeless resident of the park, limp toward a park bench. He shooed the dogs away, and they ran in opposite directions. The end of a brief park romance.

I flung my housecoat on the chair and approached my bed, drawn by a woman's flat belly, erect nipples on two mounds, a smile, and extended hands. I accepted Rita's hands and straddled her body. My tongue explored her mouth, trading wet kisses. As my hand traveled below her navel, she twisted her body around and exposed two bigger mounds. My hands traveled over her sculpted rump. Moans and whimpers followed.

When Rita's arm reached around my chest, the location of my wound from the accident, I screamed. Pain traveled through me, and my eyes became wet. Loving can be painful, at times.

My elbows and knees rested on the bed. Rita wriggled her body away from under me and turned me on my back.

"Rest, let me take care of you," Rita said.

"I'm okay," I said.

"You'll feel better when I'm done," Rita said. I saw a smile on her face.

I opened my mouth to speak, but she kissed me before my words could come out. Her tongue glided over the crevices around my neck, my chest, and my belly. When she reached my loins, I used my hand to cover my mouth. I thought my hand could control my moaning, but instead I gave a loud yell.

"Oh!" I screamed some more, loud enough for the homeless man to hear it.

My body quivered and I felt dazed. Stars appeared on my walls and my ceiling. I felt my legs jerk. My thighs slapped her cheeks. I heard her laugh. My hands held the sides of my bed to prevent me from floating away.

"I'll take care of you, Babe," Rita said.

"Wow! No more. I can't take it," I said.

Panting took over me. I think I said things I can't remember. My sense of reasoning stopped as the pleasure I felt intensified. I could not process my thoughts. Blood stopped flowing to my brain.

"Pleasing my babe. That's what I want," Rita said.

I felt dazed. Floating in space. It felt as if the light had gone out in my mind. I could not remember any words, but my body continued to wiggle. She grew relentless. As her lips smacked and her tongue stroked sensitive parts of my body, I quaked. My blurry eyes watched Rita shift her hips from side to side. Her moaning became louder than mine. She let out a yell and fell out of my bed.

I climbed down from the bed and lay next to her on the cold, tiled floor. We held each other, harnessing our body heat, but all that we generated dissipated. I could not prevent the loss, so I pulled down the comforter and rolled our bodies in it. It felt good. We held each other for a long time, in silence, before sleep rolled over the rest of our night together.

* * *

My phone, followed by a car horn on Madison Street, woke

me up. There was no sunlight, but I could see my chair next to the window and my stripped bed. I struggled to release my hands from Rita's embrace. She woke up. I rolled onto my back and picked up my phone. The time on my phone was 6:25 am. The caller ID read 'Deborah Linger'. She must have felt our connection being severed, or she had a medical emergency. My concern for Deb's wellbeing, and the potential effect it would have on my relationship with Rita, worried me. Thinking about all the possible reasons for her call, my heart raced. Without further hesitation, I answered the call.

"Hello," I said.

"Are you in bed?" Deb said. Her voice was loud, so I turned down the volume.

"Who's calling this freaking early?" Rita asked.

"I'm awake," I said.

"He's not," Rita mumbled. She moved closer and placed her arm on my chest.

"Are you busy?" Deb asked.

"We can talk. Just waking up," I said.

"I won't keep you. I have a lump in my breast. I'm having a biopsy tomorrow," Deb said.

Rita turned away from me. After several sighs, she began to mumble. I repositioned my phone.

"What time tomorrow?" I asked. I repositioned the phone, and my finger accidentally touched the screen.

"Not sure yet," Deb said. I heard it over the speaker phone. I fumbled unsuccessfully to turn off the speaker. "I need you," she added, a statement that resonated inside my small dorm room. I felt sick to my stomach.

Rita yanked the comforter from my body and pushed me away. I rolled on my wound and screamed. She took the phone from me.

"I don't know who you are. He's my babe," Rita said. She turned the phone off and threw it across the room.

Rita stood up and gathered her clothes. She laid them on my bed and walked over to the window. Admiring her naked body, I could not remember what I wanted to say to her. My mind wandered to the orgasms I had received from her passion. When she turned around, my eyes focused on her breasts, but the tears threatening to roll down from her eyes again affected me with guilt and sadness. I walked to where she stood, in my nakedness, and held her. She pushed me away and walked to the bed. Tossing aside her shirt and pants, she found her underwear. It took her less than a minute to dress.

"I told you about Deb. I can't lose you over her," I said.

"Doesn't sound like it's over," Rita said.

"It's over for me. I want you."

"Your woman needs you. You know where to find me when you're free."

Rita picked up her shoes and left my room barefoot. I ran after her. Once I reached the door to the hallway, I stopped. I covered my nakedness with the door and poked my head out.

"Babe, don't go," I said.

"You hurt me," Rita said.

She disappeared from my sight. I was not sure if Brenda had returned from her hospital admission—I cupped my loins and ran back to my room.

I sat on my bed feeling lonely and sad. When I picked up the phone to look at the time, it rang. 'Unknown caller' showed on the screen. I ignored the call, remembering that nothing good came out of the last phone call I had.

It would be my first day back at the hospital after my accident. There was nothing to look forward to. Rita had left me, and, I assumed, Brenda's issues remained unresolved.

I heard my stomach rumbling and churning. I thought about the noise my stomach made. A protest. A sign of my failure to meet the basic need to feed myself. Looking around my room, I found my car keys on my desk. Keys to a destroyed vehicle, a useless possession. I had a fantasy about finding food inside one of my three desk drawers. I walked to the desk, knelt down and pulled out the lower drawer first, followed by the top drawer and the middle drawer. No hidden snack. My need was immediate. It had been a long time since I had eaten. I left my room and went to the bathroom.

While I struggled to take a shower, the idea of traveling to Knoxville to lend my support to Deb crossed my mind. With my eyes closed and water running down my face, I remembered my father's funeral. Deb stood next to me, holding my hand during the interment. I felt the need to do the same for her, to offer my support in her time of need.

Traveling to Knoxville would affect my fragile relationship with Rita. A new, floundering love affair. However, I wondered how I would live with myself if I did not support a friend who had supported me during my time of need.

Chapter 18

I SAT ON THE CURB at the hospital, leaning against the rough surface of a concrete retaining wall. Cement points pierced my wool pants and jabbed me. The pain was nothing compared to the physical and emotional pain I had experienced that week. My eyes focused on the road. Cars passed by. I wished I had one. A white Suburban stopped at the pedestrian-crossing sign, giving off a loud engine noise. James stuck his head out of the window and waved. I adjusted my backpack and approached his vehicle.

"Hop in. I'll drop you off," James said.

"I'm not going home," I said.

"Tell me where, I'll drop you off."

"I'm taking a night bus to Knoxville. Well, deciding on it."

James laughed. He looked at me as if he couldn't believe my indecision. I wanted to explain myself, but the right words didn't come to mind. We looked at each other, and he looked at his watch.

"Who is she?" James asked.

He looked at me as if he knew that a woman was involved. A coughing spell interrupted his stare. His faced turned red, as if he was choking.

"Are you okay?" I asked.

"I moved back home. Her new dog is killing me," James said.

He reached inside his glove compartment and retrieved a piece of napkin. It was a disposable one that he had saved, like his marriage. A recycled product that could be beneficial. He covered his nose with it and coughed, noisily. People looked in our direction. Physical and emotional suffering, the price we pay for love. Doing what was best for everyone involved. A sacrifice. At that moment, I realized what I had to do.

"Drop me off downtown, at the bus depot. I'm going," I said.

I opened the door and sat down with my backpack.

"You rascal. A delicious babe, I bet," James said.

"A sick friend. Nothing more," I said.

I loosened my backpack and dropped it on the floor of the vehicle—a relief I needed. James watched me.

"How about your nurse?" James asked. I ignored his question. A complex situation. Explaining my actions was the last thing I wanted to do.

He came to a stop sign and idled his car. No cars appeared from either direction, though there were pedestrians a little distance away from the road intersection. Traffic was light enough for him to have made his turn, but he waited. I watched his eyes. He stared into the distance as if he was disconnected from his surroundings. His smile faded from his face. I wondered what our medical school education was doing to us.

"James, are you okay?" I asked. He looked in my direction with a gloomy face.

"Not sure if I did the right thing. I know she'll leave me again," James said.

"She's your wife. Don't regret anything."

"I know, but Brenda was hurt."

"She knew you were married."

"I don't blame anyone. I didn't know my wife would come back."

"You're lucky. A wife, and a crazy girlfriend. I have no

one," I said. I could not contain my laughter.

"It's a burden," James said.

"I want your burden. Not with a Brenda type. I need a sane girl to love me. And be there for me," I said.

James turned left and headed in the direction of downtown. We encountered heavy traffic and lights that stayed red longer than usual. Going from an empty side street to gridlock, confronting the epitome of life: unpredictability.

Later that evening, I boarded the bus to Knoxville for a trip to my past—a journey to uncertainty.

* * *

"Next stop is Knoxville," the bus driver announced. He pulled into the bus station and applied a brake that jerked the passengers forward, a traumatic way to end the trip. My legs wobbled as I exited the bus. The bus station had only five passengers waiting in the lobby. I used the bathroom and made a phone call to Deb—a phone call to the uncertain phase of my journey.

"Hello," Deb answered.

"I'm downtown," I said. The receiver was silent for a while.

"I've never been to Memphis. What's there?" Deb asked.

"Downtown Knoxville. I took a night bus," I said. I laughed.

I heard her yawn. "You still do crazy things," Deb said.

"I'm here for you," I said.

"That's sweet," Deb said. I thought I heard her cry.

"I need to shower and change my clothes."

"My surgery is at nine. See you then."

"Can I change at your place?"

"It would be awkward."

"I understand," I said. I didn't know what I understood, but I thought I was saying the right thing.

I walked to the entrance of the bus station and looked at the rising sun. Scattered cumulus clouds shone with reflections of the golden rising sun, and the streets were empty. Close to where I stood, birds ate crumbs from the sidewalk. They chirped and appeared delighted, even though they had no permanent home. I had nowhere to go, but I felt at peace, fulfilling an obligation. Doing the right thing. I left the bus station and walked in the direction of the medical center.

When I reached the medical center, my former place of employment, I found an empty medical student call room. After shaving, I took a shower and got dressed. I left the call room and walked to the emergency room where I had been an orderly. I looked around for people I used to know, but no one seemed to notice my presence. Nurses and medical aides walked by without speaking to me. Obviously most of the workers in the ER did not know that I had left.

On reaching the outpatient surgical center, I stopped at the busy reception area. Patients and their family members occupied most of the available chairs. I adjusted my backpack and leaned against the wall.

Looking around the room constantly, I noticed as soon as Deb walked in—a man holding her hand. My stomach felt queasy. They looked at each other, and kissed at the reception area. I looked away. My heart raced, and my face became damp with sweat. I wanted to run away, but I took a deep breath and walked up to Deb. She saw me and smiled. No hug, or even a handshake, from her. Our meeting felt awkward.

"Mike, this is Ben, an old friend," Deb said. Mike shook my hand.

"Nice to meet you," I said.

It appeared that Deb did not need me as she had said. I watched Mike and Deb's display of affection. Why she wanted me to be a witness to it puzzled me.

The receptionist gave Deb some papers to sign, while I stood by, watching the interaction between Deb and Mike. Mike rubbed her shoulder while she signed her papers. Deb turned around twice to kiss him. Watching their affection for each other, I wondered why Deb felt the need to torture me, and how much pain my broken heart could stand.

After signing her papers, Deb held Mike in a long embrace. I thought about Rita who was there for me in my time of need, before Deb's phone call took her away from me. I watched the woman I had lost, embracing another man after ruining my relationship with someone else. It was a tragedy with only one victim—me. I cleared my throat. "Good luck, Deb. I hope it's nothing serious," I said.

"I'm sorry, what did you say?" Deb asked.

She held Mike's arm as if it was a lifeline for her, probably the only support she needed.

"I hope things go well for you," I said.

"Thank you," Deb said.

I watched Deb enter the secured section of the surgical center, holding onto Mike, her new man. Her actions were sadistic, but I was not ready to accept that fact. Deb could not have called me to show off her new boyfriend. I hadn't done anything to her to elicit such cruelty. Feeling humiliated, I stood in a corner of the waiting room, trying to regain my confidence. Lonesomeness, of a type I had not known before, engulfed me. There was no one left in my life I could call to talk to. My only friend hung on my back: my backpack.

I gathered enough courage to fulfill my mission: supporting Deb during her time of need. I found a chair and sat down, opened my backpack and retrieved a book to read.

* * *

Over the course of an hour, I sat on three different chairs in the waiting room of the surgical center, confused. I was aware that my relationship with Deb was over, but I wished for a different ending. My ambivalence confused me more. Hanging on to a girl that did not want me, while risking my new relationship with Rita. My backpack sat on the floor, on a table, and on my back. Constantly changing where I placed my backpack did not change my situation, however. Pacing around and sitting on the armrest of different chairs, I felt confused about what to do. I made two attempts to leave the waiting room to travel back to Memphis. Each time, I stood by the elevator without pushing the call button. I had an obligation to fulfill. A virtue. I thought about crazy things, to feel better about my sorry self.

After a long wait, Mike came through the double doors. He looked around the waiting room. Our eyes met. He walked to where I was sitting. I looked away as he came closer to me. I had no intention of talking to him.

"She wants to see you," Mike said.

"See me?" I asked. He ignored me. "Thank you for telling

me," I added.

I did not know what else to say to him, except to show my gratitude. I waited for him to lead the way to where Deb was recuperating, but he sat down. Mike watched me while I stood next to him, waiting. He looked angry and jerked his legs constantly.

"She wants to talk to you alone," Mike said. He looked away while talking to me, avoiding eye contact.

I looked at the electronic patient board for Deb's location. There was a Deb in one room and a Deborah in another. Mike watched me. I could not decide which one to pick, so I approached the secretary. She directed me to room four. I flung my backpack on my shoulder and walked to recovery room four. Deb was reading her hospital papers when I entered her room. She smiled when she saw me.

"Thanks for being here," Deb said. She reached out, and held my hand. I could see tears in her eyes.

"You helped me a lot. I will always be grateful," I said. I tried not to cry, but my lips quivered when I spoke.

"Mike and I are seeing each other," Deb said.

Her verbal confirmation felt more painful to me than what I already knew. I tried to retrieve my hand from Deb, but she held on to me.

"Let me go," I said.

She loosened her grip and removed the necklace around her neck. A birthday gift from me.

"It's yours. Take it," Deb said.

Her nurse came over and took her blood pressure. The nurse looked at me and frowned. No words were necessary. I knew what she couldn't say to me. Time to leave.

"I'm sorry. I'll leave your patient alone," I said.

Deb held up the necklace. It showed one half of a heart symbol, my heart. The symbol of my love for her. A gift I had spent a week's wage from my summer job on. My broken heart.

Standing at her bedside, I felt pain on the right side of my chest. I closed my eyes and sobbed.

"Sir, you need to go," the nurse said.

I held my returned heart in the palm of my hand. My broken heart. I wanted to ask about her surgery, but could not. Her nurse held my backpack up. I took it and walked away. The side door led me to an empty overflow parking lot, awash in sunshine and humid weather. My breathing and heart rate increased. With an unsettled stomach, I heaved, but there was nothing in my stomach, except for water.

I took a footpath toward downtown. As I exposed my body to the hot and humid weather, sweat poured down my face. Twice, I drank from a bottle of water in my backpack. After walking for two blocks, I unbuttoned my shirt.

My phone rang once and stopped, indicating a missed call from an unlisted number. I sat on a bench at a bus stop and stared at my phone. I wanted my phone to ring again. Only one person crossed my mind: Rita. For more than a minute, I brought her number up several times, but decided each time not to call her. A musty smell permeated my nostrils while I fidgeted with my phone. When the odor became stronger, I looked up. Standing close to me was a man wearing torn clothes. He had leathery skin, was barefoot and exposed his poor dentition when he smiled. A homeless man looking for a friendly gesture, I assumed.

"Give me a dollar," the man said, extending his cupped hand.

I reached inside my pocket and retrieved my last dollar bill and a nickel. I placed the dollar bill in his hand and returned the nickel to my pocket. It was the only money I had. Feeling the nickel in my pocket made me feel good; financial security with no purchasing power. I reached out to shake his hand, but he ignored me. After I left the bus stop, I thought about the homeless man, and the last time he ate. I turned around. Once he saw me return to the bus stop, he reached in his pocket and pulled out the dollar bill I gave him. He waved the dollar at me. His right hand trembled, but he tried to steady it with his left. He was aware that he needed to support his trembling hand. A lesson I learned. Understanding a need and implementing the solution to it. Making the right decisions. It would be only a matter of time before I would be tested.

"It's yours," I said.

His eyes glistened. He sat down and pressed the dollar bill on his thigh with his palm, straightening out the wrinkles. He was performing an unneeded task with the wrong tool—this was one of the lessons I learned from a homeless stranger. I thought about my life, and homelessness. Without my scholarship from the state government, I could not support myself. There was nothing different from me and a state-welfare recipient apart from my medical education. When I thought about it, receiving a medical education rescued me from homelessness. After sighing, I unzipped my backpack to inspect my belongings.

I looked in my bag. A phone and a return bus ticket to Memphis. A bottle of water. I had two granola bars: one for lunch; the other for dinner. Enough of a snack to nourish my body until I returned to Memphis. I retrieved a granola bar and removed the wrapping. The homeless man watched me take the first bite. He moved closer to me. His eyes focused on my granola bar. Reaching inside my bag, I retrieved the remaining granola bar and gave it to him. He spoke no words, but smiled as he tore the wrapper off. His first bite, a piece fell off. As he searched for the piece, I walked away. I knew he would find the missing piece. I had to find my own missing piece—a love that had eluded me.

Chapter 19

A DAY LATER, one block away from the hospital, I felt raindrops on my face, a few spots falling on my shirt. Droplets slid off the waxed surface of my critical care medicine textbook, an unintended benefit. Worried about ruining my expensive book, I tucked it under my arm. Apart from the expense of my medical education, my textbooks were the only investments I had. Protecting the textbook under my arm seemed reasonable until it began to rain. Torrents soon soaked my hair and clothes, and dampened my enthusiasm to return to the intensive care unit as a medical student, instead of a patient. I was back in the doldrums.

Pedestrians quickened their pace as the intensity of the falling rain increased. The rain had already soaked my clothes, so there was nothing left to protect by accelerating my pace. Looking around me, I saw there was no one left on the sidewalk. I was alone. The reality of my life became clearer to me. Without Rita, I had no one to rely on.

With the torrential rainfall, water gushed down the steps at the rear entrance of the hospital, turning them slippery. Remembering the worn soles on my shoes, I had to take careful steps climbing up. The fear of falling stayed in my mind. 'Be careful, Ben,' the words my mother used to say to me. I heard it while climbing the stairs, but it was my own voice. It was not voices in my head—which had initially worried me. I was not crazy. Not yet.

Inside a locker room, I changed into my green scrub pants

and shirt. With a stethoscope around my neck, I looked in the mirror and smiled. It felt good to regain some confidence. I left the locker room and entered the intensive care unit. Two nurses huddled by a desk, exchanging handwritten clinical notes on their patients. My eyes wandered around the ICU. No Rita. The unit secretary looked up and smiled.

"Have you seen Dr Peterson?" I asked. I wanted to ask for Rita, but out of pride I asked for my tormentor.

"You're the first house-staff this morning," the secretary said.

"Is Rita here?" I asked, finally.

"Nurse Rita? She's not working."

I left the ICU and walked to the conference room. The thermostat on the wall read 67. A cold, desolate room. I adjusted the setting to 72 and sat down. I was alone.

After I had been sitting alone for five minutes, James walked in and sat next to me. We shook hands.

"How was Knoxville?" James asked.

"Nothing to report," I said, and faked a smile.

"I'm glad my old lady came back. Life's better for me," James said. I was surprised, after his complaints about the dog allergy before my trip. It wasn't my responsibility to remind him about his misery.

"I'm happy for you," I said.

"I know what you're going through. Been there," James said.

Dr Peterson and Brenda walked in. Brenda was wearing a long-sleeve blue dress, covering her wrists. When she looked in my direction, I smiled. I was not surprised when she frowned and looked away. I wondered what she had been telling Dr Peterson about me.

Dr Peterson sat opposite me. We made no eye contact. He

scribbled on a piece of paper. James shifted around in a squeaky chair. Despite the noise his chair was making, James focused on his phone, his finger flicking over the surface.

There were four of us in the conference room, but no one spoke. We ignored each other. I thought about how dysfunctional we were. Looking up, our eyes met—mine and Dr Peterson's—trading cold stares. I felt the tension deeply. Moisture formed on my forehead, as I perspired in a cold room. The thermostat read 69. I wondered what I could do to alleviate the tension in the room, but the fear that Dr Peterson would ruin my life persisted.

"I'm grateful for my time off," I said.

Dr Peterson sighed, "You're entitled to it."

The conference room door opened. Dr Trophy and Andrew walked in. Dr Trophy looked around the room and came over to me. Andrew followed him and sat on the chair next to James.

"Four admissions last night. One overdose, sepsis, and two dialysis patients. The overdose has deep lacerations. Self-inflicted," Dr Peterson said.

"I can't stand losers. Attention seekers. Yeah, I'll take pills and call 911. Please rescue me," Dr Trophy said, with a mocking voice. He chuckled. Brenda shifted around in her chair.

My eyes wandered to the others' faces. There was silence in the room. I watched tears fall from Brenda's eyes. Her nose ran. When she lifted her arm, she accidentally exposed a bandaged wrist. The place where her scalpel had sliced her open, to release the demon inside her. I stopped judging her, and immediately felt remorse. She wiped her eyes and nose, sighing repeatedly.

"The overdose is a 25-year-old female," Dr Peterson added.

"Don't tell me, her boyfriend left her," Dr Trophy said. He

cackled. Andrew laughed too. I felt nauseated.

"Stop. Please stop," Brenda said, sobbing, and bobbing her head.

"Look at you. We need stable doctors, not fruitcakes," Dr Trophy said, pointing his finger at Brenda.

Brenda laid her head on the table. Her eyes closed, and she rolled her head around. I felt cold chills inside me. Suppressing my tears, I watched Brenda suffer. I wanted to go to her and hug her, wipe her tears away. But sexual harassment lectures filtered into my mind, and the fear of being inappropriate with a female held me back. Fear of dismissal from medical school.

Dr Trophy and Andrew laughed. They exchanged glances, and bubbled with more laughter. My stomach felt worse as their laughter resonated in my ears. I stood up and covered my ears. With my ears covered, I still heard Brenda crying. My breathing and heart rate increased. It felt like a sledgehammer was pounding on my chest. My hands trembled. I wanted to wring Dr Trophy's neck. The thought of strangling someone horrified me. It was the first time I'd had such a feeling, and it troubled me.

"Stop. Where's the compassion? You're cruel," I shouted.

Dr Trophy stood up and approached me. He was so close to my face that I felt his warm, smelly breath. The thought of strangling him came back to my mind. I struggled with my anger.

"You're done. Finished. Get out," Dr Trophy commanded.

"You're a sadist. Heartless," I said. My voice faded.

"I'm the attending. And you are a piece of shit, a stupid medical student. Call security. Get his ass out of here," Dr Trophy said, his finger touching my face.

I wanted to snap his finger like a twig. Standing next to Dr

Trophy, I wanted to punch his face. Instead, I stood on the spot looking around. My body temperature rose to boiling point, fortunately my profuse sweating dissipated the heat from my body. Brenda stopped crying. No one looked up. The room became quiet, except for my heavy breathing.

Dr Trophy left the room. Walking swiftly as if he was rushing to the bathroom.

I felt dizzy and nauseated. My legs wobbled and I felt weak. James stood up and eased me down onto my chair. My palms were wet, and my hands trembled. No one moved. In the silence of the room, we waited for doom. Brenda sneezed. I looked at her, and our eyes met. Her eyeballs were sunken and rimmed with dark circles. She jerked, as if in fear. Our eyes drifted apart. It appeared as if the clock stopped, but my heart did not—it pounded. I remembered that the clock on the wall was broken. I was not crazy. There was no fight left in me, but my heart was slow to adapt to my mentally spent state.

* * *

As we waited for Dr Trophy to return, two hospital security guards entered the conference room, their hands clutching their Taser guns. I remembered cases of deaths from Taser guns. Cases presented during medical school cardiac-arrest lectures. Deaths caused by the Taser guns' electrical activity. They looked around the room. One guard approached me. He pushed my textbook aside and picked up my phone. He turned my phone off and returned it to me. I wondered how he knew it was me. My heart raced.

"Get up," the security guard said.

I stood up and reached for my book. He knocked the book out of my hand.

"Is that necessary?" Dr Peterson asked.

"I'm following orders," the security guard said.

He felt the pockets of my scrub pants without asking my permission. His partner watched with his hand on his Taser gun. James approached the security guard.

"Stop harassing him," James said.

The security guard pushed James, and he stumbled.

"James, it's okay," I said.

"We'll escort you to your car," the security guard said.

"My car is broken down," I said.

Dr Peterson left the room, followed by Andrew. James went to Brenda and whispered to her. She punched his chest. James showed her his fist and returned to his chair.

The security guards held my arms in a firm grip. Sandwiched between the two guards, I was walked out of the conference room. We entered a crowded hallway, filled with hospital workers and guests. They slowed their pace and watched as the two men escorted me to the elevator. I heard their giggles and whispers. I imagined their thoughts and conclusions. A criminal. I bowed my head, gripped by the fear of Rita seeing me.

The elevator door opened, and they dragged me in. A guard pushed the ground floor button, and the door closed with a screech. I worried about Rose, the woman with liver cancer. Her reaction—and decision about chemotherapy—if she saw me. I heard footsteps and huffing noises outside the elevator. The sound of someone running to a code blue came to mind, but there was no overhead announcement.

I heard a shout. "Hold the elevator!" Another witness to

laugh at me, I thought. Maybe I needed a witness, I would if the security guards decided to abuse me physically.

The guards ignored the shout. I reached out and held the door open. Dr Peterson stood in front of the elevator, gasping for air. He pushed my hand away as he entered. He stooped, gasping, and placed his hands on the wall of the elevator.

"Which floor?" a security guard asked. Dr Peterson ignored him.

"The dean wants to see you, now," Dr Peterson said.

"In hospital scrubs? Things can't be worse," I said.

"Better get there now. Your ass is in enough trouble already," Dr Peterson said.

"What a freaking day," I said.

"It's all your fault. Trouble maker. Sticking your nose in crap," Dr Peterson said. I had no pep left in me to argue with him. He had won. He could have Rita.

The elevator door opened on the ground floor. As people rushed to get in, we struggled to get off before the elevator door closed. We took the hallway past the cafeteria. The place I found solace. A nurse from the ICU, a friend of Rita's, passed us. It appeared as if she wanted to speak to me, but when she saw the security guards, she walked on. I imagined how she would break the news about me to Rita.

Once they'd escorted me through the rear entrance of the hospital, the security guards stopped and released my arms. I looked behind me several times as I walked down the steps. The two security guards stood by the door, watching me. Although I was curious about how long they would watch me, I was worried that I might tumble down the steps. I watched each step I took until I reached the sidewalk. Public property. Freedom for me, until I remembered the request to see the dean. The judge to pass my sentence. A case between an attending physician and a student. A demigod of medicine and a mere mortal. I knew the verdict, but I still had to go to the dean's office. To receive the proclamation. Not the Hippocratic Oath I desired.

Walking down a lonely path, I looked up to the sky, searching for a divine intervention. There was neither sunshine nor rain, just slow-moving, dark clouds. The weather reflected my state of mind, which was gloomy.

At the street junction, I turned toward the medical school administration office, a faded brick building, the windows framed with stone. Next to the administration building was an interfaith chapel. God's house.

'Your time has come. The hour of reckoning,' flashed intermittently on the chapel's digital display board. It was not the message I desired. I walked away. After taking a few steps, I entered the administration building. I held on to the railings as I climbed the flight of steps to the second floor.

I passed a student walking down the steps wiping her eyes. I sighed. I entered suite 200 on the second floor, an expansive office with empty seats in the reception area. Behind a mahogany desk, a woman held a telephone receiver as she punched in some numbers. When she saw me, she hung up the phone and gave me a smile with a closed mouth.

"I'm Ben Ava," I said.

"You're here already?" she said. She lifted the receiver and dialed three numbers. "Dr Cleaver, Ben Ava is here," the secretary said.

Not long after the secretary hung up the phone, the inner office door opened. A bald man stood by the door, wearing a bow tie, and a white shirt tucked into khaki pants. He reminded me of my father. I felt at ease.

"Hi Ben," he said. We shook hands. He had a firm, reassuring handshake.

"Benjamin Ava, Sir," I said. I wanted to feel important.

"Sorry. I thought they called you Ben," Dr Cleaver said. He gave me a smile and patted my shoulder. I felt comfortable with him. A reprieve for me, I imagined.

"My friends call me Ben," I said. Dr Cleaver looked at me, and his smile disappeared.

Thinking about my last statement, I felt that it came out wrong. My legs trembled and my palms were sweaty. I felt my heart rate increase.

Dr Cleaver watched me as I looked around his office. Certificates and commendations covered the walls. A framed picture on his desk showed Dr Cleaver, a woman about his age—his wife—and a younger woman, their daughter. I thought about my mom and dad, gone forever.

A piece of wood with a word carved on it occupied the front edge of the desk. My fingers caressed the word: 'Empathy'. A word used routinely by all the doctors at the medical school as representing the epitome of patient care, the essence of moral goodness. Most academic doctors, the gods of medicine, believe that they possess the virtue. A sham. Gullible medical students marvel at their feats and aspire to reach that pinnacle—dispensing medical care with compassion.

"There has been a serious complaint against you. You

challenged your attending," Dr Cleaver said.

"It's not true. He verbally abused Brenda. I asked him to stop," I said.

"You report issues like that. Don't challenge them. You're a student," Dr Cleaver said.

"He was mean. Saying hurtful things," I said.

Dr Cleaver picked up a sealed envelope from his desk and gave it to me. Since he did not instruct me to do so, I did not unseal the envelope.

"You're suspended until the disciplinary council meets," Dr Cleaver said.

"For asking him to stop?" I asked.

"Always remember, the university holds every student accountable. The council meets in two days to review your case," Dr Cleaver said.

He walked to the door and held it open for me. I held back my tears. The anger in me swelled, but I controlled myself. My breathing rate increased. Hyperventilation crossed my mind, but it was too late to alleviate the problem. My eyes could not focus, and my vision blurred. I shuffled to the door.

"Are you okay?" the secretary asked.

I held on to the door frame and held my breath, but there was no improvement. I stooped, and felt for a chair. I lowered my body onto the chair and closed my eyes.

Catching a whiff of perfume, I felt air on my face, and heard the crackling of papers. My eyes opened. Dr Cleaver's secretary was fanning me with an improvised fan.

"Thank you," I said.

She stopped fanning.

"Who do I call?" she asked.

"I have no one," I said.

"It's my lunch anyway. I'll walk with you," she said.

The phone rang. She ignored it, and it took four rings to stop. Dr Cleaver's inner office door was closed. I thought about Dr Cleaver. A father. A doctor. My medical school dean. His word, 'Empathy', eluded him that day. I wondered if medical school had anything useful to offer me apart from hollow rhetoric.

Chapter 20

LATER THAT DAY, the lobby was bustling with students returning from class. Most were in a hurry to return to their rooms, to sleep or reflect. I was heading to my room for the latter. I took the elevator to the sixth floor. On reaching my dormitory suite I discovered a note on my door. I peeled the note off my door. 'Report to the housing office.' I looked around. There was no one in the common area of my dormitory suite. I inserted my key in the door knob and turned it to the right three times, but my door did not open. I shook the door knob. After several attempts to open the door, I took the elevator to the first floor. I was mentally exhausted from my encounters with Drs Trophy and Cleaver.

The housing office door was closed. I knocked twice.

"We're at lunch," a woman's voice announced from inside the office.

"I'm Ben Ava. I need help to get in my room," I said.

"Come back in ten," the voice said.

"Ma'am, I need help now," I said.

The office door opened. She held the inside door knob, and stood with her legs planted apart. Her lunch announced its presence—before my eyes were a wrapped burrito on the desk and a can of Coke. My stomach churned, and I licked my lips. I could not remember my last meal. I was hungry. In the process of admiring her burrito, I forgot the urgency of my visit.

"You're locked out?" she asked.

"My key won't work," I said.

I gave her my keys and the note from my door.

"You're the one," she said.

"What do you mean?" I asked, confused.

"The school administration informed us," she said. She hesitated before she added, "About your suspension."

"Why is it your business?" I said, my voice rising.

"You have to move out. School policy," she said.

"I have things in my room," I said.

"I'll call campus security. They'll let you in to take your things," she said.

She closed her office door. I stood outside the office pondering what to do next. Where to go. Who to call. My mind even flirted with going back to Knoxville. I had no friends or family to call for assistance. I had just become homeless in Memphis. My future looked bleak. Survival became paramount for me.

Chapter 21

MY BACKPACK WAS SECURED in place, one strap on each shoulder, and my possessions were inside. Missing, were a pair of pants and a shirt I forgot in the hospital call room. It was one day before the disbursement of my monthly scholarship money. I walked to the ATM in front of my dormitory. My former dormitory, according to the school authorities. My fingers chose 'Account balance' instead of 'Withdrawal'. I was not sure how much was left in my savings account. The last time I checked, it was less than one hundred dollars. After noting the balance, I withdrew 40 dollars. I placed the money in my pocket and walked away from the place that was my home.

Sunshine laid prickly burns on my skin. The morning's torrential rainfall had been forgotten. Humid air traveled through my nostrils to my lungs, which was at times suffocating. In desperation, I searched the sky for clouds that could cover the sun. As I searched for clouds I could not control, my eyes wandered away from the heavy traffic on Madison. Cars turned into side streets on red lights, breaking posted traffic rules. Realizing that crossing the street was dangerous, I deferred my comfort and focused on surviving the traffic madness; the search for clouds would have to wait.

I walked to the bank of the river, the rapidly flowing Mississippi, a broad band of muddy water. I slipped twice on the rocks that formed the river embankment, trying to get closer to the water. Fortunately, I didn't fall. My feet trembled, so I sat on a rock, I felt the hot rock burning through my scrub pants. I had to learn how to avoid inflicting pain on my body the hard way.

I returned to the walkway and followed the path to a park, performing an aimless trek. Hungry and exhausted, I sat on a bench that was shaded by a tree. A warm breeze caressed my face, and my eyes watered. I retrieved my phone and scrolled down the list of my contacts. My fingers reached out to dial Rita's number, but my brain reminded me that I had nothing to offer. I was a suspended medical student, broke and homeless. A loser. I placed the palm of my hand on my forehead and closed my eyes. The sun, and my exhaustion and hunger, had imposed a meditation on me. I fell into a trance. Time passed slowly.

"You're sitting on my bench," a voice said. A dream.

I opened my eyes. He stood in front of me, wearing two coats and carrying trash bags. The homeless man I had seen wandering around.

"You own all the benches?" I asked.

"I sleep on benches," he said.

Two people walking by stopped and watched us. I thought about what it looked like. Two homeless people fighting over a bench. I rose from the bench. The two observers walked away. I returned my backpack to where it had been resting.

"Where's home?" I asked.

"I live here. Mission House kicked me out," he said.

"Be safe, Sir," I said.

He looked around as if he was searching for someone.

"You called me Sir," he said.

"You are," I said.

"I have never been called Sir," he said. He smiled. "Lost my job, my home, my wife," he added.

"I am sorry for your losses," I said.

My mind wandered to the Mission House. A place I could stay. Each time I opened my mouth, I could not find the courage to ask him for the location. A jogger ran by. His phone rang. I remembered my phone, which I could use to find the location. I became worried about my dulled brain. It was taking me too long to figure out how to survive.

I left the park in search of the Mission House.

* * *

Searching for the Mission House, I walked along the concrete sidewalks, exposing my body to the unrelenting sunshine. Heat radiated from the asphalt-covered street and the cement walkway—roasting heat. I felt my body baking inside. My feet, although covered, steamed inside my shoes. The distance to my destination appeared ever longer. I rested under any tree I could find along the way, standing in the shade for less than five minutes each time, before continuing. When my journey became intolerable, I sat on the ground with my shoes and socks off. My fingers massaged my toes while I took small sips of water. Each time I lifted the bottle of water to pour it on my head, I resisted the temptation. I had to choose between heat exhaustion or dehydration. Either could kill me.

Finally, I reached my destination, a red-brick building identified by a hand-painted sign secured to the ground, close to the steps that led to a glass door. No windows were visible from the front of the building. I stood and read the sign, before climbing up the three steps.

Mission House.

Temporary lodging for homeless men.

Helping people in need, physically and spiritually.

I entered the building. A peculiar smell filtered through my nostrils: stale air. Bug-infested beds crossed my mind.

A registration window with a sliding door was on my right. I approached the window with apprehension. A sign-in clipboard sat on the counter. My fingers lifted a pen. Too unsteady to sign my name, I deferred the task.

Hearing the sound of a television to my left, I turned. Worn couches and love seats had been arranged to create five sections, a kind of family room. When my reasoning returned, I remembered why people like me were homeless. No family, or family support. Instead of a family room, it could be a lounge. Four men watched television in silence, each man in a different section, thereby achieving privacy in a public place.

I slid the glass window open. A secretary sat on a bar stool close to a bench, which formed a makeshift desk. I tried to form a grin, but produced an agonized smile. I improved what I imagined was a blasted facial contortion, by showing my teeth. She squinted, looking at me.

"Welcome to the Mission House. A place of serenity. Here to volunteer?" she asked. A smile lingered on her face.

"I am looking for a place to stay," I said.

"Passing through Memphis?" she asked.

"No, Ma'am," I said.

"We only cater for homeless men," she said.

"I'm homeless," I said.

There was no shame left in me. I was tired and hungry. She

wiped her eyes and looked at me again.

"You look like a clean kid," she said.

"I may be clean, but I'm homeless. I need a place to stay," I said. I was getting angry with her assessment.

"Here's a form to fill out. You need a government ID and social security card," she said.

"Thank you, Ma'am," I said.

One of the men watching television, a bearded fellow, walked by, his eyes darting around. He looked at me before he approached the door, then he looked through the glass. Occasionally, he glanced at me. After his second look, he squeezed his forehead as if he was in pain. I heard him sigh before he walked back to his couch. I held on to my backpack tight. I could not afford to have it stolen.

I sat on a chair close to the entrance to fill out the form. My hand shook from hunger, and I scrawled jagged letters on the form. The man walked by again, and I watched him. He must have been aware that I was watching him because he turned around and came over to me. I became worried that I could not physically stop him if he tried to steal my bag. I was hungry.

"You're a doctor. I saw you at the hospital," he said.

"I don't remember you," I said.

"You came, with other doctors, to my room," he said.

"Sorry, I forget," I said.

"You'll take care of us?" he asked.

I rubbed my head and thought about what to say. He was waiting for my answer.

"I need a place to stay. I'm having problems," I said.

"Your old lady kicked you out?" he asked, and laughed.

"No. Just school problems," I said.

"Good people here. No violence."

"Good to know."

"I'll leave you alone, Doc."

"I'm a medical student," I said, loud enough for everyone to hear. I wanted him to stop calling me Doc.

"I understand, Doc," he said and walked away.

I finished filling out the form and took it, my driver's license, and social security card, to the window. The secretary looked over the form and circled some areas on it. I watched her but could not figure out why she had circled the areas.

"We have another location for working men," she said. She gave me a piece of paper with the address of the location. "It's six blocks from here," she added.

"I'm tired and hungry. I can't walk anymore," I said, shaking my head from side to side as I spoke.

"Lunch's over, but we have sandwiches," she said.

"I don't care for one, if you're going to send me away. I need some rest, to sort things out in my head, and I need a job, to survive," I said.

"I'll talk to my manager," she said.

She left her desk and passed through a door that she closed behind her. I stood by the counter. My legs trembled. My stomach churned and felt like it was tied in knots. I thought about walking six blocks in the sun. Death from sunstroke worried me. I waited for the manager's decision.

*   *   *

While waiting, my eyes closed. I saw images of Deb, flashes of her smiling face and a kiss on my cheek. She spoke to me.

Her lips moved, but I could not hear the words. I was delusional, the effect of hunger and stress. I could not tell how long it lasted. Daydreaming about a girl who had left me.

"Ben, are you okay?" she asked.

I thought it was Deb asking. I felt a tap on my shoulder. My eyes opened, my forehead was leaning against the wall. I wondered why I did not see Rita's face in my daydream. The thought of losing Rita permanently worried me.

A tall woman stood next to me. Of a slender build and with short hair, she wore a tracksuit and tennis shoes. I looked for a basketball under her arm and a whistle in her hand. I realized I was judging someone by her way of dressing and her physical features, the same mistake my attending physician had made about Brenda. A lesson for me.

"Sorry, Ma'am. I dozed off," I said.

"I'm Marjie. We've a room for you. More like a bed in a closet. I'm sorry."

"I'll take anything, Ma'am," I said.

"Follow me," Marjie said.

She walked ahead of me. I watched her steps, her athletic moves. I placed her in a basketball court, dribbling. I was losing my mind.

The men in the lounge area watched as we walked by, showing faces with no expressions. No smiles or frowns. Interested but indifferent. They were attracted to an event around them but had no feelings about it, a kind of conflict. Realizing I was a dismissed medical student making a psychiatric diagnosis, I chuckled. Marjie looked at me.

"That's my doc," the bearded man said.

"You're stupid. A doc in a homeless shelter?" another man asked.

"He was fooling around. His old lady kicked his ass out," he said, exuding assuredness. His fabrication worried me. I began to worry about what Dr Trophy would say about me. Falsehoods, to protect his reputation while ruining mine. Would I get a fair hearing with the disciplinary committee?

They carried on with their conversation as Marjie and I left the area. We passed a hall with several bunk beds. The floor was clean, and the beds were made, the sheets tucked in. I'd had a different impression of a homeless shelter, which I'd thought had dirty rooms and bug-infested beds. I sighed, feeling a little relief from my worries.

We entered a small cubicle. A twin bed sat to the side, and there was a desk at the end. Two wooden hanger strips were nailed to the wall. My dormitory room came to mind, except there was no window. No opening to the sky to gaze at the moon, and no opportunity to look out of a window to watch the homeless man. It did not occur to me until then that I had become the homeless man's guardian, from a distance. Watching out, from my window, for bad things that could affect him. I dropped my backpack on the bed. Marjie stood by the closet door and watched me. When I remembered that the homeless man kept all his belongings close to his body, I picked up my backpack.

"Your things are safe here," Marjie said, and smiled.

"I can't thank you enough," I said. Though my voice quivered, I had no tears to shed. I believed I was dehydrated.

"Dinner at five. Prayers at six in the morning. Follow the smell of food to the dining room," Marjie said, and walked away. She returned after a few seconds and added, "Clinic on Monday. Volunteer, if you're here."

"Clinic?" I asked.

"We have volunteer medical staff every Monday," Marjie said.

"How can I help? I'm just a medical student," I said.

"They'll find a way to use you," Marjie said, and left.

I took my shoes and socks off. I placed my backpack on the bed. The leftover sandwiches came to mind, but my body was too weak to leave my room. I lowered my body to the bed, where I rested my head on the backpack. After a while, sleep rescued me from my worries.

Chapter 22

THE FOLLOWING MORNING, a high-pitched, whistling sound woke me. Darkness surrounded me. When I searched for my phone inside my backpack, my fingers felt my surgical dissection kit first. Of all the things in my backpack, a surgical scalpel and a pair of surgical scissors were the least beneficial to me in a homeless shelter. When I retrieved my phone, it displayed a half-charged battery, and the time, 6:01 am. I was already one minute late for the prayer meeting. I felt my way to the door and joined the rest of the homeless men in the hall.

I counted 20 men, and one woman wearing a track suit: Marjie. She held a prayer book in her left hand. While Marjie was inspecting everyone in the hall, a man sitting next to her nodded off. She ignored him.

"Lord, make this day a special one for all of us. We are your lost children, but thanks to you, we found a home," Marjie said.

Each time I made a wish or prayed, the opposite happened to me. I knew that things would get worse for me. More hardship.

"Amen," thundered throughout the hall. Marjie closed her prayer book. Her eyes glistened, and I saw her smile.

Some men yelled, "Hallelujah," as we dispersed.

I found the shower stalls close to my room. Shaved and showered, I dressed for breakfast before 7:00 am. At the dining area, a burly man served Egg Beaters, hotcakes, sausages, and colored water labeled 'apple juice'. He denied my request for a second serving.

After helping to clean the dining room, I left the homeless

shelter and walked to the Beale Street area to look for a job. Visiting several businesses, I filled out employment forms in ten places. At a freight company, three middle-aged men were loading three trucks. Each man had a truck to load. A man standing close to them had 'Jim' written on his shirt. He had a clipboard in his hand and spat tobacco on the ground as I approached him. I assumed he was in charge, the foreman. I thought about the man that was in charge of me, Dr Trophy, and his conduct. I hoped that Jim was a better man.

"I'm looking for a job," I said.

He looked me over without saying anything. He loaded his mouth with his chew and tapped his pen on the clipboard. I stood, and watched him ignore me. Two minutes passed. I had nowhere to go and nothing to lose. One of the men loading a truck held his wrist and wriggled in pain. His co-workers ignored him. The man in charge, the silent one, Jim, walked over to the man in pain.

"Get your fucking lazy ass out of here," Jim said.

The way he approached his worker reminded me of Dr Trophy. I tried to walk away.

"I'm hurt. I need to rest," the injured man said.

I thought about walking over to the injured man to help. I remembered that I was a dismissed medical school student and had no healthcare credentials.

"I don't need your sorry ass," Jim said.

"I need this job," the injured man said.

The remaining two workers ignored what was going on around them.

"What's your name?" Jim asked.

"Ben. Ben Ava," I said.

"Drop your bag and get to work. Finish loading the truck. I pay cash," Jim said.

I threw my backpack on an empty crate. I didn't have to fill out an employment form, nor did he ask for my identification card. I became an undocumented worker.

Looking up at the sky, I could see that no clouds blocked the early morning, Memphis sun. The temperature was warming up as I started lifting crates and placing them in the truck. Jim watched from the same spot. He sat down occasionally on a crate and mumbled to himself. I thought I even heard him curse about his 'fucked-up life'.

I filled up my truck before the other two workers had finished theirs. Sweat poured down my face, and my mouth was dry. The hunger that had disappeared after breakfast now returned. I wished the Mission House served seconds.

"Look at pretty boy. He finished before you fucking morons," Jim said.

I heard murmurs from the two men loading their trucks. I lifted a crate to help one of them. He stopped loading to look at me, giving me a scowl from below his raised eyelids. His eyes were cold under a crinkled forehead. It was a look that let me know he could kill me. I felt uneasy and scared.

"Just trying to help," I said.

"You took Ned's job, you fucker," the man said. The other man ignored us and continued to load his truck.

"I'm sorry. I need this job to survive," I said.

"You're not going to survive. We'll take care of you," the man said.

"Cut it out, boys," Jim said.

I continued to help him load his truck. We finished before noon and closed the truck's doors. Jim took out his wallet and handed 40 dollars to each of us.

"Come back tomorrow," Jim said to me.

"No tomorrow for him," the man whispered to his partner.

I looked at the man who had spoken. He showed me his middle finger. There was an urge in me to show him mine, but I restrained myself. I picked up my backpack and left. Walking to the Mission House would take a long time, and, after loading a truck, I felt that I would need more food than I would get at the Mission House—so I found a sandwich place. Three customers were ahead of me. Two men stood on the corner watching the lunch line. Looking at the two men, I realized that they were my co-workers from the truck-loading job. They were stalking me from a distance. I felt my heart rate increase. When my turn came, I ordered a barbeque-chicken sandwich and a bottle of water. Instead of hunger, my stomach felt queasy, thanks to the two lurking men.

After leaving the sandwich shop, I looked around. The two men were following me. I placed my bottled water in my backpack and quickened my pace. I made a sharp turn and took the path that led to the river embankment. Walking on loose boulders with sharp edges, I almost fell several times. Gently, I maneuvered around the unsteady boulders toward the edge of the muddy river. It appeared as rapidly flowing murk, giving off no glistening from the sun. It was no longer the shining beauty I saw from my window. The Mississippi lost its shine when I stood close to it. It was not what it appeared to be from a distance. Just like the medical profession I had once admired.

The thought of jumping into the river and drowning worried

me more than the two men approaching me. With no other choice, courage came over me. My heart raced but not out of fear; it was resoluteness. I decided to defend myself, the way a man should. I would fight for my life. I planned to lose it courageously, if that was my fate. I looked at the path I had taken down the ridge. When the two men were near to me, one of them reached inside his pocket and pulled out a small pocket knife. His fingers struggled to liberate the blade. When released, the small blade glistened in the sun, a sharp object that could cut through me.

I reached down to my feet and picked up a loose rock. My trembling fingers unzipped my backpack.

"He's cornered. I'll cut him up," the man said, as he brandished his knife.

"We'll feed him to the crows," the other man said. They laughed.

I thought about the scavengers on University Drive. Birds feeding on road kill. I looked up to the sky and asked God to forgive my sins. It would be my last prayer. My death.

I slipped several rocks into my backpack to defend myself. A good swing could kill a man, or two. Looking inside my bag, my eyes settled on the surgical instrument set on top of my clothes. A surgical scalpel and a pair of surgical scissors were inside the set. Removing the scalpel, I held it in front of me, high enough to glisten in the sun. To scare them, as their knife scared me. In one hand, I held a sack of rocks, and in the other, a surgical blade. I ascended the boulders with confidence, but carefully. The man with the pocket knife stumbled on a loose rock. His knife fell from his hand, rolled across the rocks, and logged inside a crevice.

While one man searched for his lost knife, the other man watched me run up the rocks. Once I reached a jogging trail, I slowed down. Joggers ran away from me, until I realized that I still held the surgical scalpel in my hand. I had turned an instrument used to heal into a weapon of defense, making it a perceived threat to joggers in the park. I thought about Brenda and her scalpel in the park. My situation was different. I was running from a potential harm.

I stopped running, unzipped my bag, and returned my blade to its container. I slowed down to rest. Warm, humid air filled my lungs under the punishing Memphis sun.

"There's the bastard," one of the two men shouted from a distance.

"You're a dead motherfucker," the other man added.

I removed the rocks from by bag and ran. My arms swung back and forth, propelling me forward. Increased strides helped me widen the distance between me and the two men. However, my breathing became audible. I was panting in the hot sun, on a run to save my life.

"I need help. I'm dying," I heard a man say.

The plea came from a voice behind me. I slowed down and looked back. One of the two men chasing me was lying on the ground. His friend knelt next to him.

"Please help. He's dead," the kneeling man yelled.

Two joggers stopped to help the man. The fear of dying from stabbing left me. It was an emergency. Without worrying about the fact that the dying man had vowed to kill me, I turned around. I thought a cardiac arrest might have caused the man's medical emergency. I thought about my training in advanced cardiac life support as I approached the victim lying on the ground. Kneeling next to the man on the ground, I checked for his responsiveness—but he was unresponsive. His mouth and nasal passage had no objects that could obstruct his breathing. I checked his carotid artery. He had no pulse.

"Call 911," I yelled to the people gathered around. Sweat poured down my face.

I began chest compressions, counting every time I pushed on his chest. Thirty seconds into my CPR, I heard a siren from a distance. A cough erupted from the dead man on the ground, who reached for my hand and held it. I stopped the chest compressions. When he tried to rise from the ground, I held him down. His friend helped to restrain him. The two men looked at me. None of us spoke.

Two paramedics ran to us with a stretcher.

"What happened?" a paramedic asked.

"He was running after me. I heard him yell for help. He passed out. He was out for only a minute, I think. That's all I know. His friend can tell you the rest," I said.

The paramedics checked his blood pressure, placed electrocardiogram leads on his chest, started an IV, and carted him away.

After the ambulance left with the man who had passed out, the other man that was chasing me raised his thumb for me. We exchanged smiles. I found a park bench and sat in the sun. I felt elated and fulfilled. For a moment, I forgot that I was a dismissed medical student, and homeless. It felt good to help a dying man. No. A dead man. I'm a healer, I thought. I resolved to fight to regain my status as a medical student. To become a doctor.

After 30 minutes of sitting on the park bench daydreaming, the sun stung my skin. The humid air felt like hot steam going down my lungs, warming up my insides and sapping my strength. I remembered how much I depended on the disciplinary council. Academic men, probably like Dr Cleaver, with no empathy. They would meet in a day to decide on my future. Sadness replaced my elation.

Chapter 23

LATER THAT NIGHT, my room door squeaked and woke me up. I remembered several attempts I had made, jiggling the lock before I slept—latched, I thought.

My eyes opened. Light filtered into my room. Squinting, I could see the hall filled with bunk beds, bodies lying still. My eyes roamed around my room. A desk jammed against the wall. Two shirts and two pairs of dress pants hanging on the wall. No intruders in my room. My body stayed covered. My hands and legs were limp, the muscles wilted from prolonged sun and heat exposure, and my joints ached from heavy lifting. I had aged unbelievably overnight. Defending myself would have been difficult.

"Where's Rita? My Rita," I heard myself whisper in desperation. Hopelessness had sapped my energy and wrapped me up in bed. My mind wandered to many places, remembering losses I had suffered. Dead parents, and lovers that jilted me. Deb and Rita, my last two. Medical school suspension. Homelessness. No one was missing me or looking for me. I was alone in the darkness of my room, until my door opened. I surmised that the lights had come on to help me see beyond my room, but I did not know what to look for. Desolation consumed me.

My eyes closed. Rita held my hand. The two of us were frolicking in a lilac field, which gave off a delightful, intoxicating fragrance. We embraced before our tongues met. A taste of nectar lingered in my mouth. I placed my lips on her neck and ears. I felt firmness in my loins. We reached our blanket on a cleared space. As we sprawled naked on the blanket, our hands searched for pleasurable places on each other's bodies. I heard a whistling sound. It woke me from an erotic dream, to atone with a prayer. It was 6:00 am.

My limp arms and legs were revived. I rose from my bed and walked to the prayer meeting with men I had not known for long, men with their eyes half closed, their lips moving in uncoordinated prayer. I heard, "Blessings are from God." Maybe the preacher could tell me who took away my blessings. It could not be God. Instead of asking the preacher, I walked from one man to another. I shook their hands, homeless hands. My atonement for sinning in my sleep in the Mission House. 'God's house'—the sign on the wall said so.

"I'm Ben Ava," I said to each man.

"Nice to meet you, Brother," most of the men said.

"Get your sorry self to your lockup," one man growled. A miserable man, I assumed.

It was a Thursday morning. Nothing special about Thursday mornings; however, this one was when the disciplinary council would decide my fate. My future. They would decide whether I would return to school and learn how to heal, or be banished. There was nothing left for me to lose. I remembered losing my sanity, and I was not even sure if everything in my brain was intact. The visions I had seen, awake and asleep, came back to me. There was no fear left in me. I was at the bottom of everything. My self-worth rested on my medical education; the acquisition of the skills to heal. It was the only valuable thing that I had. Feeling that the disciplinary council meeting would not favor me, I thought about things to say to the men judging me. My testament on virtues and fairness.

My stomach ached all morning. I skipped breakfast at the Mission House. Showered. Ironed my pants and shirt. Dressed. A wrinkled tie steamed while hanging from my neck. The risk of scalding myself did not cross my mind. I packed everything I owned in my backpack before I stepped into the street. Should I return to my employer to load trucks or go to the dean's office to inquire about my fate? I walked.

The church by the administration building displayed a simple phrase: 'Trust in God'. I was already a believer. One that had not been favored. I needed more than a common phrase to motivate me. I walked into the church, which was empty. Ornate stained glass windows. Polished pews. No knee-rests like they had in Catholic churches. My knees rested on the floor. With too many favors to ask God, I didn't know where to start.

"Please God take care of me. I have no one else," I said aloud. It covered everything I needed. The same prayer as before, but I had felt confident then.

My phone rang in church. I thought about God calling me. I laughed. My hands trembled as I searched for my phone.

"Hello. Hello," I answered. My forehead moistened.

"I'm trying to reach Ben Ava," a female voice said.

"I'm Ben," I said.

"Good. This is the dean's secretary. You need to be here at noon. The council wants to talk to you," she said.

"I'll be there, Ma'am," I said.

I felt happy. Excited. Then I began to worry. I wondered if the council wanted to dismiss me permanently from the school during their meeting. My breathing rate increased. Panic set in.

I walked outside for fresh air.

I sat outside on the church's dusty steps and scrolled down my contact list. When I reached Deborah Linger's name, my finger dialed her number. I heard four rings before her voicemail came on. I turned it off. I returned to my contacts' list. My phone rang while I was scrolling down the list again. 'Deborah Linger' was displayed on my screen.

"Hello Deb," I said.

"Good news from my biopsy," Deb said.

"I'm happy for you," I said.

"My friends are throwing a party for me. Close friends. Dinner. Wine. A good time, I hope," Deb said.

"Enjoy your party," I said.

"You called me. Everything okay?" Deb asked.

"Nothing important. Take care," I said. She hung up. I didn't want to spoil her happiness.

A couple walking toward the administration building stopped. They kissed. The man walked into the building, and his girl stood on the sidewalk. She watched him enter the building before she crossed the street. I felt jealous.

Love eluded me as a medical student. I needed love to find me. When I thought about my situation, that of a homeless man, I laughed. I wondered how love would find me in the Mission House.

When I returned to my contacts' list, I started from A and proceeded to Z. While I was searching for someone to talk to, a lady in blue scrubs walked by. She shared Rita's body shape, a full chest and a small waist. Squinting, I thought it was Rita. I heard a voice from my phone.

"Ben," the female voice said.

"Who's this?" I asked.

"You're crazy. You called me. Remember me. It's Rita," she said, laughing.

"I'm sorry. Going down my contacts' list. Accidental call," I said.

"Don't be. I missed you," Rita said.

I tried to talk but choked. I heard Rita cry. I tried to control my emotions.

"Sorry to disturb you at work," I said.

"I'm off today. Cleaning my place," Rita said.

"Have you heard?" I asked.

"What?" she asked.

"My suspension," I said.

"I've been off. I needed time away from you for my sanity," Rita said.

"They threw me out. I was trying to protect Brenda," I said.

"That's terrible. You need to fight it. Get a lawyer, or something," Rita said. Her voice sounded angry.

I climbed up two steps and sat down.

"They meet at noon to decide on me. I need your support," I said.

"I don't know. Not sure I'm feeling strong enough to support anyone," Rita said.

"Anyone? It's me. I need you terribly," I said. My voice quavered.

"I don't want to get hurt again," Rita said.

"How can I hurt you? Talking about hurt, I'm homeless. At noon, I report to the dean's office. For the enquiry. As if I'm a criminal." There was a silence on the other end of the line. "I'm sorry I called you." I hung up the phone.

Baring my heart to Rita scared me. I had wasted my energy—weakening myself and withering my ego. I took a deep breath and looked around, observing everything I had neglected before then. I had to find a way to cheer myself up. I needed it.

Before noon, there was sunshine, less humid air, and a wind that swayed tree branches. Leaves flapped in different directions. Deciding on the direction of the wind was impossible and only worsened my own uncertainty. It was a pleasant morning by Memphis standards, except I was in agony. I moved up and down the steps in front of the church searching for a perfect sitting position, which was a futile effort. I had nowhere to go, nothing to do before noon. I was stranded in the haze of the university medical center's power.

Chapter 24

CLOSE TO NOON, the elevator door opened. The elevator was empty. Its sliding doors closed halfway, then slid open. When I tried to get in, the elevator door closed. It remained closed. A broken door. It deprived me of a quick ride to the second floor, to the dean's office to defend myself. When I thought about the experience with the elevator, I realized that things could have been worse. If I was trapped inside a broken elevator and failed to show up for my hearing, I wondered what would have happened to my case.

Less than two paces away from the elevator, I opened the door that led to the steps. On my way to the second floor I counted the steps. Ten or 13 steps? I forgot. My memory failed me. I had more serious things to worry about. Remembering the number of steps would not change the outcome of the inquisition. A disciplinary council emergency meeting, they called it.

I stood on the landing, staring at the steps. The first step I took climbing up felt as if I was learning how to walk. A fear of making mistakes gripped me. I climbed down and started over. It was better to show grace, even during a struggle, to avoid repeating previous missteps. It was a process of learning discipline, if I needed to, before the disciplinary council ruled on my case. My action did not make sense to me, but I was under a mountain of stress. I felt hot inside and sweat trickled down my face. I held the banister while ascending. I needed the support.

My hands were trembling by the time I reached the second floor. Anticipating the worst outcome, I repositioned my backpack and tightened the straps to secure it on my back. It contained everything I owned, except the money in my pocket, which was enough money for a bus ticket to Knoxville. My hometown. The thought of returning home, without a home, terrified me. I would be homeless in a different town. It would take all the money I had to get there. I had only one job prospect there: transporting patients to the emergency room, my old job. The job I left when I moved to Memphis. The option of hiding in medical students' call rooms at night, until I saved enough money to find a place, crossed my mind. I had a plan.

It was 11:45 am. I looked around the hallway, seeing it as a deserted corridor of power. I thought about waiting for five minutes before entering the dean's office.

"Hey, Bro," a familiar voice said. It was James, ascending the steps.

"Player James, you heard. Thanks for coming," I said. He laughed.

"The dean's secretary called. We're all here," James said. Things appeared to be worse than I thought. Witnesses, needed to indict me.

Andrew and Brenda approached the landing. I waved to them. Brenda ignored me. Her response, or lack of it, didn't surprise me. Maybe someday she would tell me what I did to her. When she was a few steps away from me, I noticed that Brenda had lost more weight. It had only been two days since the confrontation with our attending physician.

"I'm hot, from climbing these stupid steps," Andrew said. He wiped his face on his sleeve.

"Always about you. We're here for Ben. Support. Remember?" James said.

"Speak for yourself. I'm forced to be here. I can't wait to get out," Brenda said.

"Happy to see everyone," I said.

"You're not," Brenda said.

"I'm scared. Trying hard to be strong," I said.

"Don't fuck with mean sons of bitches if you're scared," Brenda said. She was more vulgar than I remembered. Words flowed out of her mouth with no filter. Raw.

"So, Bro, you're buying after we save your ass," James said.

"No bribe for me. I'll speak the truth," Andrew said, showing no smile. He looked determined.

"You don't need to lie for me. I was right," I said.

"Well, you…" Andrew could not finish his words before James interrupted him.

"I'll kick your ass if you mess Ben up," James said.

Andrew showed James his middle finger, then adjusted his bow tie. He sniffled as he walked away, headed in the direction of the dean's office. He stopped midway, and came back to where we were. The four of us stood in the hallway looking in different directions. I felt empty inside. I felt my hands shake.

Tapping sounds on the staircase attracted my attention. Looking down the steps, I saw Rita swaying her waist as she climbed each step. High heels guided her body up the steps with such grace—she swayed rhythmically in her ascent.

Compelled by raw excitement, I ran down the steps without grace or caution, and was met with hugs and kisses. Soon, red lipstick was smeared all over Rita's face. Feeling joy inside me, I had tears in my eyes. I reached out and held on to Rita.

"I missed you, Babe," I said.

She was there for me. My arms encircled Rita's waist as we held on to each other. She retrieved a tissue from her purse and dabbed her lips. My classmates watched Rita and me—Andrew and James with smiles, Brenda with a frown.

"Save it for later," James said. "We'll be late. It's 11:55." He'd changed. His smile faded and a new, more serious James appeared.

Rita hugged me tightly before she loosened her grip on me. I sighed.

"I'm sorry. I forgot about your wound," Rita said.

"I forgot about it, too. I have worse problems," I said.

"I understand," Rita said.

"We'll be in the office," I said.

"I'll find you," Rita said. She walked down the opposite hallway.

"Fine babe," James said. He tapped me on the shoulder.

Andrew led the way as we walked in the direction of the dean's office. Three classmates to testify for, or against, me. I was not sure which way it would go. I crossed my fingers.

"I forgot to ask. Are you here to help me?" I asked.

"We're needed, they said. Not sure if it's good or bad for you," James said.

"I'm not here to help him," Brenda said. She avoided looking at me. Instead, she looked at James as she spoke.

"My bro helped your ass. That's why we're here," James said.

"I didn't ask for help," Brenda said.

Inside the dean's office, I leaned against the wall closest to the door. Andrew and James sat next to each other. Brenda sat across the room. She looked at me twice and squinted. My hand covered my mouth. I felt jittery inside, and was breathing fast.

My hands were moist. I tried to slow my breathing without success. The secretary looked at her watch, then lifted the telephone handset. I assumed she was calling Dr Cleaver. My breathing stopped. I sensed a bad outcome, the end of my medical education.

* * *

Doctor Cleaver and four gray-haired men entered the waiting area of his office, smiling and whispering to each other. They laughed occasionally and were loud at times. They seemed callous about my plight. I trained my eyes on them, seeing men in long white coats, symbols of purity. Their names and job titles were embroidered on the coats: 'Patrick Smith, MD, FACS, Chief of Surgery'; 'Mark Wood, MD, Chief of Psychiatry'; 'Martin Haber, MD, FACP, Chairman, Medicine Department'; 'Trenton Holt, MD, Chief of Staff'. The gods of medicine that would decide my fate. Gas bubbled into my mouth from my stomach. I burped, and nausea traveled all over my stomach. A fear of throwing up gripped me.

"We'll be in the conference room," Dr Cleaver said.

"Should I hold your calls?" the secretary asked.

"No calls for me," Dr Cleaver said.

"One student at a time," Dr Wood said.

Rita walked in. The eminent doctors all looked at the beautiful woman, their eyes fixed on her waistline. We watched the attending physicians—men that I thought were incorruptible—drool over a woman. Andrew and James smiled. Brenda looked down at the floor, ignoring the display of locker room-type antics from my fair judges. Her arms appeared limp at her sides, and her shoulders were lowered. She sneaked a peek at me occasionally. Each time our eyes met, she looked away. I walked to meet Rita, embracing this distraction from the impending judgment on my character.

"Hello again, Babe," Rita said under her breath. She reached for my hands and squeezed them.

"I need you, terribly," I whispered.

My voice quavered. She kissed my cheek, then wiped it with her fingers.

The eminent doctors looked away when Rita took possession of my hand and painted my cheek with rouge. Standing close to Rita, my body felt warm—the good type of warmness. A secure feeling, one I had not experienced since my expulsion from medical school.

"Come with us," Dr Cleaver said. Everyone followed.

"Ben first, then the rest later," Dr Holt said.

"I agree," Dr Haber said.

"Let's go," Dr Cleaver said.

I followed the five men. Judicious men, I assumed. Dr Cleaver led the way. They continued with their wittiness, saying things that were funny only to them. While they laughed, I dreaded the possibility of being dismissed permanently from medical school. A burst of laughter interrupted my thoughts, making their humor painful to me.

Dr Cleaver stood by the door of the conference room, gesticulating as he ushered his colleagues in. Rita and I waited to be ushered in. He paused, making no hand gestures pointing to the conference room like he had done for the men before us. We stood and waited for his instructions, be they verbal or indicated by gesticulation.

"Ma'am, only Ben for now," Dr Cleaver said.

"He needs my support," Rita said.

"We'll take care of him," Dr Cleaver said.

"Like you did before. I'm not leaving," Rita said. She squeezed my hand tighter. I worried about the consequences of her stubbornness, but decided not to say anything. If she walked away again, I would be alone.

"Something new for us, but you can come in," Dr Cleaver said, his tone laced with a tinge of sarcasm.

Rita and I walked into the conference room. An oblong table with 20 chairs was positioned at the center of the room, and a large atomic clock hung on the wall. Its second hand moving jerkily. Luminescent lights, one door, and no windows. A trial chamber.

Silent, the adjudicators sat next to each other. Inside the trial chamber, there was no bantering. I sat opposite the men, their eyes avoiding mine. Rita sat next to me and held my hand, squeezing hard at times. I wondered if she was anxious and needed my hand to soothe her anxiety. Dr Cleaver sat down, and opened his folder.

"Your case borders on disrespect for your attending physician. Respect is essential in our profession. We respect and learn from our colleagues. We also respect our patients. You violated the tenets of professional medical conduct," Dr Cleaver read from a piece of paper. He took deep breaths while reading, as if he was in pain. It was a painful delivery for me too, because I had to control my desire to shush him.

Dr Cleaver stopped reading and looked at his colleagues. They glanced at each other. It appeared rehearsed to me. Fake nobility.

The room became silent, except for the sound made by the second hand of the clock. My life and future were ticking away with each sound.

I had expected them to ask me about the incident with Dr Trophy, to give my side of the story. Instead, I was listening to a speech about respect, nothing more than an admonition before my permanent dismissal from school. Snorting sounds came out of my nose. There was nothing left for me to lose. I rose from my chair, my hands steady and feet firmly on the ground.

"Sir, respect has to be earned. A teacher who verbally insults his student does not deserve respect. Not mine. The Hippocratic Oath said to respect my teacher. It assumed that my teacher would earn that respect. It described a family. A medical family. Members supporting each other. A few days ago, you kicked me out of school without listening to what I had to say. I've been homeless because I defended a fellow student from a bully. I have no regrets. I don't have to be a doctor to take care of people. I'll find a way to make a difference in people's lives. Rita, let's go," I said.

"Sit down, you shit-head. My nephew told me what happened," Dr Smith said. Becoming aware of his family connection, Andrew's arrogance made sense to me.

"I love his passion. That's what we need in this dying profession," Dr Wood said.

"Not a good way to express it," Dr Cleaver said, his voice raised.

"Apologize to Dr Trophy and return to your rotation. That's my opinion," Dr Holt said.

"We agree," the rest of the physicians said.

"Write your apology. I'll call him to take you back,"

Dr Cleaver said.

"I want a different attending physician," I said.

"You can't make demands. We're being lenient," Dr Cleaver said.

"I'll take him," Dr Haber said.

"It's settled," Dr Smith said.

The men rose. Some patted me on the back. My legs began to tremble, as I realized how dangerous my course of action had been. I could have lost my place in the medical school. I held Rita's hand and hurried out of the room before they changed their minds.

We were walking down the steps before I remembered my classmates waiting in Dr Cleaver's office.

"Wait for me. I'll be back," I said.

"I'm hungry. Hurry up," Rita said.

I ran up the steps two at a time. A reclaimed vigor propelled me up the stairs, an unexpected transformation. Inside Dr Cleaver's office, my classmates rose when I entered, except for Brenda.

"I'm back. It's over," I said.

"We're not needed?" James asked.

"You're not. You, lucky son of a..." I said. I laughed, instead of finishing my vulgarity. James and Andrew laughed too.

"We'll go out tonight to celebrate," James said.

"Count me out," Brenda said.

"You're coming with us. We're like a family. We stick together," James said.

I walked over to the secretary's desk. When she looked up, her eyes spoke to me. The look simply said, 'What can I do for you?' No words were necessary. I used to see it in my mother's eyes. A few years had passed since I saw it last. While I looked at her, the secretary's lips crinkled, the way my mother's used to. Happiness and sadness, two opposing feelings at the same time, engulfed me. Another sense of loss found its way back to my life. And I had thought my miseries were over.

"I need to return to my room," I said.

"I'll ask Dr Cleaver," the secretary said.

"Thank you, Ma'am," I said.

I caught up with my classmates. James was standing close to the door. He held the door handle and cranked the door open as I walked toward him.

"Let's meet at six tonight. Your lobby. I'll drive," James said.

"Sounds good," I said.

We left Dr Cleaver's office together and took watchful footsteps down the stairs to the first floor, none of us saying anything. Rita was standing close to a working elevator when we joined her. She reached out and held my hand, pulling me closer to her. We hugged in a tight squeeze. My hand rolled down her head. Without forethought, I sniffed the subtle scent of jasmine in her hair. Brenda, who stood opposite me, frowned when our eyes met. She mumbled and left the building.

"Enough, lover boy," James said.

"Let's get out of here," I said.

"It's victory, Bro. We need to celebrate. Beale Street tonight," James said. His voice resonated.

"I deserve a good time. Can't wait to dance with Rita," I said. Rita smiled.

"No one asked my opinion," Rita said.

"I'm sorry. We don't have to dance," I said.

"I love dancing, but I want to be asked," Rita said.

"Bro, always ask your lady for a date. Don't assume," James said.

"You're right James, the Love Doctor," I said. We laughed.

I reached out to hold Rita's hand, and said, "A southern gent would love your company tonight."

"I accept," Rita said.

"Let's meet at six. The Blue Oyster," James said.

"We'll be there," I said.

"Should I invite Brenda?" James asked. I laughed.

"Good luck with that. I bet, she wants to stay away from me," I said.

"I don't want her around me," Rita said.

When we left the building, I was unsure of what to do with my time. I had no place to go. I looked at Rita's face, wondering about her state of mind. Apart from her beautiful face, the mystery of why she chose to be with a struggling medical student instead of a resident physician, Dr Peterson, eluded me. While she offered me abundant smiles, her reason for choosing me stayed hidden behind those smiles. A secret, which I was eager to discover someday.

Chapter 25

EARLY AFTERNOON SUNSHINE. Medium humidity. No wind. We set out from the medical center area. Rita and I walked to my dormitory, holding hands and swinging our arms like playful children. We had the afternoon off before I returned to my medical rotation the following day. Halfway to my dormitory, sweat poured down our faces. I felt exhausted from the heat and hardly spoke.

At the reception desk of my dormitory, the place I had left a few days before, I presented my student identification card to the receptionist. She looked me over several times before she handed over the keys to my dorm room. We took the elevator to the sixth floor, listening to the clunking sounds. A song came to mind that went with the elevator noise. I decided not to sing it, though. There might be value in stupidity, but not when I was trying to impress a girl.

I received a kiss from Rita as we disembarked, but no words. We looked at each other several times and smiled. I wondered what was going through her mind as we strolled to my dormitory suite. The common area was dark; I switched the lights on. We were alone. It felt good to be back in the only home I had. We entered my room.

Two towels rested on my bed, forgotten during my hasty departure. I pushed the towels to the side and sat down. Rita sat next to me.

"I was lost without you," I said.

"Me too," she said.

"I'm sorry I got upset. I don't want to share you," she said.

"I felt wronged, losing you for no reason," I said. I wiped sweat off my face with one of the towels. "Let's take a shower. I'm too hot," I added.

"I don't want to mess up my makeup," she said. She moved closer to me and held my hands.

"I'm talking about soapy lather. Washing your back," I said. I smiled.

"I bet. You're bad," she said.

I stripped down to my underwear, then wrapped the towel around my waist and took my underwear off. I felt free.

"Come on, let's do it," I said.

I pulled her up from the bed. She took her clothes off, grabbed the other towel, and wrapped her body in it. She giggled, childlike, excited. I took my room keys from the desk, locked my door, and led Rita to the shower.

For the first time, the shower stall felt small to me. I turned the shower on and waited until the water warmed up. Rita watched me untie the towel around my waist. I hung the towel on the shower door exposing my nakedness to her. She fumbled with the towel wrapped around her chest. It barely extended beyond her waistline, exposing her hips and thighs. Her skin was unblemished. I beckoned to her with my finger. She smiled and took a step toward me, hesitating as she got closer.

"I missed you terribly," she said. She extended her hand to me.

"I missed you too, Babe," I said.

"I should have called. Too proud to let you win," she said.

"Win? Not sure what you mean," I said.

"Sorry. I meant that I was wrong," she said.

I kissed her lips, her neck, and her ears. I stopped and looked into her eyes. A gaze. She blinked and laughed.

She loosened her towel and dropped it to the floor, revealing beautiful breasts and erect nipples. I licked my lips and took a deep breath. She smiled. I watched her eyes trail to my loins, a hard situation waiting to be pacified. We stepped inside the stall. She hugged me, and kissed my neck. Her tongue traveled to my ears, then found its way to my chest, my navel, and eventually to my loins when she knelt. I screamed, loud enough that it probably traveled all over the dormitory suite. A thrilling moment.

I turned the shower knob so the water pulsated, hoping the higher water pressure would drown out the sounds I made as the lukewarm water splashed on Rita's head. Unperturbed, she kissed what stood in front of her. She moaned as she diligently massaged sensitive parts of my body with her tongue.

"Oh!" I shouted.

When I began to lose control of myself, I reached to her head to restrict her action. She pushed my hands away and resumed her activity. I put my hands under her arms, pulled her up and turned her around. With her palms against the wall and legs parted, I penetrated her from behind.

"I need it, Babe. I can take it all. Don't stop," she said, then moaned and cursed, uttering expletives. I was in a haze.

She reached behind herself and pulled me closer. My body slammed against her wet buttocks, making a slapping sound. Her legs wobbled. I stepped back and hit the shower door, making it swing open.

"Are you okay, Babe?" I asked.

"Fuck me good. Don't stop," she said.

I heard a door slam, loudly. It sounded as if it was inside my dorm suite. Turning the shower off, I reached for my towel and wrapped it around my waist. Stepping outside the cubicle, I picked up Rita's towel from the floor and handed it to her. I slightly opened the bathroom door leading to the common area of the dormitory suite. Peeking outside the door, I saw Brenda perched on a bar stool in the kitchen area, a kitchen knife and a box of tissues before her on the counter. She dabbed her eyes and nose with a tissue. I closed the bathroom door and locked it. My heart pounded.

"What's going on?" Rita asked.

My hands trembled.

"Wait here. Lock the door after I leave," I said.

Stepping out of the bathroom, I noticed that Brenda's head rested on the counter. I walked to my room with my eyes fixed on her. I was afraid of Brenda attacking me with the knife. She did not look up. Inside my room, I dressed. I picked up Rita's clothes, walked back to the bathroom and knocked on the door.

"It's me," I whispered.

"What the heck is going on?" Rita asked, in a hushed voice.

She opened the door. I walked in and locked it.

"It's Brenda. She's out there sulking. I'm not sure what's going on," I said.

"You need to move out of here. Please," she said.

"I can't afford to."

"Move in with me."

"I can't afford here. How can I afford your place?"

"I'm frugal. You don't have to pay me."

"That would be a burden on you," I said. She frowned.

Rita hugged and kissed me. We held each other. My hand caressed her wet hair. For a moment, I forgot the urgency of the situation around us. When I heard a scream coming from the common area of the dormitory suite, I withdrew my hand from Rita's hair. Brenda cutting her wrist again came to mind. With my ear to the door, I heard only silence. I became worried that she had killed herself. My arrest by the city police for questioning about the death of a fellow student flashed before my eyes. Remembering that Rita was with me—my alibi—I felt relieved. I heard a screeching sound. The sound of a chair moving on a tiled surface.

"I'm going out there. She's got a knife. I don't know what's wrong," I said.

Rita held me, standing between me and the bathroom door. I tried to untangle myself from her grip, but she resisted. It felt good that she cared about my safety. I gave Rita the key to my room before we left the bathroom. Rita walked to my room while I watched Brenda. Ready to stop her if she attacked us.

I hesitated before walking toward Brenda. Clearing my throat, I approached Brenda with nervousness. I did not want to surprise her and risk being stabbed.

"Are you okay? I'm worried about you," I said. She ignored me. "Brenda, I'm here to help you," I added.

"You're here to help me? You don't care about me," Brenda said. I wondered how to express my care for my classmate, my former anatomy laboratory partner, a member of my medical family—if I believed in the Hippocratic Oath. I thought of ways of showing empathy, the virtue I was seeking as a medical student.

I took the knife and sat next to her. She raised her head. Tears rolled down her face. She put her head down again.

Looking around the room for other dangerous objects, I saw

Rita stick her head out from my room. I rose from the chair and walked closer to Brenda. Without forethought, I placed my hand on her shoulder. Maybe I was emboldened by a witness, Rita, observing my actions from a distance, in case there was a false accusation of sexual harassment by Brenda.

"Don't touch me," Brenda said. She poked her finger in my face.

I removed my hand from her shoulder and leaned against the counter.

"We're like family. I've known you since our first day in medical school," I said.

"Family? You don't know my pain," Brenda said.

"Help me understand," I said.

"Why should you care? Tell me why?" she said, her voice raised.

Brenda's eyes glistened, and she sneered.

"I don't want you to hurt yourself," I said.

"I'll tell you when I'm ready. I'll let you watch me die," Brenda said. She laughed and coughed, then stood up from her chair. She took a few steps away from me, then turned back. "Go back to your woman. She needs your bullshit. I don't," she added.

"I'm here for you. Always. Don't you forget it," I said.

"Real nice. A wonderful man. A fucking idiot," Brenda said.

"Please talk to someone. A therapist. You need help," I said.

She reached for my neck and grabbed my shirt collar. The buttons ripped off when she pulled my shirt apart. The only decent dress shirt I had. Watching what Brenda was doing, Rita ran over to me.

"I don't need a damn therapist," Brenda said. She reached out and scratched my face with her fingernails. Blood dripped down to my neck and soaked my shirt. I placed my fingers over the wound to stop it from bleeding. Rita rushed to my side and pushed Brenda away. Brenda stumbled, and walked toward her room. Mid-way, she turned around and added, "Stop fucking that bitch in our shower." She slammed her room door. When I heard the creaky sound of her door opening, I became concerned. I thought about her scalpel and how to defend Rita.

Brenda faced her door and banged her head on it. I approached Brenda and pulled her away from her door. Holding Brenda by her arm, I wondered what to do next. Rita stood by me, but avoided looking at my face. I sensed she was angry with me. Brenda sobbed, holding on to her door knob. My grip on her arm stopped her from going into her room, a place where I would have no control over her actions. I worried about the legal implications of what I was doing.

Realizing that my grip on Brenda's arm was tight, I loosened my hand. Brenda raised her head and looked at my face. She used her free hand to tilt my face. I closed my eyes, afraid that she would scratch me.

"If you scratch his face I'll kick your ass," Rita said. She moved closer to Brenda.

"I'm sorry Ben. I didn't mean to hurt you," Brenda said. She sighed.

"I don't know what to do with you," I said.

"I know I need help," Brenda said. She looked at her scratch marks on my face again, and added, "They're superficial."

"I'll call the crisis center for you," I said.

"Not tonight. I'll be okay," Brenda said. She put her arm around me.

"Don't you ever touch Ben again," Rita said. I released my hold on Brenda. Rita walked into my dorm room. Brenda opened her door and closed it behind her. I stood outside her room, lost in thought.

I had no experience in matters like hers. I did not know what my legal obligations were concerning protecting Brenda from killing herself. I returned to my room to face Rita. To listen to her opinion on my character flaws. If allowed, I would ask her opinion on handling the main problem, protecting Brenda from herself.

Chapter 26

FROM THE PARKING LOT of Kevin's Grill, a restaurant Rita had chosen, I could see the river and the bridge that connected Memphis to West Memphis. I stepped out of the passenger's side of Rita's car and ran over to the driver's side to open her door.

"Thanks," Rita said.

"You're my lady. I can't wait to get a new car," I said.

"Have you heard from the insurance company?" Rita asked.

"Not yet. I'll call them soon," I said. We walked to the restaurant.

James and his wife stood up when we joined them. Andrew was sitting next to a woman I assumed was his date. They were giggling and did not acknowledge our presence. Brenda was missing from our group. Our medical family.

"My wife, Kathy," James said.

"Nice to meet you," Rita and I said.

After a while, Andrew and his date smiled at us, though he did not introduce her. We sat close to James and his wife.

"We need to do this more often," James said.

"Even if I don't get kicked out again," I said.

"I'm not sure about Brenda. She didn't answer my call," James said.

"Never mind Brenda," I said.

I thought about James and Brenda. Did he tell his wife about Brenda? What would Brenda have done, sitting with James and his wife? Scalpels and knives came to mind. I looked around our table for steak knives.

Our waiter came by twice to inquire about our orders. James stood up and walked to the restaurant door area. I watched him dial a number and place the phone to his ear, I saw his lips move. Kathy left the table and walked to the restroom. James returned to our table.

"She'll be here," James said.

"You mean Brenda?" I asked.

"She's not happy with you," James said, and smiled. Even with a smile, James appeared worried. Probably concerned about Brenda. A display of empathy. An enviable quality, I thought.

"We had a misunderstanding earlier," I said.

"We'll wait for her. We're like family," James said.

"We're not family. I'm ordering," Andrew said.

"I'll wait," James said.

"Wait for what?" Kathy asked, as she rejoined us.

"Your husband is special. Waiting for his friend Brenda," Andrew said and giggled.

James frowned.

Rita and I laughed.

"Am I missing something?" Kathy asked.

"No. Your husband is a good southern gent," I said.

"I know he is," Kathy said.

"A classy man. He takes care of every woman," Andrew said.

"Enough, Andrew," I said.

"Don't. Without me talking to my uncle, your ass would have been kicked out. You owe me," Andrew said. He pointed his finger at me while speaking.

"I'm grateful," I said.

I bowed my head. It upset me that a student had to intervene on my behalf. I had expected a fair hearing. However, I accepted the end result, so I had to accept the process.

"Andrew, you're a piece of work," James said.

"Let's order," I said.

When I looked up, I saw Brenda walk in. She was dressed the same way as the last time I saw her, in hospital scrub pants and a top. She stood by the door and looked around. Our eyes met. She frowned as she walked toward our table. I looked away. Once Brenda reached our table, she pulled out a chair and sat down without saying hello to anyone.

"You're late," James said.

"Mind your own fucking business," Brenda said.

"No need to curse," I said.

"You know why she's angry," Andrew said.

"Watch what you're saying, Andrew," I said.

"Why?" Andrew asked.

"Respect. That's why," James said.

"What's going on?" Kathy asked.

"Ask your husband," Brenda said.

"Enough. Let's order, or I'll leave," James said.

"Waiter, we're ready," I said.

Everyone turned their eyes to their menus except for Brenda. She looked at James and Kathy instead of her menu. When Kathy looked up, Brenda looked away. I became worried about Brenda starting a conflict with Kathy, so I kept my eyes on her. When Brenda turned around, our eyes met. She squinted while looking at me, and mumbled some words I couldn't hear. I wondered where the tenderness she'd had earlier—putting her arm around me—had gone to.

*   *   *

Around our table, everyone had finished eating except for Brenda. The waiter came back to our table.

"I'll bring a dessert tray," the waiter said.

"I don't need it. My wife gives me all the sugar I need," James said. His attempt to entertain us. We laughed.

Brenda stabbed her chicken with her fork, then picked up her knife and plunged it into the meat. Her eyes glistened. Having seen that look before, I became worried. Everyone was still laughing, except for me and Rita.

"This mess has to stop," Rita whispered to me, her face looked worried.

I rose from my chair and walked over to Brenda.

"May I speak to you privately," I whispered to Brenda.

"Mind your own fucking business," Brenda said, loud enough that the rest of the table could hear.

"What's going on?" James asked.

"He's obsessed with me. I don't know why. I hate him," Brenda said.

"I am just looking out for you. I'm sorry," I said.

"You upset me. Belittle me. Treat me like a fucking child," Brenda said.

"Boys, leave the poor girl alone. She doesn't fit in," Andrew said.

Brenda pulled her knife out of the chicken. It fell out of her hand and landed on the floor. I stepped on the knife. When Brenda looked away, I picked up the knife, placed it on the table, and covered it with a napkin.

"I hate my life," Brenda said, barely audibly.

"Is everything okay?" the waiter asked, while looking at Brenda.

"Family quarrel," I said. We laughed. The waiter left.

I sat next to Brenda. Her puckered lips and glassy eyes gave her face an unusual look. She sniffled, instead of breathing normally. Her disdain was obvious.

"I'll jump off the bridge. Get it over with. Will that make you happy?" Brenda said.

"You don't mean it," I said.

"I have nothing to live for," Brenda said.

She left her food and walked out of the restaurant. I pulled my wallet out of my pocket and left 40 dollars on the table. The money I earned from loading a truck. A job I risked my life for.

"I'll be back," I said.

"Don't get hurt," Rita said.

I went after Brenda. She was about to cross the road when I caught up with her.

"I'll walk you to your car," I said.

"It's always about you. Leave me alone. I'll walk to that bridge and jump, if you don't," Brenda said.

I glanced at the bridge and the muddy water below. Should I physically stop her if she tried to jump?

"I won't let you do it. I care about you," I said.

"I bet you do. You've no respect for me," Brenda said.

"You lost me," I said.

"I'm going back to the dorm. I'll hang myself if I want to," Brenda said.

I heard the sound of high heels on the pavement.

"Ben, what's going on?" Rita asked.

"You should've stayed inside," I said.

"I won't leave you out here with her," Rita said.

"I don't want him. You bitch," Brenda said.

I walked closer to Brenda and put my arms around her shoulders.

"Come with me. We're going back in," I said.

"Don't touch me. I can't stand you," Brenda said.

I removed my hand from her shoulder. She opened her car door and plopped her body into the driver's seat. With a sullen face, she inspected my body from my head to my feet. Her nose crinkled. As her eyes settled on my dingy shoes, she closed them and tightened her eyelids in unconcealed mockery. My eyes wandered to the unpolished old leather, the torn straps that covered my feet. When she opened her eyes, her mien—as she watched me inspect myself—made me angry.

As I wallowed in anger, she slammed her car door and drove off. I watched her drive in the direction of the bridge. When she reached the entrance to the bridge, I became concerned.

"I think she's going to do it. She's crazy. I'll call 911," I said.

"Where's she going?" Rita asked.

"Crazy girl. Ready to jump off the bridge. She needs help," I said.

"She does not. She has you snowed," Rita said.

"Go inside and call for help. I'll run after her," I said.

Rita frowned. She stayed and held my hand, tightly. We watched Brenda drive past the bridge toward West Memphis. When she crossed the bridge, I sighed.

"She's playing you," Rita said.

"I don't think so. She really needs help," I said

Brenda's car disappeared from view. Rita loosened her grip

on my hand. She led the way as we walked back to the restaurant. I sat and watched the door, hoping to see Brenda return. Time passed. No Brenda. Trickles of sweat moistened my forehead. I heard my increased breathing rate, but Brenda's safety occupied my mind. My anatomy laboratory partner. An inseparable friend during those six months. My former confidant.

Chapter 27

AT 6:00 AM, the conference room was dark. It was the first time the lights were off upon my arrival. I wiped my eyes, but I could not see beyond the door of the windowless room. I needed a new pair of glasses. From my memory, the long table was always at the center, with the chairs scattered around the room most of the time. Wouldn't that be ironic—if I injured myself on the first day I resumed my clinical rotation after suspension. I hesitated to venture into the dark to look for the light switch.

I couldn't remember ever seeing the light switch. I felt the wall on the right for a switch because I assumed that right hands turn on lights. When I reached the mid-section of the room without finding the switch, I turned around. Close to the door frame on the left, I located the switch. I realized that I should not always expect things to fit the way I expected them to.

Incandescent lights illuminated the room on my command. Chairs were scattered everywhere in the room, and three envelopes lay on the table: Ben, Andrew, and James were written on separate envelopes. One name was missing: Brenda. I picked up the envelope with my name on it, and used the side of my hospital badge to open it. Inside the envelope was a handwritten note.

Room 421. 85-y.o. female with acute stroke and depression. Room 307. 21-y.o. college student, depressed after a three-day drinking binge. Evaluate patients and present at the morning report.

Patients, assigned to me. A validation of my clinical rotation resumption. I felt delighted. I lifted the remaining envelopes, searching for Brenda's name. I hadn't learned how to avoid trouble. After failing to find what I was looking for, I assumed that she had arrived earlier than me.

I had two hours to complete my work before meeting with the resident physicians. Walking down the hall, I said 'good morning' to everyone I passed. I felt it was a gallant walk. I had a deep sense of appreciation for the opportunity—my medical education—which I would never take for granted again. I had to stay away from Brenda and her problems.

I rode an elevator, with three strangers, to the fourth floor. Room 421 was my first stop. The door was closed. I knocked twice and waited for an answer. Receiving no response, after a reasonable wait I opened the door. An elderly woman with short gray hair was lying on her back, her eyes open. She turned her head toward me, and I could see her eyes glistening from a distance. As I approached her bed, I saw the tears that barely moistened her lower eyelids.

"Good morning, Ma'am. I'm Ben. A medical student," I said.

Feeling exuberant, I forgot about the patient and gloated over how good it felt to call myself a medical student. It was an opportunity I had almost lost. Meanwhile, my patient watched me. Recognizing my jubilation was inappropriate, I regretted it immediately.

As I walked closer to her bed, she opened her mouth and closed it. No words came out. It was a failed attempt to speak. She lifted her hand and beckoned to me. I moved a chair closer to her bed and sat down. Her eyes engaged mine, and I maintained a smile. While I fidgeted with the stethoscope around my neck, tears flowed down the side of her face. My hand departed from my neck. She looked away for a second. When our eyes met again, she looked at me intently. My facial muscles relaxed, effacing my smile. She wiped her eyes with the bed sheet.

"I'm sorry," I said, out of guilt for my egotism.

She picked up a clipboard and a pen from her table. She began to write on a piece of paper attached to the clipboard.

Can't speak. Had a stroke. Last night.

Looking at her written words, I saw they failed to run in a straight line. An effect of her stroke, or nervousness? My fault, I assumed. Patient anxiety caused by my arrogance. A quality that could ruin my future.

"I'm sorry again. I didn't know," I said. She began to write again.

Sorry for what?

"Nothing, Ma'am," I said.

I was sorry about my behavior, my arrogance, but I couldn't tell her.

She picked up her clipboard. Her hand shook as she wrote.

I am a burden. Am bad. Sorry for my family. Sad.

Her written words did not flow well. I didn't ask any more questions, though she raised her hand several times, gesturing for more. Her mouth opened as she made her hand movements, but no words emerged. Her smile faded away when she held the side rails. Her head turned from side to side as she rocked the bed. I pushed a call button for her nurse, reached out, and held her hand. She stopped rocking her bed and sighed.

A nurse walked in shortly afterward.

"What's going on?" the nurse asked. The patient picked up

her clipboard to write.

I am OK now.

I smiled at the patient. She reached out to hold my hand.

I looked at the nurse's badge. 'Mud, BSN, RN'—nurses had only first names on their badges, but physicians had to disclose their full names. I wondered why.

"I never met a girl called Mud before," I said.

"You're a cocky…" Mud said, and hesitated.

"Go ahead. Say it," I said. I smiled.

My patient's demeanor changed. I saw a twinkle on her previously somber face, she was amused by my exchange with her nurse, I suspected. I felt her hand squeeze mine tighter. Her mouth opened several times.

"She seems okay," Mud said.

"She was agitated," I said.

My patient's eyes darted from my face to Mud's. Her mouth opened several times. After repeatedly attempting to speak, she kept her mouth closed.

"Don't stay too long," Mud said.

My patient wagged her finger at Mud in protest.

"Don't worry, Ma'am, I'll stay with you," I said. She smiled.

"Suit yourself," Mud said.

Mud walked out of the room. My patient sighed, and her eyes remained trained on my face.

The patient picked up her clipboard, and her fingers traveled across it several times. She looked at me occasionally and smiled. I was anxious to read what she was writing. Sitting with her, I drifted away to the last time I was with my mother before her death, remembering the last meal we had together, my mother's sneaky smile and giggles. Loneliness engulfed me. Several thoughts went through my mind, each making me feel sorry for myself. I felt cheated by the stroke that killed my mother, and despised the heartbreak that killed my father. I had no parent to attend my medical school graduation, if they let me graduate. Accepting the uncertainties in life, I returned to being emotionally available to my patient.

I heard a knock on the open door. An elderly gentleman walked in. He removed his fedora before he approached the bed. I stood up. He walked closer to my patient and kissed her lips. She dropped her clipboard and held on to his neck. I was tempted to read her scribbles but decided to respect her privacy. I walked two paces away from her bed to avoid further temptations to read what she had written.

"I'm her husband, Ralph."

"I'm Ben, a medical student."

"How's my wife doing?"

"Not sure. This is my first time with her. I'm sorry."

"It's okay. I like honesty."

"What happened?"

"She was singing to me when she lost her voice. She tried to gargle. Choked on it."

"Sad, for her to lose her voice."

"A beautiful voice."

Ralph pulled the chair to the edge of the bed. He held her hand the way I had. She lifted her body up from the bed and kissed him. Then she hugged and held him. He began to sing for her, a soft whistling sound at first, then a baritone. It was a beautiful song I didn't recognize, a love song. Her face came alive with a smile. She hugged her own chest and moved her head from side to side. He kissed her face, her cheek, and her lips. I was an observer to a display of love, a demonstration of words I had heard many times: acceptance, adjustment, kindness, and commitment.

Feeling that I was invading a private moment, I left the room. Walking down the hallway, I felt empty inside. I began to have doubts about things I thought I had experienced. I doubted if I had ever loved anyone or been loved. That is, real love, not words. A journey to oneness with someone, like the couple I observed in the room.

My life had been about surviving, making barely enough money to live on, good grades, succeeding in school. Deb was my first serious relationship. I had avoided grieving for the loss of that relationship. Rita was the chance I had to take. My mind wandered back to love in totality. Not only as a romance, but caring for someone unconditionally. My close friendship with Brenda during our first year in medical school came to mind. My 'cadaver partner'. An inseparable confidant. A member of my medical family. I needed to find her. She deserved love too.

In my daze, walking down the hall overwhelmed with emotion, I heard, "Ben."

James stood in front of me, blocking my passage. I could not remember walking the distance to the entrance of the cafeteria.

"Have you seen Brenda?" I asked.

"Dr Peterson said she's not feeling well."

"I should've checked on her."

"She's been admitted."

"I'm not surprised. The way she was driving…"

James interrupted me, "Not an accident; emotional problems."

"I could've been a better friend, but she hates me," I said.

"It's my fault," James said.

"You're damn right. Fucking her brains out, dumping her, and then running back to your wife."

James' face changed, it became taut and his eyes bulged. I could feel the anger coming out of his pores.

"Take it easy, Bro. I didn't mean to offend you," I said.

"She needs our help, not a blame job," James said.

"Where is she?"

"Dr Peterson wouldn't say."

"I'll look her name up in the system."

"Is that legal?"

"I didn't think about it that way."

"Be careful."

"I have to find her. Remember, we came here together."

"Let me know," James said, walking away.

I stood alone in the hospital hallway to assess things. Once I decided on what to do, I looked around for Dr Peterson. Dr Peterson was the person with the restricted information about Brenda. As a doctor, he was supposed to be one of my mentors, but my relationship with Rita had turned him into an adversary. It was a dangerous situation to be in.

I went into the cafeteria to take a break from my worries. I stood in line to buy tea, to satisfy my addiction to Ceylon's special harvests and to escape, mentally, while enjoying the aroma of bliss. Not even a drop had touched my lips since my arrival in Memphis. I needed to experience the bliss of Earl Grey tea. After waiting for two minutes without being served, I left the line. Patience was not a virtue I possessed. I walked in the direction of the intensive care unit to find Dr Peterson.

Halfway to the intensive care unit, I realized that I could call Brenda's phone. I leaned against the wall and dialed her number. After the third ring, she answered. I had not considered what to say to avoid Brenda hanging up on me. I heard her breathing, but no words. Silence separated us. For a moment, my body became warm.

"It's Ben. Sorry to bother you," I said.

Silence persisted from her side. I thought about what else to say before asking where she was. I heard a whimper before a crackling sound, followed by an echo of 'shit'. I assumed that she had dropped the phone.

"Are you okay?" I asked. Silence.

"I'm clumsy. Can't even hold the phone," she finally said.

"Is this Brenda?"

"Who the fuck do you think it is?"

"I heard you'd been admitted."

I walked into one of the side rooms and closed the door. Her choice of words concerned me. Brenda always cursed more than any medical student I knew, but now she sounded worse than ever. I dimmed the lights without thinking about it. When I realized what I had done, I wondered if my action was because of her vulgarity, or had I darkened the room to shield her from public scrutiny? That would be delusional behavior. I became worried about my judgment and sanity.

"Are you still there?" Brenda asked. She sniffled, then added, "I thought you'd abandoned me again."

I remembered our days and nights together in the anatomy laboratory. Falling asleep next to each other in basic science study halls. Like a brother and sister. 'Anatomy twins', a student had called us. Something went wrong between us. I did not make time to ask her what had happened to us. I was too busy trying to survive by working two jobs. My pathetic excuse for indifference. Feeling sorry for myself because of losing my parents.

"Where are you?" I asked. More forcefully.

"Does it matter to you?" Brenda asked. I wanted to reply to her question, but I stopped.

I heard my breathing. My body felt warm, and my hands were moist. My phone felt slippery. I inhaled deeply and held it, then exhaled slowly. I repeated the process several times. I heard Brenda mumble unintelligibly.

"I don't know why I worry about you," I said.

"You lying piece of shit. You don't give a fuck about anyone," Brenda said. Her words hurt.

"I've had enough of your crap. I'll hang up," I said.

"Listen to you. I thought you said you cared," Brenda said.

"For the last time, where are you?" I asked.

"You'll never come to the psych hospital to see me," Brenda said.

I couldn't help but laugh. She had revealed the information I needed and requested a visit indirectly.

"I'll be there," I said.

"I won't hold my breath waiting for you," Brenda said.

"I hope not."

I heard the phone click. She hung up. I had assumed that there was only one mental hospital in Memphis. Remembering that Brenda drove across the bridge when she left the restaurant, I wondered if she was admitted in West Memphis or Memphis. I called her phone back, but she did not answer. Deciding on where to start searching for Brenda was a task that appeared to be more difficult than I'd anticipated. The thought of asking Dr Peterson for information about Brenda nauseated me. I decided to start from Memphis.

Chapter 28

AT NOON THAT DAY, I approached a long lunch line in the hospital cafeteria and pulled a ten-dollar bill, the only emergency funds I had left, out of my wallet. The last time I checked, only two dollars remained in my bank account. My stomach growled as I stood by the cafeteria door, trying to decide on whether to have lunch to satisfy my hungry stomach, or wait for dinner to avoid staying up all night because of hunger. I walked down the hall to the ATM to check my account balance. Two dollars. My scholarship money had not been deposited.

Passing on lunch, I stood by the hospital's rear entrance and watched cars go by on the one-way street, trying to make sense out of my situation—my poor financial state and Brenda. Sometimes in life you have only one choice. The thought of going to the bursar's office to beg for my scholarship money repulsed me, until my stomach began to hurt. I became worried. Evaluating all my options, I decided that Rita, a new girl whose love I was trying to win, was not a good choice to ask for help. My stomach churned like a grinding machine while I pondered on what to do. Feeling helpless, I walked down the steps and turned left.

A block away from the administration building, I stopped. I could not come up with any justification, apart from hunger, to beg for an advance from the bursar. It would be a second visit to the office in less than 24 hours. I looked beyond the administration building at the overpass that led to the psychiatric hospital. Crossing the overpass to search for Brenda became more appealing to me than begging for the disbursement of my scholarship money. From a distance, I could not tell if the overpass had walking paths. Also, to walk to the psychiatric hospital would require expending energy. My stomach was empty, so my body had to supply the needed energy. Such a sacrifice would cause me to suffer muscle breakdown, since I had no fat storage.

Two conflicting things occupied my mind, hunger and Brenda. Crossing the overpass prevailed.

I stayed on the left side of the road, watching out for approaching cars. Two cars blew their horns, which I ignored. My eyes remained trained on the building ahead of me, the psychiatric hospital. At the entrance to the hospital, I felt faint from hunger and dehydration. I knew I could not deprive my stomach of needed nutrition any longer, but wondered about the quality of the food in a psychiatric hospital. Strangely, I imagined that the food served in a mental institution would be of a lower quality. It was a delusional thought, appropriately foolish for a man who could not afford to spend any money on food in any cafeteria.

Sweating and thirsty, I couldn't find a water fountain in the hallway. A few hospital workers walked by, though no one talked. The crowds were not of the loud type that pervaded my hospital, and the people exhibited a different mien. I didn't ask for directions. I resolved to find Brenda on my own.

Even though I had not eaten, or drunk any liquid, my bladder felt full, and I searched for a bathroom. Everywhere I checked, I found locked hospital wards. At an intersection of two hallways, an arrow sign pointed to the left with a caption, 'Bini's Kitchen'. I followed the sign. Close to the eatery, I found a restroom. Inside, an aroma of stale urine hung everywhere. The thought I had of drinking from a faucet left my mind. My surroundings had had a negative impact on me and had affected my decision. Worrying about my physical condition, I looked in the mirror and found nothing different from the last time I looked at myself. I displayed a stethoscope, a short white coat, and my university badge—and had a somber-looking face. I saw the look of a desperate man. Food occupied what was left of the thinking part of my brain. I left the bathroom to find a solution to my problem.

Bini's Kitchen didn't have a long line. I entered, noticing that the servers were smiling. My eyes found a cheeseburger and fries. The icing on the lemon cake taunted me, saying, 'Lick me.' I imagined these words coming from the cake, as if it could talk. Apart from worrying about losing my sanity with a talking piece of cake, I had a desire to splurge.

"Cheeseburger and fries," I said.

The food server prepped the bun, dressed it with lettuce, tomato, and pickles, then placed a hamburger patty on top, and crowned it with dabs of red and white sauce. Joy overcame me, and I whistled softly.

Getting a cup of clean water, I stood in line to pay. Looking at my university badge, the cashier lifted it and inspected it.

"No charge for medical students," the cashier said.

"Really? Wow! We pay at the main hospital. Thank you, Ma'am," I said.

Since my food was free, I thought about returning to the line for a plate of baked chicken. I resisted the temptation out of guilt. The shame of my willingness to accept a free meal. A benefit from a psychiatric hospital, without an official posting there as a medical student. My decision to accept the meal troubled me. Walking to an empty table, I felt uneasy. Sitting down, I remembered Brenda and the purpose of my trip to the psychiatric hospital. The lemon cake distracted me, so I ate it first. There was nothing left to taunt me. Slowly, I savored my hamburger.

Now that I was satiated, rational thinking returned to me. I had thought of drinking from a faucet in a public bathroom. It could be that low sugar levels had been robbing me of my sanity. My desire to find Brenda intensified, and the implications of my free meal became clearer to me. I felt guilty. Receiving something I was not entitled to. Dishonesty was not a virtue.

I walked to the cashier and tendered ten dollars. Although she looked at me, her hands stayed at her sides. She ignored me and tended to those waiting on the line.

"Ma'am, I'm not one of your students," I said.

Like before, she lifted my university badge and inspected it thoroughly. She returned to taking money and giving change to those standing in line. I waited.

"You're blocking the way," the cashier said.

"I'm a visitor, not a psych student," I said.

"Free food for medical students, I'm told," she said.

"I have to honor the rules. Tell the truth and do the right thing," I said. I checked my watch and sighed. I needed to leave the cafeteria.

She picked up the phone and dialed some numbers.

"Is Greg there?" I heard the cashier ask. She waited, humming a song and tapping her feet. She looked at me and sighed twice. "Greg, a student here wants to pay for his lunch. Medical student. Yes. Yes. I told him so," the cashier added.

She looked at me while she spoke on the phone, her face

serious, unsmiling. Her checkout line grew longer. Her toes hit the base of the counter.

"I'm sorry, Ma'am. I'll leave," I said.

I replaced my ten-dollar bill in my wallet and returned to the food line to price my lunch. After totaling the cost of my lunch, I applied the 20 percent discount given to medical students at the main hospital. My plan was to donate the money to a homeless shelter, someday, when I could afford to give money away. I left the cafeteria feeling better about myself, with an improved physical and mental state. The problem of my delusions had been cured by a good meal. No drugs or counseling needed.

I found a directory. After reading the listings, I took an elevator to the second floor, the location of the general psychiatry wards. Exiting the elevator, I found a locked door with a badge reader on the wall and a camera above it. I did not try to gain access with my badge; instead, I rang the electronic bell. Hearing a buzzer sound, I opened the door and encountered a second locked door. A sliding glass window was close to the door. Sliding the glass window open, a receptionist looked at my face.

"Are you a psych student?" the receptionist asked.

"No. I am looking for a patient. Brenda Galant," I said.

She lifted her phone and dialed numbers. She looked at my badge.

"A Ben Ava is here," the receptionist said.

She listened to the person on the phone, and I waited. Time passed, more than the time needed for someone to approve my visitation. I wondered if Brenda asked them not to let me in, or her psychiatrist did not want her to see me, if she had told them lies about me. I began to worry. Locked up in a psych ward to be arrested crossed my mind. The receptionist looked at me intently. I felt like a suspect she had to study carefully. My paranoia returned, on a full stomach.

"I am just here to see a classmate," I said, frustrated at the obstacles I had to overcome. Going back to my dormitory crossed my mind. I looked around me. No escape route.

"She'll see you," the receptionist said.

"Who'll see me?"

"Your girl."

"She's not my girl."

"I thought you were…." The receptionist hesitated. She smiled. I became confused.

The door buzzed and opened automatically. I entered the secured psych ward, Brenda's new place. I looked at the receptionist. I hoped she could read the frustration on my face.

"Which room?" I asked.

"I'm here," Brenda said.

She was standing close to me, dressed in a faded brown hospital gown. She was barefoot, and her eyeballs were sunken.

"You look tired," I said.

"I'm good," Brenda said.

She staggered two steps forward. I reached out and held her, my arm around her waist. I felt her bones, which were barely covered with flesh. Flashes of my hunger came back to me.

"We need to talk," I said. My hand unwound from her waist.

"About what?" Brenda asked.

"You. What's going on with you? How I can help," I said.

Brenda walked into her room, which consisted of windowless clutter, barely illuminated by the hallway light. She found her way to a bed and sat down. I stopped at the entrance to her room.

When I found, and switched on the light, she winced.

"May I?" I asked. She ignored me. I was not sure what I was asking for. I was already in her room and had turned her lights on, so I was seeking permission for things I had already done.

I leaned on the wall close to the door. She looked at me, her eyes glassy. Even though her face looked tired, the light glistened on it. I thought her face twitched. Psych drugs or an anxious tic? My eyes wandered to her desk, searching for an answer. No medication bottles. I remembered that nurses brought pills in, when needed. Patients could not dispense them for themselves in the hospital.

On her desk, there sat a cell phone, car keys, and a blank piece of paper with a pen on it. For a suicide note?

"Sit your ass down, and talk," Brenda said, angrily. I became worried that she knew what I was thinking about: that blank paper, a suicide note.

Instead of sitting, I found a wall closer to her. Sitting would put me in a vulnerable position, one of subservience, I thought.

"I'm glad you've been admitted. You need help," I said.

"Your fake ass needs help too," Brenda said, her voice raised.

"You're right, but you first," I said.

She lay down and covered her body, along with her face. I remembered her emergency room visit in Knoxville, accompanied by a surgical scalpel and a scarf. My eyes looked around her room again. No closet, or any other place, to tie a bed sheet to hang herself. I needed to change my mindset. It was traumatizing me.

While I was watching her in silence, she lifted the cover from her face and looked at me. I pulled the chair closer to her bed and sat down. I saw tears in her eyes but hesitated to reach out to hold her hand. We were alone in her room. I could be considered a classmate with delusions, and the possibility of an allegation of sexual harassment crossed my mind. Frustrated about the limitations I had, my sigh resonated in the room.

"I'm ready. Talk," Brenda said.

"You cry at night. Don't eat. These behaviors make me worry," I said.

She sat up and crossed her legs. She looked at me, uncrossed her legs, and stood up. She walked to her door and closed it. Alone with Brenda, in a room with the door closed. My heart raced, and my body felt warm. Fear gripped me, and many things went through my mind. The most troublesome was that I had no witness to defend me, if she accused me of sexual advances. That thought terrified me. It would mean the end of my medical education and a prison sentence.

When Brenda walked back to her bed, I stood up, moved the chair away from her bedside, and sat down. She frowned.

"You're afraid of me?" Brenda asked.

"Never. Giving you space," I said.

"You always do."

"I'm not sure what you mean."

"After anatomy class, you ignored me."

"Three years ago, our first year. I don't remember."

"I asked you to have lunch. You turned me down."

"I had no money. I was working two jobs to survive."

"I asked you. Girls can pay too."

"Nah. No woman pays for me."

"Stupid ego."

I stood up, and walked to the door. I wiped away my sweat, when I was away from her probing eyes. Her assertion reminded me about my struggles after the death of my parents. I had been broke.

"Please don't go," Brenda said.

"I'm not leaving. I need to open the door. I feel trapped," I said.

"You can't. I have to tell you a secret."

I returned to her bedside. The words 'a secret' excited me. However, Brenda's face looked sad, and it tempered my enthusiasm. I became worried that she was pregnant. Pregnancy by a married man. James' baby. A scandal.

"Nothing serious, I hope," I said, pretending not to worry.

"I wanted us to be more than friends. You ignored me," Brenda said.

"I didn't know. I thought you hated me."

"That's not true. I asked you to join our study group."

"I don't remember. I worked in the ER and the library, plus I studied odd hours."

"I have nightmares. Anxiety attacks. I feel depressed."

"Worried about school? You're a good student."

"They say I'm bipolar."

I reached out and held her hand. My concern for Brenda's illness was so overwhelming to me that the thought of being accused of sexual harassment left me. We stood up and hugged. I held her tight and did not worry about breaking any bones. Visions of Mom and Dad flashed in my head. I cried for Brenda and for my loneliness.

"I love you," I said.

"Do you?" Brenda asked.

"I care about you. Not in the sense of physical love."

"I understand."

"I tried to show you, but you hated me."

"I'm scared at night. It started a long time ago. One night, when I was ten, I woke up and my father was inside me. I felt pain between my legs. He covered my mouth. Told me I was dreaming. The same thing happened many nights after that. I couldn't tell anyone, including Mom," Brenda said and sobbed.

"Son-of-a-bitch," I screamed. I felt sick to my stomach.

"I have nightmares about rape," Brenda said.

"Tell your doctor. You need counseling."

"It's a crime. I can't destroy my mom by telling her."

"I understand, but you need help."

"You need to go. I can't talk anymore," Brenda said. She covered her face with a pillow.

"I'll go, but if you ever need me, I'm here for you," I said.

I hugged Brenda and wouldn't let go. Tears flowed freely from my eyes. I thought about Brenda suffering sexual abuse from her father, who was supposed to protect her. She looked at me and kissed my cheek, a kiss that meant more to me than any gift I had ever received.

"Don't forget me," Brenda said.

"Never. You're special to me. A friend forever. Like a sister," I said.

"You weasel. You can't go out with your sister."

"I never thought of going out with you. Not like that."

"Sad to hear."

"My job is to protect you. Starting today."

"Start when I get out."

"I'll be waiting."

"I know you won't come back to see me," Brenda said. She sighed.

"You're wrong. I will," I said.

"Hmm," Brenda said.

I left Brenda's room feeling sad. Her life was worse than I'd imagined. A heart broken by a former lover was the worst thing I'd thought about, not incest. Sexual abuse by her own father! The psychological effect of the betrayal worried me; it must have left a permanent imprint of distrust in her brain, which could be a lifelong curse. All sorts of things came to my mind. The thought of a father exploiting his child sexually sickened me. Dejection followed me out of Brenda's room. I entered the bathroom on the first floor and washed my hands several times, cleansing myself of an abominable act I did not commit. My stomach gurgled, and I vomited the free lunch I had eaten.

Chapter 29

FROM A SHORT DISTANCE AWAY, I could see an empty bench by the entrance to my dormitory. It had been a long time since I had seen anyone sitting on it. Everyone seemed to be in a hurry. The empty bench was reminiscent of my life at that moment. A lonely third-year medical student. My life revolved around patient care and studying. I had no social life. I wondered how Brenda felt about the burden of rape and incest she had endured, with no one to confide in until she had spoken to me. She had living parents whom she could not trust, which was an extra burden for her. Her story made me realize that my life was not as bad as I thought.

My situation was different. My parents had been dead for some time. I tried to survive alone. Deb filled a void until she made a decision that favored her, but her decision left me lonesome. I could not fault her. Even when I thought about proposing to Deb, I could not afford an engagement ring. She had filled a void in her life by finding a committed companion, but it left me feeling lonely. Life can be complicated. Solving one person's problem can lead to problems for another.

Approaching the entrance to my dormitory, students passed me. My walking had slowed down to a crawl. My mind was burdened with life's unfairness, and the psychological load slowed my pace. Conflicting thoughts hampered my progress under the burden of mental and physical anguish.

Checking my watch, I saw Rita would finish her shift in two hours. Walking inside the building, I thought about checking my mailbox for the first time in two weeks. No one sent me mail. I reached inside my pocket, isolated the smallest key on my keychain, and unlocked my mailbox. I retrieved two envelopes. There was no return address on one, and the other had an insurance company's name on it. I returned to the bench outside the building, and sat on a corner to save the rest of the available space for anyone who might need it.

Sitting alone, I opened my mail. One was a scholarship check, the other, a check from an insurance company for my damaged car. The possibility of a new car crossed my mind. Once I had a car again, I could visit my parents' graves. Other things I'd neglected for so long came to mind, such as expanding my search for a part-time job outside the university environment and taking Rita out. I felt excited.

Instead of waiting for Rita to get off work, I decided to surprise her. I pulled out my wallet; a five-dollar bill was all I had left. Whistling on my trek to the hospital, I didn't notice anyone passing by on the road. It was my road, I traveled in short sprints, and with long paces. At that moment, the world belonged to me.

Harnessing energy from my new outlook in life, and improved financial status, I reached the rear entrance to the hospital in a short time. Having food in my stomach was not necessary. Inside the cafeteria, there was no line. Dinner had not started. Going through the all-day serving section, I bought four yogurts. Different flavors of yogurt for my girl and her friend Monica.

"My girl." I said it, loud enough that the cashier turned around, and I paid her with a smile. She returned the favor, and 25 cents change, which would be the last money I had access to. Not deterred by my limitations, I marched to the intensive care unit. In my mind, I floated on the air.

My eyes searched around the unit for Rita. At the first station,

Dr Peterson sat alone. He rubbed his eyes repeatedly and looked tired. He looked at me; I smiled.

"Have you seen Rita?" I asked. I knew it was attempted suicide, but I didn't care. It would have been a gracious death for me, I thought.

"You're an idiot," Dr Peterson said, rolling his eyes.

"Thank you for the compliment," I said.

"You haven't learned."

"Just looking for my girl."

Rita came out of a patient's room. I walked up to her and handed over the food tray.

"It's yours. That's the best I can do," I said. She looked puzzled.

"I was coming to see you," Rita said.

"I couldn't wait," I said.

"That's sweet," Rita said. Dr Peterson turned away from us.

She placed the tray on a counter and hugged me tightly. A good hug, which aroused me. I'm sure it poked her, but all she displayed was a smile, a polite pretense. All I had wanted was an emotional closeness to Rita just then, but my body betrayed me. My physical yearning manifested itself. I thought about Brenda and James. They found solace in their physical needs, and I judged them, an example of ardent hypocrisy.

Holding Rita, I was ashamed to let go because of my erection. Dr Peterson had resumed watching us. He rose from his chair and walked away. He looked back before he left the intensive care unit. My hands slipped away from Rita, who took the food tray when two nurses joined us.

"Going back to my dorm. See you soon," I said.

"Don't worry, I'll be there," Rita said.

"I forgot to tell you. I visited Brenda in a hospital. She's bad."

"I didn't know she was sick."

"Not that way. Psych admission."

"She needed it. I'm surprised you visited."

"We should go see her. She needs our support."

"Not my support," Rita said. She frowned, and turned her back on me to walk away.

"Don't be angry with me. There's so much I need to tell you. Not here," I said.

"I'll see you soon," Rita said, while walking away from me.

Rita entered the ICU conference room. I left the unit wondering how to convince her to give Brenda another chance, without discussing her childhood rape. I walked down the hall with my eyes on the floor, reflecting on the discussion I would have with Rita about Brenda. As I stayed close to the wall on the right, people walked by me.

"I was waiting for you."

I heard the voice and looked up.

Dr Peterson, my supervising resident physician stood in front of me, an exhausted man with droopy eyelids.

"You need some rest," I said.

"You can't seem to let go. You'll regret your actions," Dr Peterson said.

"I'm tired of your threats. You watched Dr Trophy abuse Brenda. You ignored it. They dismissed me from school. What did you do?"

"I'm not here to protect you. Teach you medicine? Yes. Guide your fucking ass? No. You pay when you fuck up."

"I have no respect for you. People like you make me want

to quit."

"You will quit, because my evaluation will badly hurt you."

"I'll live with it, and so will you. I work hard, take care of my patients. The nurses will bear witness for me."

"That's why you're fucking Rita," Dr Peterson said. He smiled and displayed an odd look on a haggard face.

I lifted my hand to wipe the stupid smile off his face.

He patted his cheek where I should have struck him.

I lowered my hand. "Forget the Hippocratic Oath. I'll never respect you," I said.

"The Hippocratic Oath is not for you. Your future depends on me," Dr Peterson said.

"So does yours. Destroy mine, I'll destroy yours."

"Is that a threat?"

I saw beads of sweat on his face. A worried look.

"It's what they call 'fairness'," I said.

"Ask anyone. I'm fair," Dr Peterson said.

"Maybe you were, until Rita."

"Do your work, and I'll let this pass."

When he walked away, I tried to walk, but my legs felt weak. My body felt warm. My poor choice of words bothered me. I was risking my future. Again. Fear gripped me. I decided to work on my weaknesses. I needed to practice patience and the judicious use of words.

Viewed from afar, the medical profession was enticing, but bullying was not what I'd expected. Thinking about the oppressive men that were mentoring me in such a noble profession, I had doubts about graduating.

Chapter 30

JUST BEFORE SUNSET, we arrived at the outdoor café on Beale Street. It was a warm Memphis summer evening, warmer than the previous days. It painted drips of sweat on my face, the heat and humidity combined to roast my body. Judging from the amount of sweat coming out of my pores, I was melting away. Slowly. I dabbed my face every minute. Rita watched me, a smile on her face. Together, her smile and perfect teeth were captivating, like polished white pearls. I was smitten. When I reached for her hand, she leaned close to me, kissing and nibbling. We laughed and fondled each other. It felt good to me.

Our waiter came. He stood two paces away and watched us, waiting for the right moment to interrupt. Once we loosened our embrace, he placed two glasses of water on our table. While still giggling, Rita sipped her water. I heard a gulp, and a belch.

"Oops," she said, quietly. She blinked, and her smile persisted.

I was speechless. We pulled our chairs closer and, holding each other, watched the sunset. Arrays of gold and red covered the sky, natural masterpieces, with the sun as the artist. This fleeting phenomenon reminded me of events in my life that had changed over time. However, I would not let the temporariness of certain things in life stop me from admiring Rita. She was an attractive woman and there I was, a lucky man, savoring the happiness that had eluded me. Each time our eyes met, I felt exhilarated and lost myself in the two of us, Rita and me. "Thank you for loving me," I said.

"I can't imagine my life without you," Rita said.

We kissed, our tongues caressing and exchanging sweet saliva. Our open eyes searched for the shroud of love as we felt the mystery of passion.

"Without you, I'm nothing," I said.

"I feel the same way about you. We should plan a life together. Take care of each other," Rita said.

"Two of us together is my dream. Waking up next to you every day. Can't wait to finish school. I'll spoil you rotten," I said.

"All I need is you. Nothing else," Rita said.

"Let's not ever walk away from each other angry," I said.

"Okay Babe. I love you," Rita said.

Without any warning, my mind wandered to Deb, remembering the way we were: inseparable, until Memphis came between us. The quick breakup, after we had shared what I'd thought was an enviable love affair. My hands trembled, as I felt the fear of losing Rita. At that moment, while I was unsure of our future together, Rita hugged me tightly. Her hug came when I was drifting away from her, lost in my thoughts and floating around in a space of uncertainty.

"Are you okay?" Rita asked.

"Just worried about us. I have no money. No family. I may be too needy for you," I said.

"I promise to be here for you, always. Money or no money. It's called love," Rita said.

Our waiter returned with our dinner. I couldn't remember when we ordered. Too many things were going through my mind. I looked at my chicken tenders. It was what I would have ordered in such a place, but my eyes had no desire for it. My stomach was tied in knots from the fear of a broken heart. I could not force myself to eat. Food was not what I needed at that moment.

Insecurity plagued me, and food was not the cure for it.

"I'll take mine home," Rita said to the waiter.

"Do I bore you to death?" I asked.

"No. You fill me up," Rita said.

The waiter looked at me. I saw his lips move twice, though no words accompanied the movement. He hesitated before speaking.

"Sorry to interrupt. Yours too, Sir?" the waiter finally asked.

"Yes," I said.

The waiter took away our food. He walked in the direction of the kitchen. Rita rubbed her eyes. The luster had escaped from her beautiful face. She now looked at me with red eyes, which was a big change from how she looked when we arrived. I held her hand, hoping to lend support for her tired body, as if hand holding could be sufficient. I laughed.

"You're tired," I said.

"Been up since four," Rita said.

Her eyes blinked several times. She shifted in her chair twice.

"Stay with me tonight," I said.

"Sounds tempting, but I have to work tomorrow," Rita said.

"You don't want me all over you tonight. I understand," I said. I laughed.

"I'll be better after a good night's sleep," Rita said.

"During my break tomorrow, I'll visit Brenda," I said.

She looked at me with her tired eyes, and gave me a blank stare. I waited for a comment from her. She looked away from me. Opening her purse, she took out some money and left it on the table.

"I'm grateful for the dinner," I said.

"You didn't eat," Rita said. She hesitated, before she added,

"I don't care for Brenda."

"She's been through a lot. Sexual abuse. Not just sexual abuse, incest."

"What the heck."

"You mean to say, 'What the hell.' There, I said it for you."

"She needs serious counseling."

"I agree. She needs friends, too."

"Let's talk about it tomorrow. I'll drop you off."

"I can't wait to get a car."

"We need only one car, and one place to live."

"You're proposing, aren't you? I'm a broke-ass medical student," I said. We laughed.

"Poor Ben," Rita said. She continued laughing as we left the café.

Once inside Rita's car, silence descended on us. She looked at me occasionally. I kept my eyes on her face. I was concerned about Rita falling asleep while driving. I felt the urge to talk about Brenda, but avoided it. It would have been unfair to end the evening with an issue that bothered Rita. Moreover, serious discussions would have led to talking about living together, which I thought of as a disguise for a trial marriage. Breaking up after such a commitment would devastate me. Guarding my defenseless heart was paramount.

When we reached my residence hall, she kissed me, giving a tongue-expedition type of kiss. After kissing me, she sighed.

"Are you okay?" I asked.

"I would've loved for you to tuck me in tonight," Rita said.

"That's my dream. Stay with me," I said.

"Get your things and come with me. My bed's bigger."

"Can't. Seeing patients early, before I visit Brenda."

"So, Brenda is the priority. I get it. I know where I stand."

"She needs me."

"I need you too. All over me."

"I don't think you can. You need to rest," I said, and laughed.

"Take care of me tonight. I'll rest better," Rita said.

We sat in the car looking at each other. Feigned smiles, at least on my part. Going with Rita would limit my freedom the following morning. I would have to depend on her to make it to the hospital early, which would hinder my plans for Brenda. Rita kept her eyes on me, as I pondered over what to do. Her smile faded. After a prolonged stare, it felt like her eyes were pleading for the ravenous pleasure she proposed. I thought about an all-night bout of mattress gymnastics with Rita. My arousal began to affect my thinking, including my decision making. After several sighs, pleasurable thoughts overruled my pragmatism. I yielded to my physical desire.

Chapter 31

AT 11 IN THE MORNING, Brenda and I entered a small 'private consulting room' on the second floor of the psychiatric hospital. A white door separated the room from a busy hallway. No windows, or ventilation ducts, just blank white walls. A desk and three guest chairs. No telephone or computer. The whispers from pedestrians could be heard even with the room's door shut.

Brenda sat next to me while we waited for the attending psychiatrist to arrive. After we had waited for five minutes, the psychiatrist, a graying man carrying a worn, brown leather briefcase, walked in. He walked to the empty chair behind the desk, placed his briefcase on the floor, and sat down. No pleasantries were exchanged. I became worried about his clinical competence. A dangling hospital badge on his jacket, 'Dr Benton, Psychiatrist', confirmed his qualification, but his tweed jacket—on a summer day in Memphis—left me wondering about his judgment.

Having retrieved some files from his briefcase, Dr Benton opened a folder, fixed his eyes on it, and flipped through several pages. Without looking up, he reached inside his pocket, retrieved a pen, and tapped randomly on the folder. Brenda's eyes focused on the floor. She jerked her legs in a rhythmic motion, and her breathing became audible as time progressed. However, she showed no sign of respiratory distress. I was relieved.

After a long wait, and frustrated by the psychiatrist's apparent indifference to my time, I rose from my chair. His tapping stopped, and he closed the folder. The man that had ignored us for minutes looked up. His eyes found mine. He had a surprised look on his face, as if he was not aware that he was not alone in the room. As his eyes continued to watch me, I sat down. It was an eerie feeling, a kind of voiceless communication. Thinking about hypnosis, I looked away from him, worried about mind control.

"Sorry. Reviewing some notes," Dr Benton said.

His apology was late. I was angry. Brenda, having abandoned her fascination with the room floor, now stared at him. Her face wore no distinct expression compared to the expression of her predilection for the barren floor. Her countenance was as blank as the room wall. Dr Benton's eyes trailed from Brenda to me. My worry that he had hypnotized us grew.

"I have to leave soon," I said, with emphasis. He ignored me, and his eyes remained focused on Brenda.

"Are you seeing each other?" Dr Benton asked.

I ignored him.

Brenda's hands trembled. She turned to me. I wondered if she was worried about what I would say. There was only one truth. I felt that an eye conference, Dr Benton's choice of communication, was not necessary between Brenda and me. Truth remains the same. Eternally.

"Never," I said.

"I'm not good enough for him," Brenda said.

"I'm sorry," I said.

"You're sure he's the one?" Dr Benton asked.

"The one for what?" I asked.

I turned to Brenda, but her eyes found the floor irresistible again. I heard Dr Benton sigh.

"She's due for release, but she needs someone to monitor

her progress. Family, or a close friend. She asked for you," Dr Benton said.

"I don't know why. We're not as close as we used to be," I said.

"My mistake. You hugged me. I thought you cared," Brenda said.

"I do, but to be responsible for you? I don't know," I said.

Brenda's eyes swelled, and filled with tears. I stood and walked around in the small area of confinement, a consulting room that was challenging my temperament. I yearned for a window to look out of to relieve my anxiety.

"I'll extend your admission," Dr Benton said, callously.

"I need to get out. I am going crazy here," Brenda sobbed.

I thought about all my problems, my recent suspension from school, my money problems, my need for a part-time job, my shaky relationship with Rita and the impact my closeness with Brenda would have on it. Watching Brenda sob affected me tremendously. I forgot about appropriateness, I pulled her up from the chair and hugged her.

"I'll take care of you," I said.

"Thanks. I can't make it alone," Brenda said.

"Dr Benton, she has to do what I ask of her," I said.

"Reasonable things," Dr Benton said. He smiled for the first time since I met him.

"You're not my master," Brenda said.

"I'm in charge. You eat with me, every day. You're all bones," I said.

"A wonderful idea," Dr Benton said.

"Okay," Brenda said.

A smile appeared on Brenda's face, and she wiped her eyes.

Watching Dr Benton and Brenda smile as we left the consulting room, I wondered what I would tell Rita. The impact of dining with Brenda daily, and how it would affect my relationship with Rita, concerned me. I tried to hide my apprehension and smiled. Dr Benton shook my hand before he left, and Brenda walked to her room. I was left alone to reflect on my new responsibility. My fear of being hypnotized came back to mind, another possible symptom of a dangerous paranoia.

Stepping out of the psych hospital to face the hot and humid Memphis weather, I was again reminded of the challenge I had to face, the wrath of the one I had struggled to be with, emotionally and physically: Rita. The thought of losing her terrified me.

Chapter 32

EARLY MORNING BREAKFAST at the hospital cafeteria. Brenda and I were the first two customers, a new experience for us. We stood with our backs against the food trays, watching a stream of hospital workers pass through the hallway by the cafeteria. It was better than staring at food we could not have until the servers were ready.

From behind us, the clanging sounds of metallic serving spoons dropped on aluminum counters attracted our attention, a summons by clumsiness. We turned to see smiles above glove-clad hands. It was a happy morning.

Brenda was two paces ahead of me. I contemplated the omelet and pancake from the hot plate section. My stomach growled as I pondered over the selection. With abundant portions on my plate, I joined Brenda to check out.

When we left the food line, Brenda walked to a table close to the glass window, my own favorite place in the cafeteria. She placed her tray, containing a bowl of oatmeal and a cup of yogurt, two spoons, and a heap of paper napkins, on the table. Napkins to wipe off the mess she would make of her scanty breakfast.

I regretted my thought as Brenda looked at me, placing my tray opposite hers. Mine was filled with a cheese omelet and a stack of pancakes, and a glass of OJ to wash it all down. Her hands shook. I could sense her uneasiness. It was the first time we would eat together in two years without our classmates. Our first act of civility under the new arrangement. A buddy system for mental hygiene.

Watching Brenda, several lines of conversation went through my mind, but I kept them to myself. She shifted around in her seat, clearly uneasy. Her actions made me uncomfortable. I sipped my OJ, my elixir. She watched me, and sighed.

"I'll get you a glass," I said, hoping that it would cure her jitters.

"I don't like orange juice."

"What do you like?"

"Just water."

She lifted her spoon and scooped up a small amount of oatmeal. Her lips retrieved a small portion from the spoon, like a child. When she made faces, I became worried. She returned her spoon to the oatmeal bowl. Lifting the cup of yogurt off the table, she removed the foil. Her hand shook, but she managed to place the cup of yogurt on the table. She picked up an unused spoon and stared at her tray. After sighing, she returned the spoon to the tray.

"You need to eat," I said.

"I'm trying to decide," she said.

"It's simple: eat," I said. She looked at me, a frown on her face.

Watching Brenda's indecisiveness over the simple task of eating, I began to worry about how she would function as a physician, when she would have to make decisions that could save, or kill, patients. This formed an ethical dilemma for me. My role was not to evaluate her competency to continue as a medical student. It had been simply stated, and I understood it—to be a one-student 'support group' for her. I lost my appetite as the enormity of my responsibility occurred to me. I pushed my food tray away.

"Hypocrite. Go ahead and eat. Eat your damn food," she said.

She snickered, mocking me. That was how it felt to me. I picked up my tray and walked over to the waste conveyor belt to drop it off. Brenda followed me, leaving her food on the table. We had wasted time, along with food that we needed. My stomach had to deal with deprivation because of a supposed affront to Brenda.

"Where's your tray? You need to return it," I said.

"You're enjoying this shit. Ordering me around," she said.

Three nurses walked by as Brenda berated me. I recognized two of them. They stared at Brenda and me. Two paces away from us, I heard a nurse whisper, "I heard she's a psycho."

"Locked up in the psych ward, I heard," the other nurse said. They laughed.

Fortunately, Brenda was walking away to retrieve her tray and did not hear their comments. Her hospitalization was a private affair. I wondered who told the nurses about it. The 'not-so private consulting room' at the psychiatric hospital came to mind. However, the nurses were from a different hospital. The only other source could be Dr Peterson. While my thoughts wandered, Brenda returned.

We took the elevator to the intensive care unit's floor. It was 30 minutes before Rita would start her shift. I walked across the waxed tile floor in intensive care, with guarded steps, to the nearest work station. Brenda and I huddled together, far away from the secretary's desk, experiencing a closeness that was a significant change from our previous encounters. I was happy that she felt comfortable being close to me.

Every minute, Brenda's eyes wandered all over the intensive care unit. There were subdued chats between nurses and occasional laughter as they walked by. As more nurses arrived for the morning shift, their chatter grew louder. Watching the interactions from afar, we could see the night-shift nurses seemed to be the source of most of the elation, spent workers experiencing sudden surges of adrenaline. All of them were eager to go home. My eyes returned to the computer screen to read about my patient. For a moment, I forgot about Brenda sitting next to me.

Amidst the jubilation of the early morning change of shift, I heard a thud, the sound of a fall from a hospital bed—a familiar sound from my emergency room experiences. My eyes wandered around the ICU as the chatter stopped. I could hear the beeping sounds of the heart monitors. Nurses ran into a patient's room, they were joined by Brenda and me.

An elderly man was lying on the floor next to a recliner, with blood oozing from a bleeding laceration on the side of his leg. The armrest of the chair was stained with blood. His face was crinkled shut in pain. I was relieved to note his breathing was unlabored. One of the nurses untangled his IV line and checked his eyes and blood pressure. Another nurse opened surgical gauzes and covered the wound. The rest of the nurses left the room.

"Mr Task, are you okay?" I asked. Before he could answer, I added, "I'm your student doctor."

"I got dizzy getting out of bed," he said.

"You're not supposed to," I said, and reached out to steady him.

"Don't move him, I'll call the surgery resident," the nurse said.

"I'm not trying to," I said.

A nurse walked closer, and said, "I already called the surgery resident."

The gauzes were soaked in blood in less than one minute.

Brenda left the room and returned with a pack of surgical gauzes. She picked up a pair of gloves, put them on, and knelt on the floor. I opened the pack of gauzes. Brenda retrieved some gauzes, placed them on the laceration, and applied pressure to stop the bleeding.

"I'll take care of the wound," a nurse said to Brenda.

"He's stopped bleeding," Brenda said.

The nurse knelt next to Brenda. She retrieved more gauzes and reached out to take over the application of pressure. Brenda ignored the nurse and continued to hold pressure on the wound. The two women looked at each other, with frowning faces and squinting eyes, in an unfriendly exchange. I tapped Brenda on the shoulder. She looked up. I heard a squeak on the polished intensive care unit floor. A man with short dark hair, about my height, physically fit, in green scrubs and a pair of tennis shoes walked in. The nurse rose from her kneeling position.

"Dr Green, he fell trying to get up," the nurse said.

"I'm Dr Green, the surgery resident." A soft voice, and a smile.

The patient frowned.

Dr Green knelt opposite Brenda. He examined the patient from head to toe. When he was done with his examination, he lifted Brenda's hand from the wound. She quivered, but he smiled. Her lips parted. A form of smile, I assumed.

"Good job," Dr Green said.

"Thanks," Brenda said. She staggered as she tried to stand.

I thought about the breakfast we had missed. A misguided decision.

"Passing out on me?" Dr Green asked.

"No. Weak legs," Brenda said.

"I thought it was a weak stomach," Dr Green said, flirtatiously.

"I've seen blood before," Brenda said.

Blood started oozing out of the wound. I cleared my throat. Dr Green looked around, then his eyes fixed on the patient's wound.

"Hold the pressure, I'll get a laceration kit," Dr Green said.

Brenda returned to her kneeling position and held the pressure. I watched the interaction between Brenda and Dr Green. I felt ignored during their noticeable bonding. It appeared as if my buddy was searching for a new partnership.

"Need help?" I asked.

"I'm doing fine," Brenda said.

Dr Green returned to the room with a laceration kit and two surgical packs wrapped in green towels. He opened the wrapped packs, retrieved sterile gloves, created a sterile zone, and pushed the surgical instruments to his side. Outside his sterile field, I noticed a pair of scissors and a scalpel. My heart raced watching the scalpel next to Brenda. I picked up the surgical instruments and placed them on a side table. Brenda looked at me.

Dr Green passed a pair of sterile gloves to Brenda.

"Put them on," Dr Green said.

A smile appeared on Brenda's face, and her eyes glistened. A beautiful face. The face I remembered from anatomy class.

"Really?" Brenda asked. Exuberant.

Dr Green used a sterile solution to clean the wounds, and injected the site with lidocaine solution to anesthetize the area. He closed the inner part of the wound with an absorbable suture and closed half of the skin with a removable suture. He handed the suture holder to Brenda.

"Your turn. I'll guide you," Dr Green said.

Without hesitation, Brenda began to close the remaining wound. Dr Green watched with a smile. I watched in awe as her fingers twirled around the wound, adding stitches that were indistinguishable from Dr Green's work. A surgery resident. They exchanged a glance and smiles. I could sense a spark between them.

They rose from the floor together. Dr Green walked out of the room, and Brenda followed. I remained in the room, helping the two nurses clean up. Peeking through the glass ICU door, I saw a handshake, lots of smiles, and an abundance of glimmering between the two. There was a sparkle on Brenda's face, and I sensed an awakening.

Dr Green wrote on a piece of paper and handed it to Brenda. She looked at it and placed it in her coat pocket. Her eyes blinked. They shook hands, and he walked away. She stood still and watched him leave the intensive care unit. I waited for her to return, but she stood outside the room, mesmerized.

I stepped outside the room. Her eyes were blinking rapidly and there was a smile on her face. When she hugged me, her skinny hands felt like a tightrope around me. I heard a clank, and looked around. Brenda loosened her grip on me.

An aluminum carafe lay on the floor. Rita was stooping over it, picking it up and wiping the sides with her hand. I walked over to her as she tightened the cover on the carafe.

"The floor is waxed; you can't be too careful," I said.

"I know. I have to watch you," Rita said.

"Watch me?" I asked.

"You're fucking that bitch," Rita said. I looked in Brenda's direction. She was still smiling. Unaware of what was being said about her.

"Keep your voice down," I said. I looked around us. It was hard to tell if anyone had heard her.

Rita walked away from me. She used her hospital badge to access a medicine room—a secured room accessible to only a few hospital workers. I stood outside, separated from Rita by a door that I couldn't open. Her decision to lock me out of her life, when I needed to explain my coziness with Brenda, left me in a quandary. I waited for Rita, but she did not come out of the restricted room. Her action was an effective restriction on us—Rita and me.

* * *

Later that day, close to six, I left the hospital. The sun had not set. It was hot and humid outside. Car traffic had increased on most of the side streets. Pedestrians hurried along the sidewalks. The end of the work day for some, and the beginning of a shift for evening workers. We had different timetables in our lives. Frustrated about how my day had gone, I felt the desire to get away from Memphis that evening, but I had nowhere to go, no one to visit, nor the means to get anywhere. I felt stranded.

I walked for two blocks, using a side street, and came to a dead end. A street with no outlet. Looking around, I realized that I had been to the same place before. A repeated mistake. I became concerned about my inability to make useful choices in my life. To reach my destinations in life, the choices I made had to improve. I turned around and took another side street, after looking ahead to avoid a repeated mistake. A dead-end road.

After walking for three blocks, I saw the bridge, and the

river below it. Beckoning sparkles of water. The Mississippi River and the bridge to West Memphis. A different place, and a different state. To my left was an automobile dealership with an abundance of cars. The car windshields displayed sales prices. Some affordable, by my financial standing. A plan came to my mind. I crossed the street and walked to the car dealership. With too many cars to choose from, I had to make the right decision. My choice from the many cars in the lot had to take me to West Memphis. A new frontier, an adventure for me, and an escape from the doldrums. Euphoria took over me.

Chapter 33

TWO PROTEIN BARS and a bottle of water. My medical textbook. All the things I needed to survive for the day. I thought about a second bottle of water before I zipped up my backpack. I would be trading my lunch time for volunteering at the Mission House clinic. One bottle of water would be sufficient.

I searched for a new thing: my car key. I had purchased a used model two days earlier. After checking my bag for my phone, I turned my room lights off and locked my door. My morning routine, except that the urgency of time was no longer an issue. I had a quicker way to get to the hospital. A car. An improvement in my life.

In the common living area of my dormitory suite, Brenda perched on a stool. She had her eyes focused on her phone and did not see me until I was standing in front of her. It was obvious that she was enthralled by what she was observing, or reading, but I did not have the desire to snoop. Instead, I checked my watch. It was five minutes earlier than our agreed meeting time.

Brenda rose from the stool, and her keys jingled.

"I'll drive today," I said.

"Go for it," she said. She continued to look at her phone as she spoke. Her fascination with the phone made it obvious that she was not interested in what I had to say, but I felt obliged to explain my decision to drive.

"I'm volunteering at a clinic," I said.

"Since when?" she asked. She put away her phone.

"I have thought about it for a long time, but had to wait

until I got a car," I said.

"An STD clinic?" She started laughing before she could finish her question.

"Yep, I'm Doctor Love," I said. We laughed.

Brenda flung her backpack onto her shoulder and walked ahead of me. High heels had replaced her usual tennis shoes. I noticed her fitted pants. Her waist area, and below it, moved differently when she walked. Her rump was noticeable in the fitted pants she was wearing. It appeared as if she had grown one overnight. I marveled at the impact of a change of outlook on life. She blossomed with all the enviable assets of womanhood. My admiration was selfish because I ascribed Brenda's improved physical outlook to my efforts on her feeding, and my companionship. I forgot about Dr Green, her new interest. He was spending more time with her than I was.

I followed her bump and bounce to the elevator. She leaned forward to push the elevator call button, accentuating her rear. I slouched against the wall, watching the miracle of Brenda's physical transformation.

Brenda turned to me and said, "You're quiet."

"Just admiring you," I said. I couldn't control the burst of laughter that escaped from me.

"You're weird," she said, as we boarded the elevator.

"Just checking you out. In a good way."

"Looking at my ass again. You're a pervert."

"No, I'm not. I'm a real man. Admiring tits and ass."

"A real man who can't even keep a girl."

Her words hit me like a punch, but I faked a smile. Brenda's eyes avoided mine. She probably recognized my disappointment. I sighed.

The elevator squeaked before it stopped on the first floor. A few seconds passed before the elevator door opened, the result of a functional delay. It gave us time to settle our differences, but neither of us spoke.

Brenda's comment affected me more than I expected. I felt sad, but couldn't tell her that Rita had stopped seeing me because of my closeness to her, our new friendship. I thought about relinquishing my responsibility to Dr Green, but surgery residents were a stressed bunch, experiencing long work hours and verbally abusive attending physicians. He would be an unreliable confidant, judging by my experience with Deb.

Once inside the car, I turned the radio on, and we hummed along with the songs. We looked at each other occasionally and smiled, which was an improvement from the elevator experience. I took the one-way street behind the hospital to the parking garage. There was no way of turning back on the road. A decisive move. I needed such an approach in my personal life; I needed to be resolute.

"I'm sorry about my lewd remark," I said.

"You're a good man. Don't let anyone take that away from you," she said.

"Thank you," I said.

She squeezed my arm.

Brenda did not wait for me to open the car door for her, but exited the car before I did. She appeared to be in a hurry. Since she was ahead of me, my eyes focused on her marvelous buttocks. Her pants squeezed her cheeks into a tight package, leaving barely enough room to move with each step she took. I laughed as I watched Brenda climb the steps. Although it was not intentional, it was funny that I chose the rear entrance steps to the hospital to watch her buttocks' gymnastics.

As we approached the glass entrance, I saw a man in green scrubs standing by the sliding door. Brenda quickened her pace. I held my breath, afraid that she would fall because of the way her pump action set her bouncing. When the sliding door opened, Dr Green reached for Brenda's hand, and they walked down the empty hallway. Brenda forgot about me. I entered the cafeteria alone, where I would eat alone. Instead of standing in line to be served, I claimed an empty table by the window. Reflecting on my activities that morning, I realized that I had a new problem. A serious problem. An obsession with Brenda's body. It was not the new direction in my life that I had envisioned.

Chapter 34

A FEW WEEKS LATER, when I entered the emergency room, I approached the reception desk. Oblong in shape and surrounded by patients' rooms, it occupied the central portion of the emergency room, creating an open area providing easy visual access to the rooms. It served as a command center for all the activities related to patient care. Three secretaries were on the phone. While one hand held the phone, the other hand's fingers nestled on the keyboard. With their eyes fixed on computer monitors, they ignored me. I stood in front of the three secretaries, waiting for some recognition of my presence, but willing to wait my turn, whenever it arrived. I understood the fundamentals of priority. Dealing with emergency room departments required patience, a virtue that was necessary to everyone's survival.

Each room, except for one, had a nurse or a doctor examining a patient. In that one room, there was a doctor and two nurses. Each appeared to be busy. From mere observation, it appeared the patient in that room needed more resources than all the other patients. A common thread in our lives was the goal of identifying what everyone needed and providing it, even when it was only words or compassion. The ability to do this was a necessary skill that every doctor had to acquire.

Whispers and grunts emanated from several rooms. Ambulance attendants wheeled in patients. There were even four policemen standing around. Nurses ran in and out of rooms, and cries could be heard from babies and adults. It was the sound of manageable chaos. Emergency rooms were the same everywhere. I had to mentally arrive at that conclusion as I was there for a job interview as a part-time, emergency-room medical assistant-cum-orderly—to supplement my meager allowance as a medical student. I was in Memphis, but it reminded me of Knoxville. I missed home and the life that I had left behind.

As I stood at the reception area waiting for attention, Deb and Rita came to mind. Previous relationships. Even my friend Brenda had found someone who occupied her free time, Dr Green. I was back to where I started when I arrived in Memphis: alone. My mind wandered back to why I was in the emergency room—a job interview. Even with limited time, as a third-year medical student, I felt that I needed money to supplement my meager scholarship fund. Although I did not accept it initially, I needed a job to occupy my free time. I was in yet another of the lonely periods of my life.

"I'm looking for Julie, the head nurse," I said to the first secretary available.

"Is she expecting you?" the secretary asked. She began to dial a number before I could answer her.

"I have an interview," I said.

"That's Julie in room four," the secretary said. She looked away from me and carried on with her telephone call.

In room four, there was a nurse, a woman lying on a bed, and two teenage girls. The nurse appeared to be talking to the two girls. Since everyone was smiling, I assumed that the patient's medical problem was not serious. I walked closer to room four to attract Julie's attention, but I stopped when I remembered the implications of violating a patient's privacy, even if they were probably having a non-medical conversation.

While I stood in the middle of the walkway, an ambulance siren sounded. The blaring sound stopped as the ambulance pulled up near the entrance of the emergency room. Two men wheeled in an elderly woman on a stretcher and stopped at the reception area. The nurse in room four came out carrying a clipboard. I waved to attract her attention. She came closer to me, her hospital badge had 'Julie, RN' on it.

"I'm here for my interview," I said.

"I'll find a place for us," Julie said.

Another nurse approached Julie and whispered to her, and Julie's demeanor changed. First, she sighed more than once, then frowned. She flipped through the papers on her clipboard. Her state of mind, at that moment, worried me.

"Mom, I'm here. Are you okay?" A familiar voice said.

I turned around. Dr Peterson stood next to the newly arrived stretcher, his dreary eyes focused on the woman lying on it. "Mom," Dr Peterson said again. Their right hands clasped. Mother and son. Tears hung on his eyelids. Watching Dr Peterson holding his mother's hand, I concluded that he was human, like the rest of us. I remembered my mother, and my eyelids tingled, a sensation I knew well. At that moment my interview with Julie escaped my mind.

I approached Dr Peterson. Without even knowing why his mother was in the emergency room, I said, "I'm sorry about your mom," and extended my hand to him. We shook hands. I patted him on the shoulder. He looked at me with a frown. I became worried that I had taken liberties.

"How did you know?" Dr Peterson asked.

"Know what?" I asked.

"I thought you were here for me."

"I'm interviewing for a job."

"Mom had a stroke. Again."

"I'm sorry. I'll stay with you."

"You don't have to. Do your interview."

"I'll reschedule."

"Don't. I'll be okay."

I heard a sigh and turned around. Julie was standing close to Dr Peterson and me.

"He's done," Julie said.

"I'm sorry, Ma'am," I said. I felt that my actions had been irresponsible.

"Don't be. I saw how you comforted your friend," Julie said.

"I understand what he's going through. Been there," I said.

"I need someone like you working for us. It's good to be selfless," Julie said.

"So, I get the job?" I asked. Excited. When Dr Peterson looked at me, I sighed.

"The job's yours. Look for me when you're done," Julie said, and then she walked away.

The ambulance attendants wheeled Dr Peterson's mother to a room, and drew a curtain to protect her privacy. A nurse walked into the room and disappeared behind the closed curtain. Dr Peterson and I stood outside. He looked at me without saying a word. I felt uneasy.

"Thank you again," Dr Peterson said, after we had stood together for more than five minutes in silence.

"My mom had a stroke. Lost her speech. Died the same day. My dad died three months after. I knew he gave up the day Mom died," I said.

"I didn't know. I'm sorry," Dr Peterson said.

"I miss my parents terribly," I said.

"I can't imagine not having my mom," Dr Peterson said.

I tried hard to hold back my tears, not to fall apart inside the emergency room. It was more than losing my parents that troubled me, it was losing everyone I cared about: Deb, Rita, and Brenda. The only thing I had left was medical school, which I had almost lost.

"You can come in," the nurse said. She pulled the curtain aside.

Dr Peterson walked in. I watched him hold his mother's hand and caress it. I sat on the floor outside the room, covered my face, and wept. People passed by and probably did not realize what I was going through. When I had enough of crying, I wiped my face and walked out of the emergency room. While I was standing close to the entrance, Dr Peterson joined me.

"I saw you leave. I just want to thank you again," Dr Peterson said.

He extended his hand to me. We shook hands and hugged. Tears rolled down our faces. Two adult males crying for different reasons. I was mourning my losses. Deaths and breakups—the loss of loved ones, no matter how you look at the events themselves.

"Call me if you need me," I said. I was talking to a friend, not the resident physician I used to know. A member of my medical family.

I walked away from him and followed a path for a walk to nowhere. After walking around the hospital, I remembered my car, a new thing in my life.

The parking lot was across from the hospital. I entered my

car and sat in the driver's seat for more than ten minutes before I started the engine. When I reached the park by the river, I couldn't remember how I got there.

Looking in front of me, I saw familiar areas. The Mississippi. I walked down the boulders to the edge of the river bank. I sat on a rock and watched the muddy river flow. The mud would settle as sediment, but the river would continue to flow. It would join bigger bodies of water, forming a union.

Sitting alone by the river, I realized that I was watching life from the sidelines, as a spectator. I resolved to be a participant. I would return to Rita to beg for forgiveness, or move on. However, the word forgiveness repulsed me. I had not done anything wrong. Twice, Rita had left me over minor misunderstandings. Our future together did not appear to be workable. I wished that I could forget about her.

I rose from where I was sitting and walked toward my car. Driving away from the parking lot, I set out on a new mission to find my destiny—my life without Rita.

Chapter 35

A DAY BEFORE the end of my first clinical rotation, in mid-September, I decided to visit Dr Trophy's office, my erstwhile attending physician. I flipped through the pages of a worn faculty directory lying on one of the nursing stations in the intensive care unit, and found the location of Dr Trophy's office: 'Suite 301, Professional Building', a four-story building connected to the hospital by a glass-covered walkway.

After an early lunch, I followed the hospital guide to the Professional Building. Double doors separated the hospital from the glass enclosure straddling the busy road. The double doors opened automatically when I approached them. As I stepped inside the walkway, suffocating heat bathed my body, and stifling air flowed into my lungs with each breath I took. It was tempting to quit breathing or return to the hospital. I was also apprehensive about my unscheduled meeting with Dr Trophy.

Mid-way through the glass-covered walkway, my hair felt like it was on fire. Sweat flowed from my face to my neck, and soaked my shirt. I had not seen Dr Trophy since the day I was suspended from medical school for confronting him, after he made disparaging comments about Brenda in the conference room. I wondered how he would react to seeing me. There was a possibility that things would not go well between us. I was on probation, and my adventure could lead to permanent expulsion.

When I reached the third floor of the Professional Building, I stood in front of Dr Trophy's office, contemplating opening the door. My heart rate increased, and I rubbed my sweaty palms together. The office door opened, and Dr Trophy stepped out. I wiped my sweaty hand on my white coat. I wasn't sure if he would shake my hand. We stood in front of his office, looking at each other. A few seconds felt like a day. Another mistake I could have avoided.

"I'm here to apologize," I said.

What I said surprised me. My plan was to discuss what had happened between us. I had not planned to apologize, because I felt I had done the right thing. Looking back, confronting him was wrong, but supporting Brenda was right.

"Apologize to the fellow students you disgraced," Dr Trophy said.

"Brenda needed our support. She's been through a lot," I said.

"She's not stable. She's dangerous to patients."

"She's getting help."

"I'm glad," Dr Trophy said. He checked his watch as he spoke.

"I didn't mean to waste your time," I said.

"I'm glad you came. You have potential. Don't throw it away," Dr Trophy said.

"Thank you," I said.

Dr Trophy walked away from me. I could sense that he had been uncomfortable while we were talking. I wanted to follow him and continue the conversation. However, I stood in front of his office and watched him walk away.

'You have potential. Don't throw it away,' stuck in my mind. That was the best advice I had been given so far. Most importantly, it was from someone I despised. I couldn't change the things I had done wrong, but I resolved to be more careful with my actions and words—to be resolute, but respectful.

Chapter 36

DAYS LATER, in surgery rotation, my daily routine involved scalpels, scissors, and iodine-soaked packing gauze. Scalpels to cut and expel. Folded, long gauzes to pack the wound. A pair of scissors to cut away any excess. Tools too familiar to medical students in surgery rotations. Although the medical students' roles were limited, we absorbed the necessary information, including how to collect a detailed medical history from patients, and read laboratory results, and vital signs. We cleaned and dressed wounds. On better days, we drained abscesses, guided by a surgery intern—a reward for being good surgery students.

Surgery interns were our heroes or villains depending on circumstances that were changeable daily. Regardless of the intern's tendency, Brenda and I appreciated the time they spent with us—the two out of the original four from our previous rotation with the same surgery team.

Brenda was proficient with the surgical tools. Every time the interns deferred an abscess drainage to us, she rushed for the scalpel. Trying to avoid conflicts, I watched and aided her.

One day, she sat on a stool, put her gloves on, and cleaned the abscess area. Lifting the surgical scalpel, she cut into the abscess, drained and rinsed the evacuated pocket, and then packed the space with gauze. She exhibited skills that were beyond the scope of a medical student. The surgery interns watched her and whispered. I could not help but remember her emergency room visit in Knoxville when she was found in a park, along with a scalpel and scarf. I joked to myself that she was in the park to perfect her skills.

One Friday evening, the trauma team called our general surgery team for assistance. Accidents and gun-shot wounds had overwhelmed their team. Close to the operating suites, six of us stood listening to instructions from the trauma team's attending physician. Our group consisted of two senior general surgery residents, two surgery interns, and two medical students. If I was a surgery intern pretending to reward medical students, I would have used the term 'surgery medical students', which, within some groups, was a revered label.

"We'll let you handle simple cases," the attending trauma surgeon said.

"Dr Green and an intern will cover," a senior resident said.

"I'll keep a student," Dr Green said. The senior residents and the attending physician conferred, at a distance from the rest of us. We watched them huddle together. The interns stood a short distance from the conference of the elders of surgery. The two of us, the surgery medical students, watched from a distance.

Thinking about Dr Green's request for a medical student, I knew who he wanted on his team; his girl, Brenda. Watching Brenda smile while we waited, a dirty thought ran through my mind. What would happen if an emergency call came for Dr Green while they were making love in an on-call sleeping room? Would he run out of the room half dressed? I smiled. Brenda turned to me with a puzzled look on her face.

"What's funny?" Brenda whispered. I wanted to tell her what I was thinking.

"You don't want to know," I said. A wider smile appeared on my face.

"Try me."

"A dirty thought."

"I know you look at my ass."

"No, I don't."

"That's why I walk in front of you. To tease you."

"You're weird."

"Call me names, but you want a piece of my yum-yum."

"I'll throw up. You have a man."

"That hasn't stopped you from looking."

I felt a sudden onset of nausea, and a flash of heat, while Brenda spoke. Initially, I thought I felt sick because of her comment, but the symptoms persisted. Using the back of my hand, I felt my forehead. A dab of perspiration bloomed on my face. Brenda watched me take two steps backward, putting me just two paces away.

My stomach growled loudly. I remembered selecting salad and a tuna sandwich from a local grill, the late lunch I had after the hospital cafeteria closed. There was nothing else in my stomach that could mount a noticeable protest. I knew what to expect. The unfortunate thing was that I had no control over my activities. To leave, I needed permission. Unfortunately, surgery interns could not grant such permission. Out of desperation, I rubbed my back against the wall, though it didn't offer any relief. I waited for my gut to spill its contents from either direction, vomiting or diarrhea. An agonizing wait.

Brenda approached me, grinning as if she knew what was about to happen. I wanted to be left alone. My eyes searched for the closest toilet in case I had to answer a call that I could not delay, a call to evacuate my stomach. It appeared that Brenda's closeness made things worse. My stomach burbled more, and its contents felt as if they were traveling up faster than I expected. I concluded that the best thing was to find a restroom, a place to sit and wait for my lunch to pass through me, or be expelled from my stomach. Brenda moved closer to me, making me feel uncomfortable.

"I need my space," I said.

"Space for what? You're a damned student," Brenda said. She giggled.

"You're crowding me," I said.

"I don't know what the fuck that means," Brenda said.

"Okay. I don't feel good," I said. I felt the need to run to the bathroom. There was no time left for resting anywhere. Sweat ran down my face.

"What's wrong?" Brenda asked.

"I ate the wrong stuff, I think," I said. I tried to hold myself together but felt overwhelmed. "I need to go. Right now," I added.

"I'll cover for you. Go," Brenda said.

"I'll pay you back," I said.

I ran to the closest bathroom. Vomiting and diarrhea ensued, the price I paid for consuming leftover food from a small diner. I realized that I would have been better off going hungry than torturing my stomach.

After volumes of liquid passed from my body, I washed my hands several times, then my face. A cleansing ritual, I suppose, instead of the necessary shower. I looked at my red eyes in the mirror, remembering, 'Always replenish what the body has lost,' a phrase from one of my medical school teachers.

When I opened the bathroom door, Brenda was leaning against the wall.

"Heard you in there. Are you okay?" Brenda asked.

For the first time since I met Brenda, I saw her being concerned about me.

"Why should you care?" I asked, borrowing from her previous words to me. I was angry because she had listened to an embarrassing event that I thought was private: flatulence.

"Aren't we friends? I care about you," Brenda said.

"You care about Dr Green. I have no one."

"You made that choice."

The senior residents and the interns walked toward us. They were smiling as they approached where we stood, which was a new phenomenon. It was the first time I saw any surgery residents smiling after breakfast.

"Hit your call rooms," Dr Green said.

"Is it okay if I take Ben back to the dorm? He's not feeling well. Too weak to drive," Brenda said.

"I've been throwing up," I said.

"Tell him you have diarrhea, too," Brenda said, and laughed.

Dr Green laughed, too. "You can't be in the OR," he added.

"Should we leave?" Brenda asked.

"Yes. I'll let the interns know," Dr Green said.

Dr Green looked at Brenda and smiled. She blushed. This was a new Brenda, sensual and caring. I felt that Dr Green was being considerate regarding our wellbeing because of his relationship with Brenda.

"Let's go," Brenda said.

"I'll get my stuff from my locker," I said.

"I have to make a stop, too. Be back here in five minutes," Brenda said.

Brenda took the stairway, her destination unknown to me. I retrieved my books and keys from my locker. I was too weak to stand, so I sat on a bench outside the entrance. Ten minutes passed without Brenda showing up. I became worried after 30 minutes had passed. When I stood up to walk to the cafeteria for a bottle of water, I saw Brenda walking down the hall, smiling.

"I was worried," I said.

"Nothing to worry about. It's a beautiful day," Brenda said.

"I don't want to see a bad day if today is beautiful."

"Trust me. Things are good."

We left the hospital and found her car. She whistled while driving. Speeding down a side street, she cursed at the slow drivers she passed. She looked at me multiple times, with an interesting smile on her face. I wondered if she was possessed or had taken a 'happy pill'. I'd heard of them from patients, but didn't believe that medication could confer happiness on anyone.

Once we reached the dormitory, Brenda parked close to the entrance of the building. When she flung my backpack onto her shoulder, I reached to retrieve it, and she slapped my hand.

"It's heavy," I said.

"You looked tired. So, let me help you," Brenda said.

We took the elevator to our floor. She stood in front of my room while I opened my door. She laid my backpack on my desk, pushed the chair in, hung up two shirts I had left on my bed, and fluffed my pillow. I watched her, surprised at how she was taking care of me.

"What has gotten into you?" I asked.

"What do you mean?" Brenda asked.

"I don't deserve all this attention," I said.

"Why not? You're kind too," Brenda said.

She left my room and returned in less than one minute with two bottles of water.

"Thanks, Mom," I said. We laughed.

"You need to replenish," Brenda said.

"What I've lost," I said. We laughed more. "I need to change. I'm tired," I added.

"Go ahead and change," Brenda said.

"I need privacy," I said.

"I'll look away," Brenda said and laughed.

"I'm not joking. I need to lie down," I said.

When she tried to unbutton my shirt, I slapped her hand.

"I'm trying to help your tired ass. I don't want you," Brenda said, a serious look on her face.

Worried about offending her, I took off my pants and shirt and crawled under the covers. When she tried to tuck me in, I got out of bed.

"I need a shower," I said.

"I'll help you," Brenda said.

I heard a phone ring outside my room. I thought it was Brenda's phone until I heard a voice answer, "Hello." A female voice. Silence then ensued until the voice added, "I'm at University Tower, I'll call you back later." My heart raced.

"Someone out there to get you," Brenda said, and laughed.

A knock sounded on my door. I could not imagine who would be knocking at that time. While I was worrying about another eviction by the university administration, Brenda opened the door. Rita stood outside my room.

"Aren't you going to invite me in?' Rita asked.

"Come in, Mademoiselle. Take good care of him," Brenda said.

Brenda walked out of the room, Rita walked in.

"Don't go," I said to Brenda. She stood outside my room, holding on to the door handle.

"Brenda came to the ICU. Told me you're sick," Rita said.

"She didn't tell me that she spoke to you," I said.

"She was very concerned. I became worried. I'm here to help."

"You're only around when I need help."

"There are too many women in your life. I can't handle a broken heart."

"The only one with a broken heart is me. I can't count on your love."

"Brenda explained your relationship. I'm sorry."

"I have never been lucky in love. I am learning to rely on me."

Rita came closer to me. She hugged me and kissed me.

"I'll always be here for you," Rita said. She turned to Brenda, and added, "Thank you for everything."

"Don't thank me, he's been good to me. I owe him a lot," Brenda said.

"I'm sorry I misjudged you," Rita said.

Brenda walked over to Rita and hugged her. She hugged me before she walked away from us. Rita and me. She hesitated before she left the room.

"That's what I want. Friendship between us," Brenda said. She closed my room door behind her.

After Brenda had left, Rita took her shoes off and joined me in bed with her clothes on. Facing each other, we hugged, our lips met, and so did our tongues. In less than two minutes, while swapping saliva, I heard Rita snore. I watched her sleep until I joined her slumber—without knowing when my transition started.

I heard a phone ring. My room was dark. Looking around the room, I realized that it was Rita's phone that was ringing. It was after nine. I picked up the phone. Rita woke when I brought the phone closer to her. She sat up in bed before she answered the phone.

"Hello," she said. Holding the phone to her ear, she answered 'yes' several times. Before she ended the conversation, she added, "I'll be there in the morning."

"What's going on in the morning?" I asked. Rita stood up and stretched. She yawned.

"They need me to cover for Monica. She's sick," Rita said

"When do you get to rest?"

"I'll rest tonight. I hate to leave you, but I have to go."

She sat on my bed and put her shoes on. I wrapped my arms around her waist.

"Stay with me tonight," I said.

"I need to change my scrubs," Rita said.

"I understand," I said. I got out of bed and tried to put my clothes on.

"You're sick. I can make it to the car alone," Rita said. She hugged me tighter.

I walked Rita to my door before our final kiss that night. After locking my door, I returned to my bed. To my solitude.

I closed my eyes to sleep. To escape from my loneliness. I heard a knock on my door, and ignored it, thinking that I was dreaming. After a second knock, I became worried. Brenda came to mind. I thought about her. The reason I came up with for her return troubled me. Approaching the door, I was unsure about the best way to turn down Brenda's sexual advances.

I opened my door halfway. Rita was standing outside my room. I became excited and opened the door fully to let her in.

"I'm not coming in. I forgot to tell you that I love you," Rita said. She turned around to leave.

"I love you too, Babe," I said.

"We're spending the weekend together."

"Can't wait to be with you."

Rita walked away. Thinking about why she had come back, I smiled. I closed my door and returned to my bed feeling excited. The loneliness that gripped me earlier had set me free.

*   *   *

Rita and I saw each other every day. We ate together and slept together. My dorm room or her place. We were inseparable. She wore my shirts to sleep in every night. I forgot about loneliness. Things were going well between us, but I kept wondering when it would end.

Chapter 37

ONE MORNING, I heard knocks on my door—multiple and loud—followed by banging. "Ben, Ben, get up. We're late." I turned around in bed thinking that I was dreaming. The banging became louder, and my door shook.

"What the heck," I shouted.

I reached for my phone, which I had left on my desk before I went to bed, set to wake me up at 4:30 am. It was 5:30 am. My eyes were blurry, and my brain was too foggy to figure out what had happened. I had slept through the alarm, or it had not gone off. Brenda and I were supposed to be at the hospital by six—our daily routine—and I did not have enough time for complex mental exercises to try and figure out what had happened to my alarm.

It was the last day of our trauma rotation, and the end of my surgery clerkship. I was not fond of surgery rotations. I wondered if, subconsciously, I had ignored the alarm when it went off.

While pondering over what had happened, I heard, "Get your ass up," a scream from outside my room. It was Brenda with her foul mouth.

I turned over in my bed and fell on the floor. My legs felt weak when I tried to stand. I dragged my body to the door. Opening the door, I realized that I was only wearing my boxer shorts.

"My alarm didn't go off," I said.

"Did you set it?" Brenda asked, her voice louder than usual, and angry.

"I'll hurry," I said.

"You'd better. I believe I heard your damn alarm," Brenda said.

"I must have been dead," I said.

I scampered around my room. Once I found a towel, I left the room. Brenda followed me.

"I'm leaving. I'll take care of things until you get there," Brenda said.

"Thanks. I'll be there soon," I said. I watched Brenda leave our dormitory suite.

I rushed to the bathroom, turned the shower on, and brushed my teeth while the water dripped on my head.

*   *   *

Later, I met Brenda at the entrance to the emergency room, at 6:45 am. She inspected me with her eyes.

"We have two patients left to see before morning rounds," Brenda said.

"I'll take care of it," I said.

"Let's work together. It'll be faster."

"You dress wounds, and I'll write notes."

"You dress wounds, and I'll write notes. It's your last dirty rotation," Brenda said, then laughed.

"You love playing with scalpels and debriding wounds," I said.

"I love to cut," Brenda said.

"I know you do," I said. Brenda looked at her wrist. Her scar. "I'm sorry. I didn't mean that," I added.

"That was the old me. Counseling has been good for me," Brenda said.

"We're wasting time. We'll talk later," I said.

We left the emergency room area. Brenda walked ahead of me, and occasionally she looked back.

"You're slow," Brenda said.

"I'm not looking at your ass," I said.

"You have a better ass to fawn over: Rita's," Brenda said. We laughed. "By the way, how are things with her?"

"Going well. You're hardly around. Always with Dr Green."

"You mean, Paul."

"You and men with biblical names."

"He's a good man. Understanding and kind. Good skills."

"You mean bedroom skills?"

"You're a pervert."

"Aren't you doing it?"

"None of your business."

"I'm sorry."

We reached our first patient's room. The floor was crowded with nurses pushing computer carts around and morning-shift nurses arriving from every direction laden with coffee mugs and lunch bags, some big enough to contain all the lunches for the nursing staff. The ward was awash with coffee and food, the two most important commodities for the medical staff on 12-hour shifts. The patients' needs were different: get well and get out. Eating was not as important.

Brenda and I walked into the room. Our assignment stated:

24-y.o. male involved in a motor vehicle accident. Traumatic amputation of left leg below the knee.

The patient pulled on the bedspread when we walked in. His eyes inspected his leg area, eliciting a sigh.

"I'm Ben Ava. This is Brenda. We're medical students."

He looked at me and frowned. I waited for him to acknowledge our presence verbally. He turned onto his side—away from us—without saying a word. Brenda used her fingers to signal to me that she was walking to the other side of the bed. I followed her.

"We're here to change your dressing," Brenda said.

He reached out and held on to his blanket, taking an uncooperative stance.

"I'm sorry about your accident. We can help you," I said.

"Help me? Like how? By asking my girlfriend to keep her invalid boyfriend?" he asked. He sat up in bed and threw his pillow across the room.

"She will accept you just the way you are," Brenda said. She walked closer to his bed.

I watched his hand tighten around a corner of the blanket.

"You doctors ruined me. You cut off my leg," the patient said.

"They were trying to save your life," I said.

"I'm useless. I'm thinking about killing myself," the patient said.

"Talk to your girlfriend. You'll be surprised. She loves you, even without a leg," I said.

"I guess you know my girlfriend," the patient said.

I regretted my comment—I had overreached, guaranteeing a result that I had no control over. I had given a dishonest representation.

"I don't know her. I was wrong. Talk to her. Tell her how you feel. You owe her that," I said.

Tears rolled from his eyes. He wiped away his tears with the blanket, exposing his amputated leg.

"Do what you need to do, and leave me the hell alone," the patient said.

Brenda pulled over a chair and sat down. She unwrapped the dressing, her eyes focused on what she was doing. The patient watched her clean the wound. While dressing the wound, her fingers twirled around it. She wrapped his stump aesthetically.

"Good job," the patient said.

"We'll be back later," Brenda said.

When we left the patient's room, his nurses were standing by the door.

"He's thinking about killing himself," I said to the nurses. "Watch him. I'll let the attending know."

As we were walking down the hallway, Brenda stopped. With tears running from her eyes, she looked at me.

"He'll be okay," I said.

"I'm crying for me. I've been thinking about telling Paul," Brenda said.

"That you cry?" I said. I laughed, thinking that my question was witty.

"Shut the fuck up. I want to tell him everything. About me being bipolar. My father. Every fucking detail. Then he'll leave me," Brenda said.

"Not if he loves you," I said.

"I want you with me. When I tell him, I'll need your support," Brenda said.

"I'll always be here for you," I said.

"You'd better be. You owe me," Brenda said, wiping her eyes and her running nose. She was crying and smiling, offering evidence of a unique disposition.

"One more patient to see," I said.

"Let's hurry," Brenda said.

We left the surgery floor, walking at a slower pace. As always, I trailed behind Brenda. My mind drifted to Rita. I thought about my commitment to her, and my vulnerability. I wondered who I would depend on if I had a devastating accident. I had no parents or siblings. My pace quickened, and I caught up with Brenda as she entered the general medical floor.

"Brenda, if you marry Paul, will you forget about me?"

"What's eating your brain?" Brenda asked.

"You never know. Fall in love, get married, and forget your friends," I said.

"Never. I love you. I mean, like a brother," Brenda said.

I tried to hug Brenda, but she pushed me away.

"Not here," Brenda said.

"Paul will think we're doing it?"

"He knows better. He even wants to take us out tonight."

"I didn't know."

"I'm not sure if it's a good idea."

"I won't even ask why."

"I want to spend more time with him alone."

Dr Paul Green and two other residents walked by. After they passed us, Dr Green turned around.

"Better hurry, we'll let you out early. It's your last day with us," Dr Green said, then walked away. Brenda and I remained—the two of us.

My mind traveled to Beale Street. Blues and broken hearts. I thought about the homeless man. He had no one to depend on. I remembered my nights at the Mission House.

"I love you too, Brenda. Like a sister. I'll never look at your ass again," I said. I smiled.

"You still can. We're not blood relatives," Brenda said. We

laughed.

We knocked before we entered our patient's room, a quiet space with no lights, a windowless pit. I reached for the switch on the wall to turn on the lights. I heard a hiss, like the sound of a snake. Instead of being afraid, I laughed. I was too happy about ending my surgery rotation to let a snake stop me from finishing my assignment for the day.

"No lights. My head is about to explode," said a voice in the darkness.

I flipped on the lights. A man dressed in a snake outfit jumped on me. When he unmasked his face, I recognized the surgery intern. Brenda laughed. She didn't appear to be surprised and was probably a conspirator in the prank. The rest of our surgery team joined us. Throwing their hands up in the air, they congratulated each other, including Brenda. She was a budding surgeon, an accepted member of the surgery team.

I watched them have fun at my expense, an excited group with a common predilection for scalpels and sutures. Brenda pulled me by the hand to join them. She exuded their confidence, and I knew I did not belong with them. After all, cuts and stitches were for the ones that had the calling. The ones with skillful hands. My interest was talking, and comforting people. My thoughts focused more on why things happened, and how to stop bad events from happening. The ones gifted with surgical skills focused on solving problems. Cutting and stitching to heal.

Paul and Brenda came to me. Smiles on their faces.

"I'm off tonight, let's have dinner," Paul said.

"I'll check with Rita," I said.

"I'll call her and plan the evening," Brenda said.

"I'll wait to see what you come up with," I said.

Brenda and Paul left together. I turned around and walked in the opposite direction.

* * *

Most of the patrons had left Toni's Bistro, it was close to midnight, and we were celebrating the completion of our third-year surgery clerkship. Dr Paul Green, Brenda, Rita, and I sat in a corner booth, a semicircular compartment. We had occupied the space for three hours. Most of our conversations were about the medical profession and patient care. We laughed freely. Two unopened bottles of wine sat on our table. Our waiter approached our table and picked up the used plates and glasses.

"Ready for your wine?" the waiter asked.

"We'll take the bottles of wine home," Dr Green said. He sounded as if he knew what the rest of us wanted. No one opposed his suggestion. Our waiter left.

When Dr Green looked at his watch, I raised my wrist at the same time. Midnight. Two days of rest ahead of me, before the next clinical rotation. There was no rush to get back to the dormitory. I thought about Dr Green's work schedule, but he didn't appear to be worried about the time.

Brenda moved closer to Dr Green and placed her head on his shoulder, snuggling her head into his neck area. It was a perfect fit, a move she had probably perfected from repeated practice.

"Cozy," I said.

Brenda raised her head. Her face showed no discernible emotion.

"I'm not comfy. I'm stressed," Brenda said. She turned to Dr Green and added, "I can't keep the secret any longer. You need to know."

"I know already. You cry at night. I hear you call his name—Ben. You love him?" Dr Green said.

Rita pushed me away, an angry look on her face. She stood up and slapped me hard, before she turned to Brenda.

Tears rolled down Brenda's face.

"You don't understand," Brenda said.

"I understand. You've been lying to me," Rita said. She looked at Brenda while biting down on her lip. Her nostrils flared on her scornful-looking face. I became afraid that she would bleed from a self-inflicted wound, the result of misplaced anger.

"Listen first, before you judge," I said, raising my voice.

Paul wiped his lips vigorously with a napkin. A cleansing ritual, I thought. Truth had to come out of clean lips. He threw the napkin on the table.

Rita sat down at a distance from me, as if I was afflicted with a communicable disease. A cheat had to be avoided.

"Paul, you know I love you," Brenda said, her voice barely audible.

I heard Paul sigh. He looked at Brenda, then reached for her hair and stroked it.

Rita stood up, turned to Dr Green, and said, "You're a good man. Forgiving and all, but I'm not. They lied to me."

"Please, let me say what's on my mind," Brenda said, interrupting Rita.

"Go ahead. You can have him. I'm done this time," Rita said. She wagged her finger at me.

"Nothing like that. It's worse. I don't know how to tell Paul my father raped me throughout my childhood. I've struggled with it. I tried to kill myself," Brenda said.

"I'll kill him," Dr Green said, his voice raised.

Rita covered her gaping mouth with her hand. Her eyes filled with tears.

Paul pulled Brenda closer and hugged her. Her head nestled in his neck. I heard her whimper.

"I'm struggling with being bipolar," Brenda said, and sniffled as her nose ran.

"Why didn't you tell me?" Paul said.

"I've been in counseling. Doing better. Ben's been supportive," Brenda said.

Rita bowed her head and rested it on her clasped hands, her eyes closed. I reached out to her and put my arm around her waist. Even in that position, I felt her heart beating fast.

"I'm sorry, Brenda. Count on me. Whatever it takes," Paul said.

Everyone wiped their tears, except for Rita. With her head still bowed, she shook it from side to side. Brenda, Dr Green, and I looked at each other. I wondered if Rita was still angry with me.

"Forgive me, Rita," I said. I was afraid of losing her again.

Rita lifted her head. Her eyes traveled from me to Brenda. Brenda started crying again.

"I was 12 when he first raped me. My own father. The man who was supposed to protect me," Rita said. Her voice quavered. Brenda got up and sat next to Rita. They hugged, and wiped each other's tears.

"Useless fathers betraying their kids. Purely evil men," Rita said. "I know. I can't trust anyone either. I run from closeness. I was afraid to love," Rita said. She moved closer to me and added, "Look at Ben. A beautiful man, and I was scared to love him. I ran away twice. I'm sorry, Babe."

"Stop running. True love is beautiful," Brenda said.

"I need help. Counseling, therapy, I don't know what," Rita said.

"I'm here for you. You're my babe," I said.

"Brenda's going home with me. No more dorms," Dr Green said.

"You're taking away my friend," I said.

Brenda extended her hand to me. The hand with the winged ankh bracelet that she told me on the first day of medical school was a symbol of being 'battered but still standing'. The symbol of her abuse and survival made sense to me now.

"You have me now, Babe," Rita said, as she stepped between Brenda and me. Separating us. Taking control.

Dr Green took Brenda's hand. We laughed, our tears drying.

*   *   *

During the rest of the third year of medical school, I saw Brenda occasionally, mostly in conferences for medical students. We had different clinical rotations and she rarely came by the dormitory. We spoke on the telephone several times about getting together, but our time constraints prevented it from happening. I stayed at the dormitory. On the days that Rita worked, she stayed with me. During the weekends that we were free, we visited historical places in Tennessee, and Mississippi. It was interesting that we only crossed the bridge to Arkansas twice.

Six months into my fourth year of medical school, after completing my required courses, I scheduled an appointment with a psychiatrist, Dr Living, a renowned psychoanalyst at the medical center. It was my first time seeing a shrink, and I didn't tell Rita about it. I felt the need to see one, but didn't know why.

The appointment was for nine o'clock on a Tuesday morning. I arrived at Dr Living's office at 8:45 am. The waiting room was empty. Looking around, there were ten chairs, two side tables, and a water cooler in the waiting room. A clock on a blank white wall. No paintings or pictures on the wall.

"Good morning, how can I help you?" the secretary said.

"Here for my appointment with Dr Living," I said.

She handed me a clipboard with papers and a pen attached to it.

"Have a seat, fill in the forms and let me know when you're done," the secretary said.

I had no medical problems to report on the forms. When I reached the mental illness part, I left it blank. I was there to be analyzed by the expert.

At nine, the secretary ushered me into a small consultation room. No windows. Two chairs in the room. I had barely sat down when a short man with a prominent belly walked in. Clean shaven. Faded blue jeans and an Oxford shirt. He decorated his casual presentation with a smile.

"I'm Oscar Living."

"Ben Ava, senior medical student," I said.

"You're counting the days to graduation," Dr Living said, still smiling.

"Can't wait. It's been a long four years," I said.

"Really? How about the friends you'll leave behind?" Dr Living asked.

"Well…" I hesitated.

Dr Living interrupted, "It's not important. Tell me why you want to see me."

"I'm not sure. I guess I want to be checked out."

"I'm a psychoanalyst. That's all I do."

"That's what I need," I said. I felt foolish, and tried to improve it by smiling.

"Anyone in your family with mental illness?" Dr Living asked.

"Not that I know of, my parents are dead."

"Let's talk about your childhood first."

For 45 minutes, we talked about my childhood, the death of my parents, my responsibilities, my fear of commitment, isolation, and love. We had five minutes left in the session when he pulled his chair back, away from me. His smile faded away.

"Apart from being a doctor, what do you want most in life?" Dr Living asked.

"To be loved," I said, without hesitation. He turned his notepad over and smiled. "When do you start my psychoanalysis?" I asked.

"We're done," Dr Living said.

"That's all you need? Do I get a report?" I asked.

"Nothing to report. You are the psychoanalyst, the only one that knows what you desire. To be loved," Dr Living said.

He stood up and shook my hand. We left the consultation room together. I decided not to share the information with Rita.

Chapter 38

ONE WEEK BEFORE MY GRADUATION from medical school, I drove to Knoxville and went directly to the cemetery where my parents were buried. After inspecting their headstones, I visited a florist for my mother's roses. Instead of a dozen roses, I bought three dozen to make up for the time I was absent. Returning to the cemetery, I placed the roses on my mother's grave.

I retrieved a note from my pocket, a note I had written, and stood facing my parents' graves. I began to read my note, loudly enough that anyone around could have heard me.

Dear Mr and Mrs Ava,

This is to officially inform you that your son will graduate from medical school, with honors, on May 21 this year. It is unfortunate that you cannot attend. However, he plans to return to Knoxville one week after the graduation ceremony to display his certificate by your graves.

Rest well until he returns,

Ben Ava

After reading my note, I entered my car and traveled to the university medical center in Knoxville, where I used to work. When I reached the surgery center, I found a vacant chair in the waiting room and sat down. I pulled a note I wrote to Deb out of my pocket to review.

Dearest Deb,

I know you are busy, so I decided to leave you a note. I hope you are doing well and getting enough rest. I know how surgery residencies can be, but remember to make an effort to spend time away from the hospital. In

*our busy lives, we forget to spend time with our friends and family. I hope
you are an exception to that habit.*

*I apologize for not writing to you before now and ask for your
forgiveness.*

*On May 21 this year, I will graduate from medical school. Since my
parents are gone, I have only two people to invite to the ceremony as part of
my family. You were once so close to me that I considered you a member of
my family. I hope it would be okay with your fiancé if you decide to attend
the ceremony in Memphis.*

*In case you didn't know, I am returning to Knoxville for a combined
residency in internal medicine and psychiatry in July. I need to return to
Knoxville because I feel like an unworthy son for leaving my parents'
graves unattended for so long.*

*Forgive me for intruding in your life, but I needed to let you know how
I feel. You will always be special to me,*

Ben

I approached the secretary's desk to leave the note for
Deborah Linger, MD. I waited while the secretary was on the
phone. While I was waiting, Deb came out of a patient's room.

"I'm going into operating room three," Deb said to one of
the nurses. Our eyes met, but she kept walking, past the double
doors leading to the operating rooms. Maybe she didn't recognize
me, it had been close to two years since I last saw her.

I dropped my note on the secretary's desk and left the
medical center to return to Memphis. I knew she would not
make it to my graduation ceremony.

* * *

One week later, the medical school graduation ceremony was

to start at noon. I stood in front of the university conference center at 10:00 am, waiting for Brenda. It had been six months since I last saw her. While waiting, I pulled out a piece of paper from my pocket to look at the names of the people I had invited to my medical school graduation ceremony. Only the names of Rita and Deb were on my guest list for the university. I knew that Deb would not travel to Memphis to attend my graduation ceremony, so I was expecting only Rita.

At 10:30 am, Brenda climbed the steps in front of the conference center. We hugged and held on to each other. Neither of us wanted to let go. Eventually, we separated.

"I missed you terribly," Brenda said.

"I missed you too," I said.

"Where's Rita? Did you break up again?" Brenda asked. She laughed. Instead of answering her, I smiled. "Something's wrong," Brenda added.

I felt a tap on my shoulder. I turned around. Deb was standing close to me, in her academic gown. I was surprised to see her, and even more surprised to see her wearing academic regalia.

"I asked the dean if I could place the doctoral hood on you," Deb said.

"I didn't think you'd come, let alone take part in the ceremony. Wow!" I said.

She hugged me, the way she used to. She buried her face on my shoulder and sobbed.

"I hope you forgive me someday. I never meant to hurt you the way I did," Deb said.

"He was a mess when we came to Memphis," Brenda said.

"How would you know? We didn't speak to each other then,"

I said.

"I heard you cry at night, calling her name," Brenda said.

"You heard yourself cry, not me," I said.

The procession line started to form inside the conference center. We were about to enter the building, when I saw Rita walking up the steps. I ran down to meet her and hugged and kissed her. Deb and Brenda watched us walk up the steps. Before I could introduce Rita, Deb reached out to shake her hand. Brenda winked at me and stepped away from the three of us.

"So, this is your new lady?" Deb asked. I looked at her and smiled. "New love intoxicates like wine," Deb added. She smiled.

"Why does it matter to you?" Rita asked.

"Where's Paul? I need to get out of here, before someone gets hurt," Brenda said. She laughed.

"I'm Deb Linger, Ben's ex. It's my lucky day. I've been chosen to place the doctoral hood on Ben," Deb said. Her face was decorated with a smile.

"He didn't tell me!" Rita said. She frowned.

"Because he didn't know. I asked to," Deb said.

"Haven't you hurt him enough?" Brenda asked.

"I'm here to support him. Don't worry, I'm getting married next week," Deb said.

"Congratulations, Deb. I'm happy for you. I hope to do the same soon with Rita," I said.

"You're proposing to me?" Rita asked.

"I was going to ask you at dinner tonight," I said.

"I accept," Rita said.

"I don't have the ring here," I said.

"Who needs a ring when you're in love?" Deb said.

Deb hugged me and hugged Rita too.

"I'm sorry for what I said to you," Rita said.

"Take care of each other," Deb said.

"We're moving back to Knoxville," I said.

"We are?" Rita asked.

"Brenda and Paul too," I said. "Brenda's doing her surgery residency at the medical center and Paul has a job offer. Surgery attending physician."

Paul joined us. He was late. We hurried to join the rest of the participants inside the conference center.

* * *

Later, during the ceremony, the dean of the school of medicine finished his speech and read the names of the recipients of special awards.

"A special award for the Best Surgery Student of the graduating class, Brenda Galant," Dr Cleaver said. He handed Brenda a framed, gold-plated scalpel and placed a gold medal, suspended on silk material, around her neck. Brenda bowed several times while the crowd clapped for her. "Our next award is to be presented by Dr Ezekiel Trophy," he added.

Dr Trophy walked to the podium. He picked up the microphone and cleared his throat.

"The Humanitarian Award in Medicine, and World Peace Medal, will go to a fine young man and an exemplary student, Benjamin Ava," Dr Trophy said.

Tears of joy overwhelmed me. Rita hugged me and cried. I walked up to the podium to receive my awards. Dr Trophy hugged me before he presented the awards to me.

After the awards ceremony, the issuance of certificates and

hooding started. When my turn came, I marched to the podium, climbed the stairs to the dais, and bowed my head.

Dr Deborah Linger climbed the dais behind me and placed the hood around my neck. When I turned around to shake her hand, she hugged me, and whispered, "Tell your girlfriend I was the first, and always will be." We laughed.

I watched Rita while walking down from the podium.

When I returned to my seat, Rita said, "Next time she hugs you, I'll break her hand. I'll never give you up for anyone. You're mine forever."

More books from
Harvard Square Editions:

People and Peppers, Kelvin Christopher James

Gates of Eden, Charles Degelman

Love's Affliction, Fidelis Mkparu

Transoceanic Lights, S. Li

Close, Erika Raskin

Anomie, Jeff Lockwood

Living Treasures, Yang Huang

Nature's Confession, J.L. Morin

Love and Famine, Han-ping Chin

Dark Lady of Hollywood, Diane Haithman

How Fast Can You Run, Harriet Levin Millan

Appointment with ISIL, Joe Giordano

Never Summer, Tim Blaine

Parallel, Sharon Erby